Praise for Rachel Hauck's p

Lost in NashVega

"Rachel Hauck not only writes a charming and humorous story, full of down-to-earth people, she writes about Nashville better than most travel guides."

—lifeway.com

"Packing witty dialogue, quirky characters, and a rocking "country vibe," her story will make you laugh as it plunges you into the world of today's country music industry."

—Christianbook.com

"Thoroughly down-home delightful."

—best-selling author Stephanie Grace Whitson

"Move over Jennifer Weiner—a new voice has just hit town! *Lost in NashVegas* gives us a fun peek at what it might be like to be a struggling songwriter in the heart of the South. Hauck's storytelling is a rare and luminous gift. I'm her number one fan."

—Colleen Coble, author of *Fire Dancer*

"A highlight of my reading year, *Lost in NashVegas* receives . . . my highest recommendation."

—novelreviews.blogspot.com

"*Lost in NashVegas* strums the heart strings with humor and a girl's search for purpose. For Robin McAfee, finding the spotlight isn't easy, but always fun."

—DiAnn Mills, author of *Lanterns and Lace*

"Fun, funny and full of good ol' country charm, *Lost in NashVegas* grabbed me on the first page and didn't let go. Pour yourself a tall glass of sweet tea, sit back in a comfortable chair, and get ready to meet one of the sassiest Southern chicks in Christian fiction. You won't be sorry!"

—Virginia Smith, author of *Just As I Am.*

"Thanks to Hauck's masterful storytelling and characterization, aspiring songwriter Robin Rae McAfee from Freedom, Alabama lingers in my mind like a lifelong friend. *Lost in Nashvegas* breaks through genre lines so smoothly that anyone with a heart and a sense of humor will love this story."

—Christine Lynxwiler, author of *Arkansas* and the Pinky Promise Sisterhood series

"Perfect! Beautifully written with perfect Southern charm, Rachel Hauck superbly captures the world of NashVegas—the fears, the hopes, the people, and the aspirations of a wanna-be songwriter. I found myself cheering for Robin Rae: a brave, spunky, good ol' country gal shouldering not only her dreams, but the dreams of the people she loves. Encore, Encore!"

—Susan May Warren, award-winning author of *Everything's Coming up Josey*

"With a lively cast of characters and a Southern setting so real I feel like I've just returned from a visit, *Lost in NashVegas* grips the reader from start to finish, offering a fun glimpse into the world of songwriting and a storyline that's as good as warm apple pie on a lazy afternoon."

—Diann Hunt, author of *RV There Yet?*

Lost in NashVegas, an ACFW book club selection.

Diva NashVegas

Rachel Hauck

NASHVILLE DALLAS MEXICO CITY RIO DE JANEIRO BEIJING

Published in Nashville, Tennessee. Thomas Nelson is a trademark of Thomas Nelson, Inc.

Thomas Nelson, Inc. books may be purchased in bulk for educational, business, fund-raising, or sales promotional use. For information, please e-mail SpecialMarkets@ThomasNelson.com.

Publisher's Note: This novel is a work of fiction. Names, characters, places, and incidents are either products of the author's imagination or used fictitiously. All characters are fictional, and any similarity to people living or dead is purely coincidental.

Library of Congress Cataloging in Publication Data
Hauck, Rachel, 1960-
Diva NashVegas / Rachel Hauck.
p. cm.
ISBN-13: 978-1-59554-191-8 (pbk.)
ISBN-10: 1-59554-191-8 (pbk.)
1. Women country musicians--Fiction. 2. Nashville (Tenn.)--Fiction. 3. Musical fiction. 4. Chick lit. I. Title.
PS3608.A866D58 2007
813'.6--dc22

2007008341

Printed in the United States of America
07 08 09 10 RRD 6 5 4 3 2 1

To Javier LaBoy, for calling me a diva.

MUSIC

1995—*Willing to Make a Change*

1997—*Aubrey James*

1999—*Better Left Unsaid*

2001—*Dandelions & Daffodils*

2003—*This Way to the Parade*

2005—*Borrowed Time*

2007—*At Last*

BIO

At eighteen, Aubrey James, the daughter of gospel icons Ray and Myra James, rocketed to the top of country and pop charts. An overnight sensation with her first album, *Willing to Make a Change,* she quickly found the platinum road to superstardom comes at a very high price . . .

1

"Aubrey James is the holy grail of celebrity interviews. Whoever gets her to sit first wins."

—*Beth Rose, Inside NashVegas*

On a warm June night, I stand stage left among a swirl of activity—the stage crew, band members, and music artists coming and going—waiting to go on. Closing my eyes to rehearse my entrance, I have an odd sense of suspension, for a moment unable to determine time or place.

Ladies and gentlemen, Aubrey James . . . Run out smiling. Grab the mike. Wave and greet the fans. Hear the opening bars of "Borrowed Time."

Done it a thousand times. All over the world. Before queens and rednecks. Tonight is no different.

Except I'm utterly exhausted.

You're the CMA Fest's closing performer, Aubrey. Don't let the fans down. Don't do it.

Opening my eyes, I expect—I hope—the fans' excitement will jump-start my adrenaline, washing away the cloak of weariness.

It always has.

But tonight, the electric excitement charging the Titans Coliseum fails to touch me. My thoughts wander, and my heartbeat fires like a worn piston. Tiny beads of sweat prickle under my arms and across my forehead. I try to focus on the opening number again.

Walk out . . . Drummer counts down "Borrowed Time," bass comes in, then the electric. On the downbeat, I sing. Engage the crowd. Find the sweet spot.

Six months on the road with my all-girl band.

Hear the smooth call of the steel guitar, the whine of the fiddle, the exquisite, elegant harmony of my background singers. Can do this . . . By pure grit and grind. Come on, Aubrey.

Tonight's performance also ends my eleventh tour—sponsored by a hip new bottled-water company, FRESH!. A brilliant partnership orchestrated by my business manager. Music, I've had to learn, is as much about business as it is art.

Rolling Stone magazine put me and the band on the cover of their January edition with the headline "Aubrey James Gets FRESH!"

The swirl of activity around me increases. Roadies and techs finalizing the stage before we go on. CMA Fest cameras moving in. The show is being taped for television.

Are there half as many people in the coliseum as there are back here?

My drummer hurries past with her cymbals and snare. "I'm late."

"You have time," I say, watching her step up to the drum stage. From the corner of my eyes, I spot my manager, Zach Roberts, observing me with an inquisitive expression, his arms crossed over his lean chest. "What?"

"You're sweating, and don't tell me it's the Nashville heat. You have dark, puffy eyes, a frog voice, and you're pale."

"What's your point?"

"You're sick."

"I'm going on, Zach." Six months on tour, a hundred cities, can't end with a sore throat, fever, and puffy eyes. Besides, the fans deserve their final CMA Fest performance.

Zach rubs his forehead, doubt shadowing his brown eyes. "You look like a bag of bones, Aubrey. Did you lose weight on the tour?"

"Haven't you heard? It's all the rage. The Tour Diet. I'm writing a book about it this summer." I pat his cheek. "I'm fine. Trust me."

The stage manager passes by, flashing his palm. "Five minutes, Miss James."

Five minutes. Where's the familiar rush of preshow adrenaline? Without it, I'm not sure I can manufacture enough energy to carry me through the set.

Zach curves his arm around me. "This is your last performance. Then you're free as a bird for the summer."

"Free. Right. Besides this little gig here and that little gig there. A new photo shoot for the FRESH! campaign . . ." I lower my chin and gaze at him from under my brow. "Not to mention concluding the renegotiation with SongTunes and finishing my next album, and wanting to sleep until fall."

He smiles. "We're working with SongTunes, and if you have to cancel a few appearances to get rested, then do it. Besides, if you're sleeping, I can work with some of my other clients for a change."

"Oh, please. I'm your favorite and you know it."

"Some things go without saying." He winks, but his merriment fades. "Hard tour, wasn't it?"

"Incredibly."

"At least the tabloids have backed off."

"For now."

How could one tour have so much controversy? Stolen equipment and personal items like jewelry. Missing money. A bus fire. The fired bus driver, who is now threatening to sue.

Worst of all, I parted ways with my musical director, Melanie Daniels. Midtour she announced she wanted more control, more money, and a solo spotlight. We argued. She left.

Angry.

A few days later, the tour arrived in Dallas amid the swarming media. Frustrated, tired, and hurt, I just *had* to make a pithy remark about Mel to a nosey journalist, didn't I? The B-word slipped out. Along with a few other choice phrases. Once the tongue gets loose . . . This is why I *never* do interviews. Never. Words get said, ideas twisted.

My comment about Melanie leaving the band made celeb magazines and tabloid headlines around the world.

Remembering causes my pulse to pound and my middle to constrict. I fall against Zach.

"Aubrey, you can't go on," he says, pressing a fatherly hand to my forehead. "You're burning up."

"I'm going on." The rest of my band emerges from a dark corner of the stage, and I move away from Zach, forcing my lips to smile. "All set?"

Vickie Campbell, my bass player, puts her hand on my shoulder. "Let's do it."

"One minute." The stage manager passes again, flashing a finger in our faces. "One minute." Rascal Flatts is performing on stage two and coming to the end of "What Hurts the Most."

I breathe deep, shaking out my hands, stretching my neck, wiggling my legs. Tom Petty sang it right—the waiting *is* the hardest part. Closing my eyes, I take a deep breath, and . . .

A firm hand slips over my shoulder, and soft lips nuzzle my neck. My heart races as I whirl around.

"Car, what are you doing here?" Nervous energy fires through me. "I'm about to go on."

His smile fades as his expression darkens. "I thought you'd be happy to see me." He pulls me to him. "Surprise." Then, Brown "Car" Carmichael the Third kisses away my lipstick.

Gently, I struggle free. "Car, honey, I thought we were meeting at the house later."

"This isn't the welcome I expected, Aubrey." His tone is clipped.

The stage lights go up and the crowd's rumble deepens.

"Car, what *did* you expect? I'm thirty seconds from a performance." Stepping backward toward the stage, I hold my expression, pressing the corners of my lips upward. "Can we talk about this later? I'll be all yours then."

He props his hands on his belt, the sharp edges of his handsome face softening. "Sure. Knock 'em dead, Brie."

The announcer is on the mike. "Ladies and gentlemen, please welcome the queen of country soul, Aubrey James!"

2

"Once she realized she could capture and hold a crowd, Aubrey became consumed about delivering the perfect, standout performance. She demanded it of herself, her band, and her crew. She drives herself hard and expects no less from everyone working with her."

—*Greg Leininger, CEO of SongTunes Records*

"Hello, NashVegas!" Dashing out, I find enough of a spark to brighten my weariness. With an album-cover expression, I wave to the crowd. The coliseum is a sea of glow sticks, but the exertion cost me my last ounce of energy.

Come on, Aubrey, buck up.

Digging deep, I try to find my diva-self, quite sure she's hiding under a mountain of blankets, sipping a cup of homemade chicken noodle soup.

So very tired.

The cheering mounts. Poster boards declare, *We love you, Aubrey.*

"Are you having a good time tonight?"

The crowd's response is enthusiastic, but instead of spurring me on, it exhausts me more. Two sentences into the performance and my throat burns and aches. No way will I hit the big notes of the "Borrowed Time" chorus.

Wondering why the band is not counting down the intro, I turn around to see Reba McEntire walking out from backstage.

My smile drops. Reba? What's she doing here? While it's an honor to see her, I'm not sure why she's strolling my way, grinning. Did I forget something? Please don't tell me I'm supposed to sing with Reba. How could I forget?

"Look who's here." I motion to the country legend. "Give it up for the first lady of country music, y'all."

In contrast to Car's unexpected appearance, seeing Reba is the kind of surprise I like. While the fans give Reba her due, I slip my arm around her, hoping to tap into the country legend's incredible strength.

"I know a secret about you, Aubrey," she says in her famous twang while flashing her famous smile.

"Me? Y'all know I don't have any secrets. Just read the *National Inquirer*."

Laughter balloons among the fans, accompanied by a barrage of hoots.

I try to focus on the crowds, but the stage is bright, and my eyes start to water. Faces are melding with the light.

Reba gives me a squeeze. "This is the last night of Aubrey's hundred-city FRESH! tour"—more cheering— "and her *thirtieth* birthday."

Well, there's *that* secret. "Shhh, Reba, no one is supposed to know."

Dozens of *Happy Birthday* signs pop up. Camera flashes explode around the coliseum like tiny white bombs. When a couple of stuffed bears and wrapped boxes fly at the stage, the coliseum's security team move into action.

Reba sweeps her arm wide and, looking over her shoulder at the band, begins a rousing rendition of "Happy Birthday."

The fans sway and join the song, their voices chasing around the coliseum.

"Happy Birthday, dear Aubrey . . ."

Cheers and whistles rise as the song ends. The band holds out the last note, crashing the cymbals and whining the electric. Laughing, I face them, cutting the air with my hand. The music stops. But now Car appears from the shadows, walking toward me with a lopsided smile that makes my heart skip a beat. For the first time tonight, I notice how amazing he looks. Clean-cut and all-American.

But what is he *doing* out here?

"This is Aubrey's sweetie, Car Carmichael," Reba announces. "Vice president of Carmichael Financial right here in downtown Nashville. He has a special surprise for our birthday girl."

This news jump-starts my adrenaline. *Car, what are you doing?*

Reba hands him her microphone and disappears into the shadows. Car bends slowly to one knee.

The fans go bonkers.

"C-car? Get up." My legs and arms tremble.

He pulls a small blue box from his pocket and holds the mike to his lips. "Aubrey Jo James . . ." His voice thunders around the coliseum.

Tugging on his hands, I will him to stand up. *Please, Car, not here, not now.*

". . . will you marry me?"

He opens the Tiffany box to reveal a dazzling, brilliant diamond. A cameraman butts in between us, zeroing in on the prize. Over my shoulder, the ring is splashed up on the Jumbotron. The crowd hoots and whistles.

This is ridiculous. How can a man ask a girl to marry him—at least ask *me* to marry him—in a fan-filled coliseum? I'm *working*.

Car slides the ring onto my finger.

Words escape from my heart. "Oh my gosh."

The ring is like a fireband, hot and suffocating. A chant rolls forward from the fans: "Yes. Yes. Yes."

My arms feel weak, my feet numb. The roar of the crowd swirls around me as if I'm trapped in the belly of a dark cave. A drop of sweat runs into my eyes and burns.

"Car, I—"

Before I can finish, he swoops me backward for a long, crowd-pleasing kiss. When he sets me upright, all I can utter is, "Wow."

Cradling me like a pet puppy, Car raises the mike again. "Y'all want to come to the wedding?"

The fans roar back a "Yeah!" making my blood run cold.

"Stop! You're giving ideas to the wackos," I hiss in his ear.

Car frowns, leaning down to my ear. "Brie, have fun with this. They'll forget by the time we get married next spring."

You've picked springtime? And no, they won't forget. You have no idea.

Car bends me back again and stares me in the eye for a lingering moment while the folks work up another raucous cheer. Then, with a sudden jerk, he plants his lips on mine. The louder the crowd, the harder he kisses. All I can do is hang onto him with stiff arms until he lifts his face and stands me upright. He bows and waves to the crowd.

Like they're here to see you, Car.

As he walks off, still waving, I watch his straight back and square shoulders. What do I do now? How do I segue from here?

"Guess I'm engaged," I say with a light laugh, the diamond like an anchor on my hand.

The fans applaud, but I can tell, they're ready to move on.

"Borrowed Time" blasts into the night air, and I morph from stunned girlfriend into a country diva.

"We've had a blast meeting so many of you on the FRESH! Tour. Country fans are the best fans anywhe—" My voice cracks.

A field of fists pump the air above the crowd. One of the cameramen moves in front of me as I start to sing. I wink, flirting with the camera. My voice isn't strong, though, so I push a little. But two measures into the first chorus, my voice breaks and quits. No volume. No energy. No sound.

Immediately, my backup singer takes over the lead with my bassist rounding out the harmony while I carry on as if the whole vocal exchange was planned.

Blinking, I try to focus, but all I see is purple and green. My steps are awkward, my movements clumsy. I keep walking, clapping, trying to sing.

Then, the lights fade. The noise drifts. Everything . . . goes . . . black . . .

I open my eyes. Sunlight warms my bedroom with bright light. Outside my window, white puffy clouds float along a perfectly blue Nashville sky.

Oh, thank goodness, I'm home, in my room, in my snuggly, comfy bed.

I slip further under the covers and nestle against the pillows. Peace settles over me. Pure, unfettered peace.

This is the perfect place. The other side of the rainbow.

A light knock resounds, and as I poke my eyes out from under the covers, I see Momma's pretty, smiling face peeking around my door. "Hey, baby girl. How're you doing?"

"Good, Momma. Good." I motion for her to sit on the edge of my bed.

"You're tired, Aubrey Jo." Momma sits, her back straight, her shoulder-length hair layered around her face. She looks me over with her lips pressed tight.

"I am tired." I can't help it—despite my best efforts, water spills from my eyes. "There's no rest for the diva, you know. Everyone counting on me—"

Instantly Momma cradles my head in her arm and presses her velvet-like fingertip against my lips. "Shhh, don't worry about it now. You push yourself too hard. Birthday girls shouldn't worry."

"Did you feel this old and tired at thirty?" I run the heel of my hand over my eyes to stop the tears.

She thinks, absently stroking my arm. "I had Peter at thirty. You at thirty-two. Your daddy had just signed the record deal with Myrrh, and we had tour dates booked out for the next year and a half." She moves her hand to her high, lovely forehead. "Oh, that man of mine . . . Never stopped."

"See, I get it legitimately. Don't blame me. Blame Daddy."

"Yes, you're like him—driven, born with music in your soul." She brushes wisps of my hair aside—her soft show of affection.

"Tell me the story again."

"Well . . ." With a smile, she wraps her arm around me a little tighter, and I burrow down. "I was about seven months pregnant with you and, oh, out to here." Her arm extends as far as possible. "We were on the last leg of a five-month tour and had just landed in Florida for a Gospel Fair at this big Baptist church on Merritt Island. After a quick sound check and a light dinner, the show started at seven o'clock sharp."

She chortles, lacing my fingers with hers. "The music started and you came alive, jumping and kicking. Oh, my poor bladder." With a laugh, she tosses back her head. "You didn't quit dancing until the last note was sung, the lights shut off, and your daddy and I had crawled into bed. Then you scared us all half to death when you didn't move for another twenty-four hours."

"Wore myself out, did I?" I trace her fingertips.

"Like you're doing now. You don't have to hold on so tight, Aubrey."

"If I don't, I might spiral off into space."

"Remember what your daddy says: God is always in control."

"You don't know what it's like, Momma. So many demands, a posse of people to support."

"God is more than able. And willing. Hold onto faith and hope, girl."

"Hope left me a long time ago."

"Oh, Aubrey, impossible. You always have hope whether you choose to recognize it or not." She kisses my forehead, her gentle touch watering the dry places of my soul. "Why do you put your light under a bushel?"

"There is no light anymore."

My comment is dismissed with a flip of her wrist. "There's plenty of light. You just need to let it shine."

"You don't understand. Ever since the accident—"

"All things work together for good."

"Not all things." I peer into her hazel eyes. "Not all things . . ."

"It hurts me to hear you feel this way." With a sigh, Momma rests her head on the pillow next to mine and quietly begins to sing. "All to Jesus, I surrender . . ."

3

"I'll never forget her first recording session. First song, first day. It'd been awhile since she'd done music, but when we started playing, she started singing with energy and soul. Sang that song down in one take. It was something else."

—Mark Wallace, session guitar player

*"How many people does it take to watch a diva sleep?" I peer at the whis*pering crowd huddled at the foot of the bed.

"She's awake."

"Aubrey, honey, how are you feeling?"

"My head is throbbing, but other than that . . . Did my diva dive spice up the show?"

"About gave a hundred thousand people heart attacks." Connie Godwin, my adopted mom, settles on the bed next to my legs. "Some girls will do anything to get out of turning thirty."

The glint in her eye makes me smile. "Not me. I *love* turning thirty."

Connie pats my leg, looking around at the rest of them. "The dive didn't hurt her none. Same ole Aubrey."

In the room with Connie are Zach and my friend and assistant, Piper Cantwell. "What day is it?" I ask.

"Sunday morning. You're in Baptist Hospital." Zach steps around Connie. "You were dehydrated, exhausted, and underweight."

"Underweight? Impossible these days." My response inspires no smiles.

"Sweetie . . ." Connie's tone is motherly. "This is serious. The doctor wants you to rest this summer, take some time for yourself."

"Sounds like good doctor advice." Speaking makes me realize how very thirsty and weary I am.

Piper flashes her Palm Pilot. "I need to talk to you about a few things. I've cancelled as many appointments as possible, but—"

"Sandlott." The one word takes all my effort. "Don't cancel the Fourth of July Sandlott concert."

Piper smiles with her dark eyes. "I already told them you'd be there."

She's worth every penny I pay her, and then some. "Thank you." I reach for Zach's hand. "Did I make the tabloids?"

He grins. "Not yet. It's only been thirty-six hours. Give them time."

"However," Piper chimes, "the picture of Car kissing you made the front page of *The Tennessean's* CMA Fest coverage, and Heather Byrd wrote about it in her celebrity column."

"Gerry House wanted to know how you convinced Car to do an onstage proposal with a mega kiss," Zach says. "And *Inside NashVegas* ran a short piece. Just the facts, no speculation."

"Did you guys know?" A heavy feeling settles on my chest, and my tongue feels dry and thick. "Can I have a sip of water?"

Piper fills a cup and holds the straw up to my mouth. I take a long, cool sip. "I tried to tell him," she says. "But once Car decides something . . ."

The cold water washes away some of the heaviness. "Yeah, I know."

"FRESH! sent two dozen get-well roses to the house already." Piper sets the cup on the stand beside my bed, then wraps her fingers around my forearm.

"They've been really good to me."

She gives me a squeeze. "Fans are starting to drop cards and flowers by the front gate."

"My fans . . . the best. What would I do without them?" I pause, then add a low-toned question. "Where's Car?"

"Working, where else?" Piper's remark is snide. She stands back, crossing her arms.

I glance up at her. "He runs a demanding business."

"Maybe so, but his fiancée is in the hospital."

"Apparently dying of thirst." I smirk.

"No excuse." Piper refills the water cup.

In the slim, streaming sunlight, I catch the brilliance of the ring on my left hand. The white diamond casts a prism of pure colors against the hospital wall. "What's the reaction to my engagement?"

"What you'd expect. Congratulations. Speculation. Some are happy, some are dubious." Zach rocks back on his heels, hands tucked in his pants pockets. "Though there's been some poking fun of such a public ordeal. Leno fast forwarded a clip of Car's last kiss, then rewound it, then showed it fast forward again." A suppressed grin tightens his lips.

A prickly warmth spreads across my cheeks. "Car has no idea, does he?"

Piper curls her lip. "No, but he thinks he does."

Connie walks around to sit on other side of my bed. "He did play to the crowd remarkably well for an amateur."

"Did I look surprised?" My hand is slightly chilled, so I slip it under the blanket, the tip of my thumb touching the smooth platinum band.

"Just a tad."

I drop my head against the pillow, staring at the ceiling. Somewhere, somehow—I'd felt a profound sense of peace. When? Where?

The dream.

I sit up. "I dreamt about Momma."

"Recently?" Connie asks.

"Yes, but I can't remember . . ." I brush my hand through my hair, yearning for the profound sense of peace I felt in the dream. No worry, no pain. All the gaps of loneliness completely filled. "I was in my old room, at the old house. Connie, you remember how bright and sunny it was and . . . so incredibly peaceful. Momma came in and sat with me—" My voice falters. "She sang, 'I Surrender All.'"

There's a watery sheen in Connie's eyes as she nods her head, tipped to one side as if hearing Momma's voice. "One of your mom's favorite hymns."

"She was trying to tell me something . . . I think . . ."

"Your momma always carried the wisdom of the ages in her soul," Connie says.

I rest my arm over my eyes. "But it was only a dream."

For a long time, we're silent. In my mind's eye, I picture Momma over and over, trying to recapture the intimacy and peace of the dream, but I can't.

Zach and Piper are whispering to each other. "Did you tell her?"

Raising my head, I peer at them. "Tell me what?"

"She's lying in a hospital bed, for crying out loud." Connie stands by my head as if to protect me. "You can't tell her while she's in this weakened state."

"Tell me what?" My range of motion is tethered by an IV stuck into my left arm. Nevertheless, I do my best to sit up and, holding my tired eyes open, form a smile. "What's going on?"

Zach glances at Piper. "You're her assistant and best friend from high school. Tell her."

"So"—she makes a face—"you're her manager. You get paid big bucks to do this sort of dirty work."

"Is it about Peter?" My eyes roam their faces. "If you have news about my brother, spill it now."

Zach shakes his head. "No, not Peter."

"Then what?"

"Aubrey." Zach walks over to his briefcase and pulls out a tabloid.

"I thought you said I didn't make the tabloids yet."

"No, not for the engagement." He hands me the slick newsprint. "Melanie sold her story of the FRESH! tour to *Star*. And she's making the rounds with some of the B-rated talk shows."

"What do you mean she sold her story—" The paper shakes in my hand. There I am with uncombed hair, red eyes, and a wide-open mouth, pointing at one of the crew members. "Holy cow, I look like a lunatic."

"Exactly what the story implies."

A wave of nausea shoves me back down into my pillow. "I can't believe it. Why would Melanie stoop so low? This isn't like her."

"Honey, she's angry. You were angry. Said things in Dallas you didn't mean."

Without demand, the bitter words of our argument replay in my mind. "Melanie's not the type." I toss the tabloid aside.

"Apparently, fifty thousand dollars makes her the type."

A cold surprise washes over me. I glance at Zach. "Fifty thousand? Dollars? To dish about me and the tour?"

"Not only to *Star*, but the British tabloid *Daily Mail*. You have a big fan base in England."

"I can't believe it . . . yet I said all those awful things about her in Dallas." I close my eyes. "She felt justified."

Zach winces. "It gets worse."

I peek at him. "How worse?"

He presses his fist against his lips. "She signed a record deal with SongTunes."

"What?" I jerk forward. "She's signed with my label?"

Zach tucks his hands into his pockets with a big sigh. "This isn't going to be your best day, Aubrey. BMG fired Greg Leininger last week from heading up SongTunes and hired Nathan Brack."

My eyes begin to water. "Stop. I don't want to hear another word."

Zach rests his hand on my blanketed foot. "I've got more to say, and you're not going to want to hear this either, but Aubrey, Melanie's angry and out for revenge. She's been jealous of you for a long time, and now that she's earned some leverage, she's going to use it."

"I've weathered worse and survived. Only made me stronger." A sharpness stabs my chest. Piper jots a note in her Palm. What, I can't imagine.

"Does Melanie know about the Boot Corral incident?"

I make a face. "The Boot Corral incident? You're kidding—"

Piper's smile sits at half-mast. "Sorry, I was trying for funny."

With a sigh, I remind her, "The Boot Corral incident was entirely your fault."

Her mouth drops open. "I beg to differ."

I smile. "It was funny, though, wasn't it?"

"Very."

Zach's expression is stern. "Can we get back to the issue, please?"

Connie looks over her shoulder at Zach. "Any chance we can negotiate with Melanie? Put an end to the feud?"

Zach shakes his head. "I've tried to call her. She doesn't respond."

"What does it matter?" I stare up at the ceiling. "If she's decided to do this, she won't stop. Besides, ever since she started dating Bo Candler, her attitude has worsened. I'm sure he's feeding her jealous thoughts."

Piper touches my arm. "Aubrey, it's time."

I stiffen. "No. I'm not doing an interview. No."

Ignoring me, Piper faces Zach. "What about getting her on a big venue like *Oprah* or a Barbara Walters' interview? A spread in *People*? Why can't we get her on the A-list talk-show circuit?"

"Hello, Pipe? Aubrey talking. I said no. If I've learned anything over the years, it's ignore the gossip and it'll go away. Most people won't buy Melanie's crap."

If I was exhausted before . . .

Zach paces in a small circle. "We could get her on *Oprah* and other A-list talk shows. But they won't air until the fall or winter. Which"—

he stops with a shrug, his expression twisted with thought—"wouldn't be so bad because the *Star* and *Daily Mail* stories will be old news. The B-list talk shows? Forgotten. So it won't look like Aubrey is attacking Melanie, but all the while, we're replacing her lies with Aubrey's truth."

"Betrayal is the worst." I cover my eyes with my arm again.

"Never mind all this strategizing. Aubrey is resting this summer." Connie trumps Piper's suggestion with her *Mom* card. "She's not going traipsing all over the country taping talk shows just to undo Melanie's foolishness."

"Forget Melanie, then, and the tabloids. You're right, we've dealt with them before." Piper's movement is animated with enthusiasm. "Aubrey, you just came off your eleventh tour. You are one of the few artists who forged a deal with a sponsor. Your fifth album sold eight million copies. Your boyfriend proposed at the coliseum in front of CMA Fest fans. Do you know how many requests for interviews we got yesterday? Fifty. Ten more this morning."

She leans on the foot rail. "Let's repay evil with good. Turn this around. Do an exclusive with a reliable news source. Get your story out there so people won't care about Melanie's story. Aubrey, your parents were gospel icons. People still buy their music. Their daughter grew up to be one of country music's biggest success stories. Now you're engaged to one of Nashville's elite, respected sons. Tell your story, your way. Let's hear from you."

Zach stares out the window as Piper speaks. By the furrowed lines on his forehead I know he's listening, and thinking. "Piper's right. You need to tell your story."

"Please, there's no story. The studio press releases sum me up nicely. Twelve years in the business, five albums, thirty million units sold. Other than that, it's all about my private-life screwups. Dumped by a Hollywood hunk, rebounded with a rogue drummer. Label disputes and how I dislike a big Music Row execs like Nathan Brack who try to hog-tie my career. Then there're my private tragedies. Dead parents and missing brother, and all about how the Christian girl went wild. No." The litany leaves my sore throat burning.

"Aubrey, you got it backwards. Your story isn't about mistakes, it's about triumphs," Piper counters.

"I agree," Connie says.

My wise counselors wait expectantly. *What should I do?* "This will impact all of you."

Piper grins, tugging on the hem of her blue top. "She's softening."

"Also the Carmichaels."

"Are you saying you want to do this?" Zach presses.

"Yes, but"— I hold up my on-one-condition finger—"I'd want to sit down with Beth Rose from *Inside NashVegas*."

Zach's pinched expression warns me he's not keen on the idea. "*Inside Nashvegas*? A local show? Melanie went international."

"I thought this wasn't about revenge?"

Zach laughs. "Yeah, well, it's not." He glances at Piper. "But we should at least get outside of Nashville."

"*Inside NashVegas* has been wanting an interview for years. They can do, 'Inside the Life of a Diva' or something equally as corny. Hometown girl, hometown show."

With a shrug, Zach agrees. "Piper, why don't you—"

"I'm on it. They're going to flip."

4

"Aubrey James is not at all what you see. She's manipulative and selfish, and if she could get rid of every female artist in town, she would. Take it all for herself."

—*Melanie Daniels, Star interview*

Scott Vaughn

Friday, June 15

In the middle of coordinating interviews for a piece on the Sandlott Wood Bat league, my producer, Olivia McConnell, raps on my office door.

Her knock is distinct. Never changes. *Knock, knock, knock-knock.*

Phone to my ear, I motion her in. "Yeah, can we get with him before the game? I heard he signed a letter of intent with Lipscomb University." I scribble "Tom Hayden" on my desk calendar. "Four o'clock."

Olivia sits in the adjacent chair, elbows resting on the arms, fingertips pressed together, looking every bit like she just stepped off a page from some female how-to-look-good magazine. *Glamour*, *Vogue*—one of those.

"Lovely Olivia, what can I do for you?" I hang up the phone.

"Beth's out."

"Out? What are you talking about?"

Olivia spies my mini baseball bat from the Nashville Sound's game opener and reaches for it. I snatch it from under my computer monitor before her long, frightening fingernails scar the wood.

"Her doctor has put her on complete bed rest. He's concerned she might lose the baby."

"Whoa. How's she taking it?" I lean back, swinging the bat with one hand.

"Scared, but willing to do whatever she has to do." Olivia recrosses her legs. "Hannah Warren is your new temporary cohost."

I knock a phantom pitch out my office door and down the hall. *It's Vaughn with a home run!* "Great. Love working with Hannah. Sorry about Beth and the baby, though."

She twists her lips, making a face. "There's more."

"Lay it on me." I swing at another phantom pitch. *Swing and a miss. Strike one.*

"Piper Cantwell called. Aubrey James has finally agreed to give us an exclusive."

Another pitch, another swing. Out of the park. My fake crowd cheers. *Waaaaaah!* "Good for our team. Beth is going to hate missing this one, but great coup for Hannah."

Olivia stands and leans over my desk. The way her head curves down from her neck reminds me of a vulture. *Never, ever say that out loud.*

"Not Hannah."

"Then who?"

"Scott Vaughn." She snags the bat from me—my defenses were down—and swings at her own phantom pitch. "Out of the park. McConnell beats Vaughn's all-time batting average." She drops the bat to my desk and lifts her waxed eyebrows. "You're spending July with Aubrey James. Sam's orders."

"What?" I go to shoot out of my chair, but the arm is stuck under the front desk drawer. "I can't. I refuse."

"If you want to keep driving that Porsche of yours, I'd rethink your position." She smiles with that ha-ha sort of look I hate and walks out, slamming my door behind her, shaking my ceilingless walls. I hear, "McConnell one, Vaughn zero."

Ever since I called her out when she slid into home base during the company softball game . . .

She *knows* I can't interview Aubrey James. I can't. Besides, I'm *Inside the Game*. Beth, now Hannah, is *Inside the Music*.

Shoving back the chair, I free myself, in the process pulling the top desk drawer out and onto the floor. The contents spew all over.

"Crap." I consider the pens, pencils, paper clips, gum wrappers, old sticky notes layered with dust and dirt, and various other various junk items lying on the floor, then raise my foot and step over them to head upstairs.

"What's this about me doing the Aubrey James interview?" I barge through the door that reads, *Sam Watson, Executive Producer.* "I'm *Inside the Game*." I slap my hands to my chest. "Beth and Hannah are *Inside the Music*."

Sam looks up. "Scott, good to see you. Come in, take a seat."

I pace. "This interview is perfect for Hannah. She'll probably poison my coffee if you don't give her this piece."

The creator of *Inside NashVegas* reaches for a pencil from the silver holder by his computer. Not that he needs a pencil, but to make me wait. He taps it against his palm a few times.

"Here it is in terms even you can understand, Vaughn. I'm not sending in the second string when I have you. We're hot on the heels of going national on CMT, and I'm not taking a chance on lousing up this interview. This is the break we've been looking for to get CMT's final buy-in."

I swing my arms wide. "Third string, Sam. I'm the third string here. Beth is first, Hannah second."

"Beth is benched, Hannah's a substitute. *You* are now first string. Besides—and I'll deny this if you ever repeat it—you're actually better at human-interest pieces than Beth. Part of why *Inside the Game* has a huge female following."

"Ah, shucks, you mean it's not my wit and good looks." I drop to the chair.

Sam laughs low. "Keep dreaming."

"What about the pieces I'm working on with the Sandlott teams and the Nashville Sounds? Not to mention football season is around the corner, beginning with training camp and preseason games."

"Not asking you to drop those. I'm asking for a few hours a day, a few days a week. *Capisce?*"

"Okay, okay, I see. This is *you* getting back at *me* for benching you during the softball game against the Fox 17 morning crew." I've got to stop heading up company sporting events. First Olivia, now Sam. "You wanted to show up Charlie Chase. I get it, I get it. Look, I'm sorry, okay? I was a competitive jerk. My bad." I look at him square. "Won't happen again. Cross my heart, hope to die, stick a needle in my eye."

"I'm still ticked about you benching me. That payback has yet to come."

Is it hot in here? I loosen my tie and unbutton the top of my oxford.

"This is about *Inside NashVegas* going national." Sam dips his silvery head as he speaks, looking pleased. "We'll earn a midseason slot on CMT *if* we wow Viacom's head honchos. Aubrey James is the perfect 'wow' factor."

"So, you think I'm the one to help get us to CMT?"

"You'll have a great rapport with Aubrey. If all goes well, we'll debut in November during sweeps week, then pick up a slot in January."

I shake my head. "Sam, I'm not your guy for this one. Trust me. Send Hannah." For a split, honest second, I consider confessing my crash-n-burn date with Aubrey a year ago before she met what-a-show-off Car Carmichael. Never figured one stupid decision one stupid night would come back to haunt me like this. "Look, Sam—"

"Two weeks from Tuesday." Sam goes on. "We want to get as much material on her as possible. Thought we'd do it at her place, make her comfortable, get an inside look of her home."

"I'm not your man for this job."

"Vaughn, *Inside the Game* is going to need a national sports director once we go to CMT." A lock of salt-and-pepper hair falls over his forehead as he rises from his chair. Tucking his hands into his wrinkled pockets, Sam walks to the front of his desk. "We'll have to consider the country music fans who live in Dallas, Seattle, Miami. Know of anyone who might be interested in the sports director's job?"

Standing, I meet him eye to eye. "You're one son-of-a-gun, Sam." Slamming his office door behind me, I jog back to my office, praying desperately for Aubrey James to have a forgiving heart of gold.

5

"We contracted with Aubrey James for an exclusive, but when her relationship with Jack Mills fell apart, she canceled on us while the crew set up in her home. An expensive disappointment."

—20/20

Aubrey

Friday, June 22

My house manager and chef extraordinaire, Gina Lacy, serves Car and me a candlelight dinner out on the covered porch, an outdoor living and dining area. My favorite part of the house.

Our dining table is covered with linen and delicate, gold-trimmed china. An expensive set Car insisted on buying last fall.

"My mom always set the dinner table with china." He beamed with confidence.

"My mom set the table with Chinet."

The reference went over his head. "*Chinet*? Never heard of it. Is it imported?"

"Yes, to Harris Teeter. Car, it's paper plates."

Recalling the conversation makes me laugh on the inside—Car never hearing of Chinet. We grew up within ten miles of each other.

My fork lightly strikes the thin, hand-crafted plate. I run my finger along the rim, making sure there's no fracture or ding. The white and gold is beautiful, especially in the candlelight, but a piece of my heart longs for the brick two-story off Granny White Pike where Momma hosted laugh-filled dinners served on oval Chinet plates.

At seven o'clock the night air is still and cool. Red and gold hues color the blue sky, and the crickets are singing their night song.

Beside the table lie my dogs, George and Ringo—a couple of German shepherd mutts and two of my best friends. They welcomed me home as if they'd been counting the days I'd been away. They followed me everywhere, and I'm not sure, but I think it hurt Gina's feelings a tad. She came to the house every morning while I was on tour, even on weekends, to spend time with "the boys." Then returned every evening to make sure they were fed, watered, and walked. She gave me a detailed account of their care when I called home to check in, yet the moment I walked through the front door, their unspoken doggy language said, "Gina who?"

Then, to Car's chagrin, they jumped into bed my first night home from the hospital—George at my feet, Ringo on Car's pillow. He growled when Car tried to remove him.

I gave him a sheepish look. "They missed me."

His wicked grin told me he missed me too. Strolling around the bed to my side, he shoved me over and squeezed in next to me. A move George didn't like. He jumped to his feet and stood over us, watching.

"Okay, I can't make love with a dog staring at me." Car rolled off the bed. "Come on, boys, let's go. Out." Car's bark sent them scurrying for the door.

But tonight, as I peer through the flickering candlelight at Car's square, perfectly chiseled face, I wonder if it is a bad thing I preferred the dogs' company that night to his.

Under the table, George moans and rolls over, resting his nose on my foot. His pink tongue kisses my ankle. Despite my busy schedule and extended days on the road, my mutts love me unconditionally.

Since my fainting away during CMA Fest, I've been home over a week, resting and healing. Gina tempts me with her home cooking and pumps me full of vitamins. I've gained back five of the twenty lost pounds I lost.

Physically, I'm on the mend. But emotionally . . . this tour drained my reservoir and I'm not quite sure how to refill.

Car shifts in his seat, cutting a bit of chicken, flipping the page of the financial periodical he's reading. Home a week and he's reading at the dinner table as if we've been married and settled for twenty years.

"If you're set here, I'll take off." Gina pokes her head through the french doors. "Feed my old man. He got used to me being around when you were on the road." She motions over her shoulder toward the kitchen. "Dishes are cleaned up. There's fruit in the fridge for later, and a cinnamon apple pie cooling on the kitchen island. Ice cream is in the freezer."

"Gina, you spoil us."

Car toasts her with his wine glass. "Wonderful dumplings."

Gina nods her thanks. "I'm happy to see the bloom back on Aubrey's cheeks."

"Bloom?" Car blurts with a laugh. "I'd say her bloom was plucked a long time ago."

I gasp. "Car."

Gina's expression falls for a quick second, but she catches it with her bowlike smile. "See you tomorrow."

Once she's gone, I angle over my plate to capture Car's attention. "How rude."

"Oh, come on. Bloom on your cheeks?" Car's expression is scoffing. "You're not an innocent schoolgirl."

"She meant I look healthy, not virginal. You really have a one-track mind."

"After this past week, I'd say you do too. Should I tell Gina about your bloom last night?" His tone and grin cause heat to creep across my neck and face.

"Don't even joke about it. Melanie's done enough damage."

He returns to his periodical. "Yeah, and who gave her all that information? You should be more discerning, Aubrey."

I shove the dumplings around my plate. Car sets his reading aside and stretches his hand across the table, grazing his fingertips over my wrist. "Honey, I know you're disappointed about Melanie." His voice is tender and embracing.

My lips twist into a sad smile. "Yes, but disappointed in myself. Our relationship changed when she fell in love with Bo, but I never imagined it would lead to betrayal."

We finish our meal in silence, Car reading while my gaze follows the gardener, Juan, as he waters a dark patch of soil along the perimeter of the security wall.

Soon, June will surrender to July, ushering in the crisp hot days of summer. Slowly, I inhale, as if air in my lungs could stir up the memories from summers past. The fear of forgetting grips me. Besides the beat-up old boxes in the library, faded images and the distant echo of laughter is all I have left of Daddy, Momma, and Pete.

"We don't laugh enough, Car." My words come out of nowhere, yet from the depths of my being.

He peeks at me from under his brow. "We laugh."

"Not enough." The smell of new-mown grass scents the breeze, and in the distance a neighborhood dog barks, drowning out the whir of a motor. Ringo lifts his head and sniffs. George hops up with guttural growl and trots to the edge of the granite porch floor, his large head swerving from side to side.

Car folds up his periodical and looks out to where Juan is shoving some kind of bulb into the ground. "Is there something out there you want to laugh about?"

At *this*, I laugh. "No. I was just thinking how much we laughed at home when I was a kid."

He nods with a jut of his chin. "Ah, I see."

I wait, wondering if he'll tell me how much he laughed as a Carmichael kid, but he doesn't. An only child of very proper blue-blood Southern parents, I'm quite sure Car's laughter was scheduled. Daily from three to five.

Pinching my lips, I exhale a laugh through my nose. Grace Carmichael is as stuffy as they come, with her white summer gloves and country club bridge parties.

"What do you think Juan's planting so late in the month?" I muse aloud to Car.

He's staring off at nothing. "Planting? Not sure."

"You're a million miles away." I prop my elbow on the table and rest my chin in my hand.

He focuses on me. "Sorry. Work."

"What's going on?"

"We had a group of investors for a SoBro condo project, but two of them pulled out today. Every time we get enough investors to move forward, someone drops out."

"Sorry, babe. I'm sure you'll find more investors. You *are* a Carmichael."

He stands, slipping his hands into the pockets of his khaki shorts. "Trying to get people to stick to renovating downtown is like trying to win an egg toss. A few good passes and we're feeling good, then, bam, someone drops the egg and it's a mess."

"Can't believe you're going to let a few cracked eggs stop you." I chuckle.

He looks down at me over his shoulder. "If I had a name . . . say, like Aubrey James, behind a project."

As I stand, my smile fades. "No. You know better."

With a shrug, he turns back to watch Juan. "Can't hurt to ask."

"Sorry, Car, but for now, we have to keep our business dealings separate." I get up to pour a cup of coffee from the sidebar, hearing for the first time the music coming over the speakers. Rod Stewart sings, "It Had to Be You." Gina must have popped in a CD before she left. She's a hopeless romantic.

"I hear you, but we're engaged. We share a bed. You can't trust me with some of your investment money?"

"Be it the luck of the draw, Car, but I've been burned and scammed by close friends, boyfriends, and one distant cousin who turned out not to be my cousin. Besides, my business manager keeps my investment funds pretty tight and tied. We just launched my handbag line this past fall, and my business account is to pay salaries, keep AubJay Inc. running, and market my products."

"What about your personal account? Your balance could buy the whole condo project."

Sweetening my coffee with Splenda and skim milk, I shiver as the hair on the back of my neck bristles. "Car, how do you know my balance?"

A year into our relationship, and me with half of that time on the road, Car and I have never been open about our finances. Does he really know my balance or . . . "Are you just guessing?"

He shrugs and closes the distance between us. "Don't get your nose out of joint over this, Brie, but yeah, I know someone over at your bank."

"And they told you?" The notion of Car snooping into my finances leaves me chilled.

Car pours himself a cup of coffee. "Brie, he was doing me a favor. I thought if you invested, we'd get the rest of the money we need, no problem."

I press my hand hard against his arm. "Don't ever do that again. Ever."

"Brie—" He smoothes his hand over my hair.

I step away. "No, Car, use your own money. I don't understand this. The Carmichael coffers are deeper than mine."

He tilts his head to one side. "It's a good investment, Aubrey."

"I've lost too much in the past. I won't lose it again."

"Aubrey, sooner or later we're going to have to combine accounts—"

"Why?"

He laughs like I'm crazy. "What? We're going to have separate accounts?"

"Sure. Create a joint household account, come up with a monthly budget, and split the amount between us."

"I'm not going to be on your accounts?"

"And I won't be on yours."

Car returns to his chair, holding his coffee cup between his hands. "Good to know we're starting out this relationship with so much trust and respect."

"Car, please—" I set my coffee aside and reach my hand to his.

He doesn't say anything for a minute, then lightly rubs his thumb over my fingers. "Piper put the Fourth of July dinner on your calendar, right?"

All is well for now, then. I settle back in my chair with a final squeeze of Car's hand. "What dinner?"

Car's expression is incredulous. "Aubrey, I've told you a hundred times."

"You've never told me anything a hundred times. Don't talk to me like I'm an airhead."

"Fine, then I told you several times. My parents *always* host a Fourth of July celebration at the Belle Meade country club. You know, the one with congressmen, senators, the governor, a billionaire or two. Mother planned to officially announce our engagement."

"Announce?" I angle toward him. "Who doesn't know after the CMA Fest? I bet even the billionaire knows. By the way, why don't you ask him to be your SoBro investor?"

"I told you I was sorry about the CMA Fest. Who knew you'd hate my surprise?"

"Um, Piper?"

"Piper's always yapping about something."

Okay, narrow road. Barrier ahead. Danger. Change the course. Getting up, I slip around the table and sit on Car's knee. "Thank you for trying to do something spectacular. We never talked about our expectations, so you did what you thought would be unique. But I live and work on stage." With my finger, I trace the straight line of his nose down to its perfect tip. "Guess I never told you I preferred something quiet, private, and romantic. Curled up on a blanket by a lake, watching the flickering flames of a small fire as it reflected on the water's surface. You'd kiss my forehead, then cheek, and whisper in my ear, 'Will you marry me?'"

His feathery kiss sends tingles down my back, and my heart swirls and melts.

"If I'd have known . . . " he says, grinning, nuzzling my neck. He chuckles into my hair. "But I've had a half a dozen women tell me they loved the proposal. Thought it was romantic. Wished their husbands had done something over the top for them."

"What would that be? An airplane flying over the coliseum during a football game with a trailing banner? 'Marry me, Judy.'"

Car laughs against my skin. "Probably." He reaches for his coffee. "That's funny."

Leaning against his chest, I slip my arms around him. "Those women don't have public lives to compete with their private ones."

He kisses me again. The strong taste of coffee lingers on his lips. "Speaking of private . . . Why are you doing the *Inside NashVegas* interview?" His hands wind around my hair.

"You know why. We talked about this."

The amber lawn lamps begin to glow as the evening spreads over us. The pool lights click on and send a wavy radiance through the water.

"Don't see how it's going to make a difference." Car takes another sip from his china cup, then makes a face. "Coffee's cold already. *Inside Nash-Vegas* is a local. Melanie went national. Shoot, she went international."

"Because I trust *Inside NashVegas*." I twist Car's engagement ring around my finger. So stunningly beautiful, but not the one I pointed out to him, in fun, while shopping last Christmas.

"This one?" he'd asked, tapping his finger against the jeweler's glass case.

"Yes, isn't it lovely? Simple, yet elegant."

So he knew. Even if we weren't talking marriage, he knew what I liked. I glance again at his engagement ring. It really *is* beautiful. Car has exquisite taste.

"If you trust *Inside NashVegas*," he says, "then go for it." He runs his hand absently down the side of my leg.

"It seems like the right time to speak for myself." I say. "It was one thing when the tabloid headlines were lies. It's another when the story is perfectly true."

From across the lawn, Juan straightens his back. Catching my eye, he waves, motioning for me to come. "Be back," I tell Car.

"See, I plant lilies for you." Juan waves his hand over an area of ground lighted by Victorianesque garden lamps. "And here, tulips. Bloom in spring."

Dropping to my knees, I pat the fresh dirt, hoping not to pet a worm. "It's sort of late in the season. Do you think they'll do okay?"

My momma planted tulips every year. Then complained when Daddy booked her on so many singing engagements she couldn't enjoy her garden.

"I don't see the fruit of my labors," she'd complain.

"Then stop laboring." Daddy loved to tease.

Juan shrugs his response. "Yes, late, but they do fine." His Spanish accent laces all of his words. "If no, plant something else. Why not try?"

I smile. "I like your thinking."

"This your garden. Juan take care for you." He thumps his chest. A refugee from Nicaragua, he's the hardest-working man I've ever known besides my daddy.

Juan is shorter than me, with black hair and eyes and a thick mustache. His light-brown skin is tanned from working in the spring sun though he's rarely without his worn straw hat.

"I go now. Wife with baby." He winces. "Two-month-old, a girl. She fussy." He shakes his head with a sigh.

Rising to my feet, I lay my hand on his shoulder. "All babies are fussy, Juan."

He removes his hat and gives me a half bow. *"Hasta luego."*

"Until later." I bow in return.

Picking up his tools, Juan heads toward the garden shed. "Wait, Juan. Let me send home some leftovers."

He turns. *"Gracias, jefe."*

Dashing past Car, who is engrossed in his periodical again, I bustle around the kitchen gathering leftovers for Juan's family. Just inside the pantry door is the picnic basket Car bought "for romantic afternoons in Centennial Park."

Romantic picnics in the park? Zero.

I scoop the dumplings and remaining salad into plastic containers, then scan the refrigerator shelves. Might as well send along the fruit too. Did Gina buy a gallon of milk? Who's she kidding? I add it to the goodies.

The basket is enormous. Car had high expectations of himself. Or me. Never figured out who was supposed to coordinate the romantic afternoons in the park.

I cut two slices of pie—one for Car, one for me—then put the rest in the basket.

"Where are you going?" he asks when I pass by again, tugging the basket along with both hands on the handles.

"Giving leftovers to Juan."

"Aubrey, you pay him well. You have to draw a line between being his boss and his friend."

I don't hesitate a step. "I choose to be his friend."

Juan's smile rivals the garden lamps as I approach. "Thank you very much. I bring basket back tomorrow. *Gracias por todo*."

"*De nada*." I wave. "Hello to your wife."

When I return to the porch, I sit on Car's knee.

"You're sweet to look after Juan," he says. "Forgive me, but I grew up with Grace Carmichael, and she enforced strict protocol between the family and the servants."

I smooth my hand over his chest. "It won't be like that around here. People are people, no matter what their bank balance. Giving the basket of food to Juan is the best feeling I've had in a long time."

He reaches for my hand and kisses my fingers. "Guess I have to give up some of my traditions to live with a wild woman like you."

I run my hands through his hair, making the sides and ends stand up. "Car, back to the Fourth . . . You know I have to do the Sandlotter concert in Music City Park. I do it every year. Besides, *Inside NashVegas* is scheduled to be there, and I invited Jennifer Nettles and Joe Diffie. It's way too late to cancel on them. It would be rude."

Car's expression darkens. "Mom sent out invitations. She'll be humiliated."

I lift my hands with a shrug. "She should've checked with me."

"How do you know she didn't?"

"Because Piper would've told me."

He sighs. "No chance of her making a mistake?"

"Sure, but in the ten years she's worked for me, she's never missed a personal appointment like this."

"Babe, sooner or later you're going to have to work the Carmichael schedule into your life. You missed Easter week at the St. George Island house because you were performing in Centennial Park for the Oasis

Center fund-raiser. You missed Grandma Carmichael's eighty-fifth birthday party for the AMAs."

My blood pumps with adrenaline. "Are you keeping score? Music City Park is not a bargaining chip. You can either come with me to the event as a doting fiancé or go to your parents, but I'm going to sing for baseball and the city's youth athletic league."

He presses his hand on my leg. "What am I going to tell my mother?"

Glancing into his eyes, I feel his dilemma, but it's not mine to resolve. "Tell her to come to the Sandlotter game. Bring her friends. She's chairwoman of, what, five charity organizations?"

He frowns, then slowly smiles and breaks into a laugh. "I can see the ladies of the auxiliary sitting in the stands rooting for the home team." He yanks me toward him and kisses me, his hands sliding low on my hips. "I'll take care of it. But please, Brie, let's work on coordinating in the future." He buries his face in the crook of my neck. "Wanna go for a swim?"

Grinning, I look over at the pool. "Guess so. I can get my suit—"

He rises from the chair and peels off his shirt, slapping his lean, sinewy chest. "Already got it on."

Laughing, I shake my head. "Go ahead. Skinny dip if you dare. But I have one word for you: paparazzi."

"What? Come on, Brie . . ."

"Nothing doing. Trust me, it's not a risk worth taking."

Smiling, he grabs his shirt, flopping it over his shoulder. "Guess you're right. Too much public exposure is . . . too much public exposure." He wraps me close and walks me inside. "Let's take this conversation upstairs."

6

"I love baseball. To me, it stands for everything great about summertime, our country, and our history. There's nothing like the crack of a wood bat."

—Aubrey James, The Tennessean, on her participation in the Sandlotter Fund-raiser

Midmorning Monday, Piper and I huddle up in her office off the great room and go over my schedule, making adjustments, canceling what we can so I can rest in between *Inside NashVegas* sessions, making sure we note the appearances I don't want to cancel.

"*Inside NashVegas* segments are going to be more like a video biography," Piper says. "But they do want to do a couple of planned segments to capture you in everyday life, the things you do around here when you're not on the road."

"Like what? Me watching you work is pretty boring TV."

She laughs. "They mentioned a cooking segment."

"What? Did you tell them?"

She shuffles through a neat stack of papers. "No." Her voice is barely audible.

"Piper, tell them. I don't cook."

"Watching you cook would be hilarious TV." She gets up to fax some papers. "Are you okay with this interview thing?"

I gaze out the window. "I am. Oddly enough. Feels like a journey of discovery."

"See, God is already turning Melanie's bad into *good*."

"Maybe." I let my devoted Baptist friend's comment glance off me.

"Maybe? One of these days you should stop and let God catch you."

With my chin in my hand, I mutter, "Maybe."

"Final thing on your summer schedule, Aubrey, the Coming Home Gospel Celebration at the Ryman with Ralph Lester and his band, plus a half dozen gospel singers. This is the one where they're doing a tribute to your parents. We gave them a tentative yes last spring."

I hear the clicking of her keyboard. Outside the window, the sky is perfectly blue. Cloudless. "What do you think?"

"It's up to you. This is the fifth tribute to your parents you've been invited to do. Turned them all down before."

"It just feels awkward, you know?" A redbird flits past and lands on the low branches of a nearby maple. "My life isn't very *gospel* these days."

Behind me, Piper's sigh causes me to glance around. Her thin, black-rimmed glasses ride low on her slender nose. "You can change your life anytime . . ." She stops, holding up her palms. "Never mind. No sermons. Do this for your parents, if you want; otherwise, don't."

I hesitate for a second. "When is the event?"

"August sixth."

"I'll do it. Find out the rehearsal schedule. Do I need to bring my band, or am I singing with Ralph's?" I turn back to the window as the redbird spreads its wings and launches from the branch into the sunlight. *I wonder what it would be like to fly.*

"That I know—Ralph's."

"Fine, I won't have to assemble the band after giving them the summer off. The Sandlott gig is their last performance until the fall."

"Ladies, top o' the morning to ya."

Zach strolls from the foyer into the great room, his fake Irish lilt barely audible amid his strong southern drawl.

"Top o' the morning?" I repeat with a laugh. "Zach, ten thirty hardly qualifies for top of the morning."

Piper closes out my schedule, and I head to the kitchen. The sweet cinnamon scent of Gina's homemade breakfast buns has been teasing my senses all morning.

Zach meets me at the island counter, picking up a plate and fork with his eye on the cinnamon buns, though his fork is poised over the pineapple and strawberries. "I've got some news for you."

"Ami's pregnant." I pick up a plate and do not hesitate to tear away a cinnamony bun.

Zach ha-has with a shake of his head. "I wish." Married three months, thirty-eight-year-old Zach claims *his* biological clock is clanging like a four-alarm fire. "You have a meeting with Nathan Brack, your new, charming, wonderful label president." He stabs a bun with his fork and drops it to his plate.

Jerking open the refrigerator for a Diet Coke—need something fizzy—I roll my eyes with an exaggerated sigh. "What for?"

Zach reaches around me for a bottle of FRESH! "To get reacquainted, I reckon."

"Should I enter with, 'Are you still a jerk?'"

Zach scowls. "Aubrey . . ."

Piper joins us in the kitchen. "You're three months late with your next album. I'm sure Nathan will mention it."

"Because we were renegotiating money with Greg," I counter, pouring my soda into a glass of ice.

Zach cuts a bite of his cinnamon bun. "Greg Leininger put SongTunes so far in the red BMG doesn't know if they can pull it out."

"How?" Piper demands. "Look at all the top artists he's signed. Greats like Emma Rice, Aubrey, Paul Kirkland. Mallory Clark—she's new, but her first album went platinum."

"Greg was the artists' friend," I say.

"Right," Zach says. "So much so he wasn't BMG's friend. Can't say as I blame them for bringing in Nathan Brack."

I swallow my Diet Coke with a cough. "Blame them? The man is all about himself, Zach. His way or the highway."

My manager shoots me a warning look. "Better get over it; he's calling the shots."

My legs quiver a little. "Zach, what will this to do my renegotiations with SongTunes?"

He swigs from his water. "Well, that's the thing."

I slide over next to him. "Zach, what's the thing?"

"He's playing hardball, Aubrey."

"I shouldn't be surprised."

"Is he calling off her renegotiation?" Piper asks, her voice moderated.

"Worse. If Aubrey doesn't deliver her next album by the end of summer, he's going to sue."

"Sue?" A string of blue words fly out of my mouth. "Cretin. I told you, he's a cretin." I kick the service cart.

Zach gently grabs my arm. "Simmer down, Aubrey. We can open up renegotiations in due time. But let's tap dance a few rounds with Nathan, hear what he has to say, give a little."

"Give a little?" I look at Piper. "Finally, he's lost his last marble." Give a little. I'm sure money from my last album bought several of the SongTunes execs new Mercedes last year.

"You have a meeting with SongTunes July third, three o'clock."

Piper retrieves her Palm from her desk. "Three o'clock . . . on the third."

"Do we have an agenda?" I ask. "Or is this just tea and cakes?"

"Let's go and find out what Nathan has to say. I've called your lawyer. She'll be there too."

The bang of french doors swinging wide interrupts us. George and Ringo bound in with their pink tongues dangling. Gina collapses against the door, huffing and puffing, the ends of her short, dyed-red hair perpendicular to her head. Her pink tongue also dangles.

"Saw a rabbit . . . Took off like a shot . . . Pulled my arm right out of the socket . . ." She bends forward, gripping her waist. "Ran . . . home . . . all . . . the way."

Laughing, I drop to the floor. "Did you guys wear out Gina?" George presses his face against my arm while Ringo leans his weight against my leg.

"Too . . . old for . . . this." Gina kicks out a stool and plops down. Even huffing and puffing, her blue eyes shine from her oval face.

She's a longtime friend of Connie's, in her midfifties, married but childless. And one of the jewels of my life. Don't know what I'd do without her.

"Young at heart, old in body, eh, Gina?" I snicker, snatching up the dogs' water dish and refilling it at the sink.

"Watch it now, sweet stuff. Fifty's gunning for you too." Gina's weariness is negated by the teasing lilt in her voice.

"Did you boys see a rabbit?" George lifts his head, water dripping from his mouth. I sit next to him on the floor, scratching behind his ears while reaching over to pat Ringo's back. I laugh when he gives me a very slobbery kiss.

"You're taking them out tomorrow." Gina wags her finger at me.

"We'll see. Last time I did, photographers followed me home."

"Hey, Piper, turn that up." Zach motions to the TV. "What's Kelly Sutton saying?"

From my spot on the floor, I stretch to see the TV as Piper aims the remote. If Beth Rose hadn't been so persistent over the years about interviewing me, I'd have given my story to Kelly Sutton of *Tennessee Morning*. We've socialized at various parties and album launchings—got along fabulously. We have the same sense of humor.

". . . the saga with Aubrey James's former musical director, Melanie Daniels, continues. Yesterday, Daniels accused the country superstar in her blog, *Life with a Diva,* of plotting to ruin her career by blocking her deal with SongTunes and reneging on a promise to let Daniels produce her last album." Kelly turns to her cohost, Charlie Chase. "Seems Aubrey James can't keep out of the news these days."

"Melanie's crazy." I get up off the floor. Piper, Zach, sweaty Gina, and I gather around the leather sofa, eyes glued to the TV. "She has a blog called *Life with a Diva?*"

"Did you read any of Melanie's blogs?" Charlie Chase asks, stacking the pages of his script. "Pretty interesting stuff. Lots of behind-the-scene pictures, stories. Even more than reported in the tabloids."

"What blog?" I wail.

Zach presses his finger to his lips. "Shh . . . Listen."

Kelly's talking. "I know Aubrey James, and I'm not sure Melanie is being fair."

Charlie tips his head to one side. "Well, a lot of folks are checking out her blog."

Hot mingles with cold, so I perspire and shiver. "How can she blog about me? She doesn't work for me anymore."

"Piper, check it out." Zach holds his plate under his chin for another bite of his breakfast bun. "She's going to milk it for all she can, Aubrey."

Piper surfs over to the *Life with a Diva* blog. I start to read . . . and gasp.

"She's evil." Piper minimizes the screen immediately.

"Wait, I didn't get to read any of it." Zach brushes crumbs from the corner of his lips.

"You don't want to see." Humiliation burns my cheeks.

"Yes, I do." Zach reaches around Piper for the mouse.

She covers his hands with hers. "No, you don't."

Gina shakes her head. "To think I served that girl my slow-roasted prime rib right here in your dining room."

Shoving Piper out of her chair, I tell Zach to step aside so I can read

Melanie's blog. As I scan her words, the prickly sensation of dread creeps over me. "She told the most intimate details of my life. About me and Jack. Derek. And Car." With a moan, I rest my forehead to the edge of the desk. "Even stuff I told her about Music Row and some of the other artists."

Gossip kills.

Zach sets his empty plate on the desk. "What were you thinking? Telling Melanie all this stuff?"

I lift my head. "Zach, she was a friend. We toured together for four years. We had a bazillion conversations." I gesture toward the scene. "Obviously she planned to blog from the beginning of the FRESH! tour."

Tears form in my eyes and I shove away from the desk. "I'm used to the lies and ugly photos in the tabloids, but not a firsthand betrayal by a friend. I didn't even know SongTunes was courting her. How could I interfere? And we never talked about her producing for me."

Piper squeezes my shoulder. "She lost sight of your friendship, that's all."

I glance at her. "What friendship?"

7

Scott

Tuesday, July 3

Parking my Porsche behind the Inside NashVegas van, I scan through my BlackBerry, reviewing the schedule one last time.

July 3rd—First sit-down, 10:00a–noon

July 4th—Music City Park concert, second sit-down (Was going to be there anyway.)

July 10th—Outdoor summer cooking segment, 11:00a–until ?

July 12th—Third sit-down, 10:00a–noon

July 19th—TBA (Planned segment)

July 24th—Fourth sit-down, 10:00a–noon

July 31st—Recording studio, songwriting segment

August 6th—Coming Home Gospel Celebration at the Ryman, 5:00p

I walk the arched driveway to the long, redbrick veranda, taking in the surroundings of a diva. Maple, oak, and elm trees shade the brick Belle Meade home. *Very nice diva digs. Not shabby at all.* Behind me, the sloping, green lawn is contained by a low stone wall.

Though my downtown Bennie Dillon loft is small and modest in comparison, it serves my purposes. Close to work, close to food, and close to sports.

Most important, no yard. If I had a dollar for every yard I mowed in my teen years—all the widowed women of the family and me the only teen boy—I'd be a rich man.

Taking the front porch steps two at a time, I loosen my tie while pausing at the front door.

You can do this. Just ring the bell and—

Rafe, my cameraman, swings open the door. "What're you doing? Get inside. Sam's neck is getting red."

In the next beat, my cell phone rings. It's Sam. "Get in here."

The diva's foyer is half as wide and half as deep as my loft. The high, sculpted ceiling arches over plain white walls, yet the floor is a fancy Italian marble. On my right, a curved staircase winds up to the second story, and on my left, a doorway leads to a formal living room.

While the surroundings are elegant, the ambiance feels sort of sterile. Very unlike the Aubrey James I met a year ago.

Rafe motions for me to follow. "We're in the great room. Aubrey gave us permission to leave the equipment set up until we're done. Nice place, huh?"

I fix my tie. "I wouldn't expect anything less, Rafe."

He leans toward me. At six-four, "Lurch" makes my six-one seem small. "Have you ever seen her up close?"

"Once, twice, maybe."

He flicks his hand like he's touched something hot. "Shew-wee, she's gorgeous. Don't believe I've ever seen a more beautiful woman. But if you tell my wife . . . I'll deny it all."

I slap Rafe on the back. "Your secret is safe with me."

On the other side, I find Olivia scurrying around with a clipboard and tight expression while Sam talks with Zach Roberts. "Scott, you know Zach."

"I do." We shake hands.

"And this is Aubrey's assistant, Piper Cantwell."

A pretty woman with long, dark hair swept up in a loose ponytail offers her hand. "Nice to meet you."

"You too." Ducking into their inner circle, I ask, "She knows I'm coming, right? Not Beth."

"Well—" Olivia starts.

Sam puffs out his chest and bellows, "What does it matter?"

Zach addresses me by tipping up his chin. "Seems in all the shuffle, Olivia forgot to tell us about Beth. But it's fine. Certainly Aubrey will understand Beth's situation. And since Olivia just found out yesterday . . ."

I peek at Olivia. *Yesterday.*

She walks around behind me, her heels clicking against the same Italian marble that's in the foyer. "Be cool, be cool," she mutters into my neck.

This is not good. Aubrey's going to flip her Dolly Parton wig. I've got to warn them. "Listen, everyone, I—"

"What is he doing here?"

They all turn—Sam, Olivia, Zach, and Piper. The diva has entered the room. *Here it comes.*

Zach pops a smile and walks over to her, arms wide. "Scott's doing the interview, Aubrey. Did you know Beth Rose is pregnant? Her doctor put her on complete bed rest."

"No, I didn't know." Her ocean-blue eyes focus on Olivia. They are soulful and concerned. "She and the baby are all right?"

"They're both fine, but she just needs to stay in bed."

Aubrey motions to her assistant. "Pipe, send her something from me, please."

"Already made a note."

Hanging on to my cool, I try not to gawk like a schoolboy, but I'd forgotten how beautiful she is in person. Photographs don't do her justice. Smooth, symmetrical features. Long, thick chestnut hair. Yet, something about her beauty goes beyond what the human eye can see.

However, right now I see she's angry. Big surprise. Zach is off to the side talking with her, hands in motion. Then, with a sharp glance at me, Aubrey walks out.

"Aubrey . . ." Zach goes after her.

Sam claps his hand on my shoulder. "Vaughn, what'd you do?"

I peer down at him. "We met once. It didn't go . . . *ahem* . . . well."

He pokes me in the chest. "Fix this. We lose this interview, you can go straight to the office and clean the toys out of your bottom desk drawer."

Olivia stands by me, her way of showing solidarity, but I shoot her a look. This is her snafu. She should've let Zach and Aubrey know Beth had a pinch hitter.

A nervous knot forms in my middle as I follow the muffled voices of behind-closed-doors arguing down a thick-carpeted hallway. Stopping in front of a wide mahogany door, I knock once. Gently. "Aubrey, can I talk to you?"

The voices stop. After a second, the door opens, and Zach motions for me to go in as he steps into the hall. He turns to Aubrey. "You gave your word. Signed a contract."

"I heard you the first time."

He regards me for a moment. "I don't know what you did, but own it, say you're sorry, and let's move on."

Aubrey stands by a window on the other side of the room, half in the sun, half in the shade. On my right is a beautiful dark-wood baby grand and a row of guitars perched on stands. Plaques, pictures, platinum records, awards of all kinds hang on the wall to my left.

"This must be the music room."

"And you must be Einstein."

"My mother likes to think so." I chuckle. "But you know mothers. Always dreaming big for their—"

She's not smiling, or laughing. Stuffing my hands into my pockets, I walk the length of the wall, feeling chilled from the iceberg of emotion between us. "Amazing. So many accomplishments."

She doesn't answer, but I smile at her over my shoulder. *Come on, melt, you coldhearted—*

Stop. Not fair. I'm the coldhearted one. "Aubrey, I owe you an apology. Long overdue. I'm sorry."

"For what?" Her expression is innocent, but her tone sarcastic.

Ducking my head, I laugh. "Guess I deserve that." Leaning against the piano, I look up at her. "I'm sorry I left the party without telling you. I'm sorry I didn't call."

"Do you know how humiliating it was for me to walk around a party of *your* friends asking, 'Where's Scott? Have you seen Scott?'"

"Incredibly rude and selfish of me." Disgusted, I shake my head, embarrassed by my actions. "I assumed you'd be okay."

"Never, ever assume, Vaughn." Aubrey folds her arms and leans against the other side of the piano. Her chestnut hair falls over her shoulders in lazy, not-quite curls. "Did you meet someone else?" Her piercing blue-green eyes make my heart thunder.

"No, no." I wave my hands. "Something came up. That's all."

"At midnight?"

"It's complicated. A personal issue of mine at the time. You—you were perfect, charming and beautiful. I had a great time." Thus, the root of my problem.

She regards me as if trying to determine if I'm lying or just wimping out.

I motion to the wall. "Five albums, five platinums."

"He can count."

I glance at her, supposing she's earned the right to fire potshots.

Beside the platinum records, the wall is adorned with awards from all the music associations—Academy of Country Music, American Music Awards, Grammys. All but the Country Music Association. If we survive today, I'd like to ask her about it.

The adjacent wall is covered with pictures of Aubrey's beautiful, beaming face, her arms around every great name alive on Music Row. Vince Gill, Amy Grant, Dolly Parton, Richard Leigh, Dan Huff, Keith Urban, Toby Keith, Brooks and Dunn, Faith Hill and Tim McGraw, Martina McBride and her family, her good friend Emma Rice, her longtime producer David Whitestone, and former SongTunes president Greg Leininger.

On the adjacent wall are awards and gold records from the Gospel Music Association, a tribute to her famous parents, Ray and Myra James.

"Your parents were pioneers in Christian music."

"Is the interview starting?"

"I grew up listening to their records." I motion to the row of eight guitars. "Is there a story behind these?"

"My dad owned seven of them. The one on the far right was given to me by songwriter Danny Hayes years ago."

Acknowledging with a nod, I walk over to her and into the fragrance of her perfume. "Please believe me when I say I'm sorry. I can't change the past, Aubrey. I would if I could. Can you forgive me and do this interview? For both our sakes?"

She steps around me. "Let's get it over with."

With the script rolled up in my hand, I sit in the club chair, ready to get started. Poised and perfect, Aubrey sits across from me in the leather wingback.

One camera focuses on Aubrey, the other on me. Rafe will also film with the portable DV, moving in and around us, capturing different angles, light, and depth.

Olivia is talking to Zach. Sam, thank goodness, left for a meeting.

Rafe indicates he's ready for me to cut my first teaser. I sit straight, adjust my tie, and clear my throat. Aubrey makes me nervous.

"Three, two, one . . . Hi, everyone. Scott Vaughn for *Inside NashVegas*, in the home of Aubrey James. Join *Inside the Music* Monday mornings this fall for our exclusive interview with Aubrey James, the queen of country soul."

"Got it," Rafe says.

I face Aubrey. "Ready?"

"Whenever you are." She looks confident though her hands are clasped and white-knuckled in her lap. After my apology, she softened, but it's unsettling that our personal business is not finished.

Standing, I address the room, pointing my rolled-up script at Aubrey. "Can we have a private moment, please?"

"S-sure." Olivia shoots a quick glance at Zach, then Aubrey. "If it's okay with you."

For a split second the diva looks as if she's going to refuse, but she answers with a smile. "Fine by me."

In a few moments, we're alone. Taking my seat, I lean toward her, crumpling the script in my hand, not quite sure how to speak my heart.

"What do you want, Scott?"

"Well, I knew a moment ago, but, um—"

"You're a journalist. Say it."

I look her in the eyes so she knows I'm serious. "This is your first big interview, and despite what happened last year between the two of us—

"Which I'm still curious about. What exactly did happen, Scott?"

"Trust me, the details would bore you. But I want this interview to go well for you and *Inside NashVegas*. Let's have fun. Are we cool?"

Aubrey thinks for a second. "Only if you're willing to tell me what happened."

"Are you two ready?" Olivia bounds around the corner, using her cheery voice and tapping her watch. "We're burning up time here."

I slide back in my chair. "Olivia's right. We should get going on the interview."

"Don't think you're going to get off this easy."

I grin. "Believe me, I don't."

8

"Aubrey James is an amazing singer, entertainer, and songwriter. I wish she'd record her own stuff. Be bold, Aubrey. Don't let the Big Dogs run you down."

—*Country recording artist Emma Rice*

Scott: *The final night of the CMA Fest, you fainted. What happened?*

AJ: Exhaustion. Took the big diva dive. The FRESH! tour drained me. In between shows, I filmed a commercial for FRESH!, had photo shoots. Plus, we did a hundred cities in six months.

Scott: *Based on Melanie Daniels'* Star *interview, you guys had a lot of drama going on. What happened between you and Melanie?*

AJ: Wow, starting off with the loaded questions. [shifting in her seat] Melanie came to work for me as my musical director four years ago. She took care of my band on and off the road and worked with me on my last three albums. She helped pull together the all-girl band.

Melanie is a great musician and brought a lot of new ideas to my team. I felt lucky to have her, and we became good friends. At least I thought we were friends. I certainly shared enough of my life and heart with her.

About a year and a half ago, a new man came into her life, and suddenly she started demanding more. More money, more influence. She wanted to be included in all my major musical decisions, right down to designing the tour show.

Scott: *What about her claim you hindered her career?*

AJ: Not true. I didn't even know she was talking a record deal with SongTunes.

Scott: *You fired her in the middle of the tour. Why?*

AJ: We'd been at odds before the tour started. While I valued her immensely, and honestly felt she deserved some of what she was asking for, her attitude was one of "You owe me." No matter what we offered, she felt it wasn't good enough. We argued a lot last year. It got very tense and heated between us. In fact, right before we started rehearsal for the tour, I wasn't sure if she would be on board as my musical director. She didn't return our calls, and we heard rumors she was bad-mouthing me on Music Row. Then one day she showed up, guitars in hand, as if nothing had ever happened. She was warm, fun, pleasant, eager to get to work.

Scott: *Didn't you think that was odd?*

AJ: For a musician, no. [grinning]

Scott: *I see. What were her reasons for disappearing?*

AJ: She said she needed to get her head together. She had taken time to hike the Appalachian Trail with her brother and then visited family in Florida.

Scott: *She seemed like the old Melanie to you?*

AJ: Yes. Sometimes she seemed subdued and distracted. Her temper was short, but it never crossed my mind she was making mental notes for a future blog or planning to diss me in the international press.

Scott: *She blogged, "Aubrey James is only about herself. Our drummer was having personal issues, but Aubrey would not even listen to her story. She sucks the life right out of a person. No matter how long the road, how hard we worked, she demanded that much more and never gave in return."*

AJ: I guess I did drive the band hard. First of all, we were an all-new, all-female band and had our share of Music Row skeptics. Second, we'd forged a huge deal with FRESH!, a young company trying to build an image. I believed we should be beyond excellent. For ourselves, our sponsor, the music industry, and really for women in our industry.

Scott: *[smiling] Pretty big burden for one female band to carry.*

AJ: [laughing] Are you kidding me? Between my bassist, Vickie, and Melanie I had two of the best musicians in town. Besides, I didn't ask anything of them I didn't ask of myself. I worked hard knowing what we could achieve. And we did it.

Scott: *You wore yourself out.*

AJ: True, but looking back, it was worth it.

Scott: *Besides keeping a blog of the FRESH! tour, Melanie sold her story about you to* Star *and to a British tabloid. Tell me about your response to this and why you think she took such a drastic step?*

AJ: My response? Hum . . . Hurt. Blindsided. Very surprised. Since the beginning of my career, I made it a point to stay out of the public eye as much as possible, which made me a huge curiosity for the media, especially the tabloids. She knew how much my privacy meant to me.

Scott: *Why'd you work so hard to stay out of the public eye?*

AJ: [shrugging] Mainly to keep some perspective on my life. Not mix up the private Aubrey James with the public one. She *can* be a demanding diva. Aubrey James the private person can't.

But in my innocence-of-youth, I became involved with characters like Jack Mills and Derek Crammer, and found myself the target of tabloids. Embarrassed, I hid. But the more I hid, the more they printed. Most of it lies and speculation with just enough truth to make it annoying. But to answer your questions as to why Melanie took such a drastic step? Fifty thousand dollars.

Scott: *You think she did it for the money? Fifty thousand isn't a lot, really.*

AJ: To me it is. The price of my privacy. But money matters a lot to Mel, and to her boyfriend, Bo. She grew up really poor and worked hard to get through college. Looking back, a lot of our arguments were over money and how she felt it all came so easily for me. In reality, she's a way better musician and singer. She's trained and educated. But I was the one with my name in lights.

Scott: *Have you talked to her since the* Star *interview?*

AJ: No, but I'd like to eventually. She *was* a friend and I'm angry about what she did, but I'd like to hear her side. I know all stories have two sides. All relationships have two points of view.

Scott: *This was what? Your tenth tour?*

AJ: Eleventh.

Scott: *With your first album you toured with Garth Brooks. What was that like?*

AJ: [smiling] Amazing. I mean, Garth Brooks. [laughing] Holy cow. He's an incredible entertainer, a generous heart, and he taught me so much about performing. He's a natural. I, on the other hand, preferred to just get up onstage, stand like a statue in the spotlight, and belt out a song. I had to learn how to engage the crowd, move around, perform, entertain. No matter how talented an artist is vocally or musically, being a performer is what separates the men from the boys, women from the girls.

Scott: *How'd you get hooked up with Garth Brooks?*

AJ: Luck. God. The brilliant mind of Connie Godwin, my adopted mom, who managed me when I first started with Mountain Music in '95. She decided I should tour with Garth and sent him my first CD, asking him to consider me for a touring partner. He did.

Scott: *You opened for him?*

AJ: No, actually, he opened for me. [laughing] Of *course* I opened for him. But, toward the end of the show, he always invited me back out to sing a few cover numbers with him.

Scott: *Glad to see your sense of humor surface.*

AJ: Contrary to popular belief.

Scott: *All righty, then, moving on. Your parents were cutting-edge gospel singers for their day. What did you learn from them about music and performing?*

AJ: [drawing a deep breath] More hard questions. I haven't talked about them in a long time. [eyes glistening] Yes, my parents were cutting edge for their day. My father was a prolific songwriter. Growing up, we had all kinds of music in the house—old-time gospel, Motown, '60s rock and roll, '70s pop, country, classical. I loved Daddy's *Bread* album because they had a song called "Aubrey."

Scott: *I know the song. Did it inspire your name?*

AJ: My heart says yes. I always meant to ask them about it, but . . . [her voice trailing off] Anyway, Daddy hung out with guys like Keith Green and Michael W. Smith. They were very passionate about their message, but doing it with musical excellence. He wanted to incorporate different sounds and rhythms into his songs.

Scott: *Was he a performer?*

AJ: A little, but Christian audiences are very different from, say, a rock audience or a country audience, especially in the '80s. They attend concerts to be lifted up or touched by God in some way. To worship. Entertainment was secondary.

From my parents . . . [hesitating, pressing her hand over her eyes for a second] From my parents, I learned how to give my all for every concert. No matter how big or small, the audience deserves my whole heart.

I remember one summer when my brother, Peter, and I traveled with them, we got to this one dinky, tiny church in the middle of Texas. Our booking agent told us it was a big Baptist church, but it turned out to be an *old* Baptist congregation and, like, five people showed up. But we gave them our best show.

[pausing, smiling softly, then shifting her glassy gaze] Daddy used to say we're all only playing for an audience of One anyway.

Scott: Jesus?

AJ: You've heard the saying?

Scott: Yes, from a friend of mine, Shawn Bolz, pastor at Faith Community Church.

AJ: I know Shawn. He was my pastor, too, years ago.

Scott: Tell us about the FRESH! sponsorship. How'd you pair with a bottled water company?

AJ: [pointing to Zach] My genius manager. It was his idea. He called my lawyer, Skyler Banks, and my business manager, Eli Davenport, and pitched the idea of finding a sponsor.

More and more artists are partnering with corporate sponsors. We wanted something different. Not typical country products like trucks or beer, boots or hats. Zach suggested FRESH!. We kept a cooler of FRESH! on stage for every concert. Gave away bottles before and after the show. It was a great partnership. Still is.

Scott: Then it was your idea to pull together an all-girl band.

AJ: Yes, my genius contribution to the project. [laughing] After a bunch of years on the road with guys, I wanted to eliminate the hassle of groupies. I mean, how do you look a guy's wife in the face when you know he's shagged a girl or two along the way?"

Scott: Can't be easy.

AJ: It's horrible. Touring has a way of lulling a person to sleep. Week after week, traveling from city to city, it's easy to find yourself in this surreal world of sleeping by day and performing by night. Makes a person feel disconnected from real life. Sociologists should study the social ramifications of a touring band. They'd get all kinds of goodies. It comes with its own set of rules and moral code, and if you're not careful, it can be as if home and hearth never existed. All your values and standards get suspended in this I'm-on-the-road mentality.

The girl band was my dream team. Vickie and Melanie were already with me, so we added a female drummer, Keeta, and keyboarder slash fiddler and steel guitar player Laura. Keeta introduced us to Alexa, who added so much to the percussion sound we love.

In my insane, warped little mind, I imagined a bunch of women on tour would be like a rolling slumber party.

Scott: [laughing] Sounds good.

AJ: Not so much. It started out fun, then PMS hit and we had it for six months. Good grief. I felt sorry for the few men on the tour—my tour manager, my bodyguard, and the roadies. There were days my rolling slumber party was more like a rolling petri dish spawning hormonal, emotional breakdowns.

Scott: Care to share specifics?

AJ: Well, there's the story Melanie referenced about our drummer.

And I just want to add that the band has backed me with this Melanie thing, and I'm grateful.

Anyway, our drummer, Keeta, was having personal issues. We were about to go on at the sold-out St. Petersburg Forum when the production manager whispered, 'Keeta is in the bathroom, crying into her cell, breaking up with her boyfriend.' Keeta is a fabulous musician and performer, but her love life is a train wreck.

The house lights were going down, and the crowd was gearing up, getting loud with excitement. But still no Keeta. I whispered a "blue" word to the production manager. "Tell her to get her [bleep] out here before she's fired."

Meanwhile, the sound engineer was looping a prerecorded intro over and over, and the fans got ansty, stomping their feet, whistling, hooting. I don't know if you've ever faced an angry mob, but it's very scary.

Then, all of a sudden, the music kicked. My heart flew out of my chest. I bet I lurched forward a good two or three feet. Keeta had found her way to the stage, and she took out her heartache on the drums. She gave her best performance all tour.

Scott: *What's your take away from this tour? I, Aubrey James, learned . . .*

AJ: [laughing] Too many lessons to name. [thinking] Here you go. A lesson for the ages: I, Aubrey James, learned women communicate on seventeen different levels, and for the first time in my thirty years, I feel genuine compassion for the male species. We put you guys through some crap, but all I can say is I'm sorry, there's no cure in sight, just love us.

Scott: *[chuckling] Rafe, did you get the apology? It has to make the cut.*

AJ: Please air it. It's true. It's downright frightening how women communicate.

Scott: *So the tour wasn't a big sisterly, woman-rule-men-drool slumber party?*

AJ: No. Women are amazing creatures, but I'm certainly glad God created men.

Scott: *Makes two of us.*

Glancing at the script, I try to find the next set of questions, realizing we left the planned conversation after page one. Peeking around the room, Olivia gives me the thumbs-up. Let's see . . .

Scott: *You're one of the most successful country artists of the past decade, and one of the most photographed women in the world.* US, People, National Inquirer, The Globe, Country Weekly, Hello, Daily Mirror, *newspapers, magazines, tabloids across Europe, Australia, Canada, Brazil, Mexico, Japan . . . I could go on.*

AJ: Are you telling me or asking me?

Scott: *Recounting a fact. How does this sort of stat impact you?*

AJ: I can't win a CMA, but the Most Photographed Woman honors, I win. [laughing] When I go into Harris Teeter, which isn't all that often, I autograph the tabloids by the checkout counter. I'm usually on two or three covers.

Scott: *Good for you. So you see this as a necessary evil and have fun with it.*

AJ: Is any evil necessary? [looks down and brushes an imaginary piece of lint from her jeans] I certainly don't take the tabloids seriously. Except when my so-called friends dish on me.

Frankly, I'm astounded by this whole paparazzi thing. I'm a country singer, Aubrey James, born and raised on the other side of town. How can I be one of the most photographed women in the world?

Scott: *You're beautiful and mysterious. Your European fan club is the second largest fan club in the world, behind Bono and U2.*

AJ: Now that's incredible. [glancing at Piper] Did you know this? I love my fans. They are the reason I tour every year. But the rest of this is a mystery. Right up there with who shot JFK, you know? I have no idea why the press follows me. Actually, I think whenever my neighbors need beer money, they camp outside my house and wait for me to come out.

Scott: *Well, beer money is important.*

AJ: Naturally. My privacy is worth the price of a six pack.

Scott: *[smiling] Okay, next fact. Five times you've made* People's *Most Beautiful list. Twice on the cover. Do you look at your reflection in the mirror and think, "I'm* People *magazine's Most Beautiful?"*

AJ: Good grief, Scott. No. And if I did I wouldn't confess it to you.

Scott: *Hey, just trying to get the* Inside *story.*

AJ: To be honest—and this is from right here [patting her stomach]—I get up in the morning and wonder why I can't find the dental floss.

Scott: *[laughing] Now that would be annoying.*

AJ: Priorities are so skewed in this world. Two-thirds of the population wakes up hungry on a daily basis, and *People* magazine is worried about who's the Most Beautiful. It's ridiculous. There's probably women in the mountains of Peru who blow me away in terms of beauty, but we'll never know them.

Scott: *Then you're not honored.*

AJ: Of course, I'm *honored*. I'm not stupid. Who wouldn't be? However, it's not a part of my résumé.

For me, I can't help but notice a Grand Canyon-sized chasm between *People* and people. Impoverished citizens around the world sell their children into slavery for the equivalent of three hundred American dollars. Where's that story? Or all of the human rights abuse around the world. People in prison and tortured for their faith. Where's that story? We only like to wave our social justice flag when the issue is comfortable.

Scott: *Is the poor your passion? The tortured?*

AJ: Justice is my passion. It's a stupid passion, but there you go.

Scott: *Why is it a stupid passion?*

AJ: By whose scale is justice being doled out? Mine, yours, the liberals, the conservatives? It's not an exact science. So, mostly I am passionate about the hypocrisy of the elite in our country who tell the middle class and the poor they aren't doing enough and to depend more and more on the government to take care of everything. It frightens me.

Scott: *You've obviously thought a lot about this.*

AJ: Touring does that to me. We see so many people, hear so many stories.

Scott: *Do I hear a future political candidate?*

AJ: No. Absolutely not. I can do more as a celebrity than as a politician because I don't have to play the games.

Scott: *You had another surprise, besides fainting, during CMA Fest. You became engaged.*

AJ: I did.

Scott: *Engaged to Brown "Car" Carmichael. Congratulations. Set a date yet?*

AJ: Not yet. But probably in the spring. He's busy with the SoBro development project downtown, and I'm tied up with this annoying interview thingy.

Scott: *[smiling] Right. It's all my fault. So, how'd you two meet?*

AJ: Right here in our little Belle Meade community. My assistant Piper and I were in Bread & Co. for lunch, and my order got mixed up with Car's. Really weird. We talked for few seconds, and I kept waiting for him to ask for my autograph, but he never did.

Piper and I left, came home to find my new furniture being delivered, and while we were watching the movers, Car drove by in his Humvee. He came back ten minutes later with an invitation to a barbecue with his parents. One year ago this month.

He was very charming, yet down to earth. Which for me and my romantic past was refreshing.

Scott: *And the rest, as they say, is history?*

AJ: And the rest, as they say, is history.

9

"I wish Melanie Daniels all the best in her endeavors."

—Aubrey James, press release response to Melanie Daniels' article

Aubrey

As Zach drives east down West End Avenue toward Music Row and the SongTunes offices, he peeks at me from the corner of his eye.

"Looks to me like somebody had a good time today." Zach brakes as a green light switches to yellow.

I smile, watching a woman with five little dogs on leashes cross in front of us. "I loved it." A trill escapes me. I slap my hand over my mouth.

Zach laughs. "What did you love about it?"

"Weird . . . everything. Even that boorish Scott Vaughn. He was professional, funny, sincere. It was exhilarating." I laugh. "What a *diva* thing to say, right? 'Loved talking about me.'"

"It's been a private goal of mine to get you sitting for an in-depth interview."

"Congratulations. You can die a happy man. You know, just expressing my heart over Melanie made me feel a gazillion times better. I'll go ahead and forgive her. What the heck." I flick my hand in the air.

"How magnanimous of you. Very Christian too." The light flashes to green.

"I didn't forget everything my parents taught me." Resting my elbow on the car door, I watch Nashville go by. "I am looking forward to tomorrow, and Thursday, talking with Scott."

"Good, good. Better than spending several days a week with someone you hate."

"I never said I hated him."

"What happened between you two, anyway?"

"We met once, last year. It didn't go well."

"But he apologized and now you're over it?"

"More or less."

Zach tips his head with a click of his tongue. "With all this forgiveness going on, we might start having church."

Laughing, I punch at him, missing his arm, batting only the air. "Maybe we will. And maybe, just maybe, I'll go to church this Sunday . . . or the next. One of these Sundays."

"Well, before lightening strikes, can I change the subject?"

"Go ahead." Looking out the window, I picture Scott Vaughn sitting across from me this morning. He was quite charming and . . .

"Are you sure?"

Turning to Zach, I watch as he shifts in his seat, adjusting his seat belt, then drumming his thumbs on the steering wheel. "About going to church? Why wouldn't—"

"No. About marrying Car." Zach slows his Lexus as another yellow light catches us.

"Oh." This explains his nervousness. Did I figure this question would come? If not from Zach, from Piper, or Connie. "Yeah, I'm sure. I mean, is anyone ever sure?"

"You've been down this road before with Jack and Derek."

"Exactly, and that's in Car's favor. He's nothing like them. He's normal, works a regular job in a downtown office. Wears a suit, plays golf to win business deals. The Carmichaels are a well-established Nashville family."

The red light is short, and we're on our way again. "In other words, he's safe."

"Zach, I'm ready to settle down, be a part of a family. I'm not getting any younger."

"Can I give you some advice your father might give if he were here?" he asks with a sideways glance. Zach never met Daddy, but this wouldn't be the first time he's advised me with Ray James wisdom. "Pray about it."

Tears pool in my eyes. I bat them away. "Daddy would've given that same advice."

"You pretend to be cut off from your religious roots, but I don't buy it." He swerves down Demonbreun toward Music Row East. "No matter how hard you fight it, I'm convinced you're still a gospel girl at heart." He parks on the street behind my lawyer Skyler Banks's car.

"It's been a long, long time, Zach." Unbuckling my seat belt, I let the nylon material slide between my fingers.

He jerks his keys from the ignition. "I'm not the most faithful person of prayer, either, but Aubrey, please. Marriage is serious business."

I study my hands, absently noting my fingernails are too long to play the guitar. "Maybe you don't understand, Zach, but sometimes the dream isn't a knight in shining armor, but a place to belong at Thanksgiving and Christmas, and on lazy summer nights."

"You have a place to go for Thanksgiving and Christmas. Ami and I—"

"It's not the same." Shaking my head, I search for the words to make him understand. "Like I'm always looking from the outside in. I'm the invited and even cherished guest, but I'm not family by blood or marriage." I look at him. "I want to be the one who looks at Car on a Sunday afternoon and says, 'Honey, call the folks. Let's barbecue.'"

Zach props his arm on the steering wheel. "Not that you've ever barbecued in your life, but I understand the dream. My question isn't the dream or the knight in shining armor, but which knight."

"At the moment, he's the only knight I know."

"Aubrey, Zach, come in, come in. Good to see you." Nathan Brack greets us at his office door with a practiced voice, holding out his arms as if hosting a reality reunion show. His angular face is lined from too much time in the sun, and his sporty grin is white and capped. When I reach him, he links his elbow with mine and escorts me the length of a gleaming conference table. A glass of ice and chilled bottle of FRESH! awaits me.

"Good to see everyone," Zach says, taking the chair next to mine, nodding to the SongTunes side of the table. Skyler Banks, my dear attorney, sits on the other side of Zach and looks amused.

Wonder what's up.

Smiling, I greet the SongTunes staff, their lawyer, Ian Carter, and the head of A&R, Aaron Littleton. For a few minutes the conversation around the table is casual—the great summer weather, May's ACM awards, the record number of fans attending June's CMA Fest, and speculation about the Titans football season.

At last, Nathan clears his throat and stands, his expression morphing from happy host to driven businessman. Under his piercing gaze, I shift in my seat, pour more FRESH! over my ice, and take a slow sip.

Nathan strolls behind his team on the other side of the table. "We're working on recasting our vision, redeveloping our objectives, putting SongTunes back on the map.

"When did SongTunes leave the map?" I ask. "You have five of the top artists in the business. Me, Emma Rice, Janie Leeds, Paul Kirkland. Never mind new artists like Mallory Clark."

Nathan stops at the other end of the table, propping his hands on the edge. "Aubrey, I need an album from you."

"Fine." I glance over at Ian. "Finish our renegotiation."

"Aubrey," Ian starts, shifting in his seat. "We—"

"The negotiations are off," Nathan interjects. "This company is in the red, and we're not giving any more money to artists already earning millions off of us."

I rocket to my feet. "What about the millions you earn off of the artist? Off of me, Nathan? What about the money you earn off my back catalog? Songs you put on compilations that sell so cheap I don't see any money."

Zach swivels toward Nathan with a glance at Ian. "Red bottom line or not, there's money being made from MP3 sales and back catalog, and Aubrey's not seeing any of that money." He motions to Ian. "We just went over all of this. You agreed."

Ian defers to Nathan. "We're putting renegotiations on hold until we see Aubrey's new project."

"The new project is on hold until I see the money," I say with fire.

Zach stands, holding his palm up in my direction. "Aubrey—"

"Zach, we're not putting the negotiations on hold. It's his way of stealing from me. I don't care if SongTunes is in the red." I glare at Nathan. "Which I find hard to believe."

"You see me standing here instead of Greg Leininger, don't you?"

"Doesn't mean anything," I say. "You probably went around telling lies about him."

"Aubrey." Now Skyler is on her feet. "Don't get personal."

"Aubrey," Nathan starts, "all I want is what's owed this company."

"And all I want is what's owed me."

Nathan crosses his arms and strolls my way. "Back to square one, are we?"

"Tell you what," Skyler interjects. "Aubrey will deliver an album by . . ."

"September first." Nathan fires the date as if he'd held it on the tip of his tongue.

"September first? That's two months away." Pressure forms at the crown of my head.

Skyler's expression begs me to calm down. "At which time, you'll agree to open renegotiations, correct?"

Nathan hesitates with a look at Ian. "Certainly, we'll consider it."

Skyler taps the table with her fingernails. "BMG would not be pleased if you held up a new Aubrey James release over a few back-catalog and MP3 dollars."

"Perhaps they would not be pleased if Aubrey held up several million dollars over a few back-catalog and MP3 pennies."

"Nathan," I begin, "I can't do an album in two months. Dave and I need to talk about our concept, go over the songs we have on hold. I want to go in a new direction. The last two albums have been the same old, same old. Me belting out songs. There was no craft, no art—"

Nathan interrupts with a hard laugh. "Don't spout your artistic-integrity mumbo-jumbo to me, Aubrey. Be a tortured Van Gogh, if you want, but give me Andy Warhol. Neat little everyday Campbell's soup cans. I want standard Aubrey James. It's too late to reinvent yourself and expect the customers to follow."

I study him for a moment. "Nathan, I have the best *fans* in the world. They will follow me. And for your information, I know this is a shocker, but music isn't always about the bottom line, branding, and marketing campaigns. Art can't be confined to black or red ink."

He tugs the crease of his slacks and sits in his high-back leather chair. Rocking back, he scans the room, stopping at each face. First his team, then mine.

At last, me.

"September first, Aubrey. And, don't come in here with a compilation you just threw together. I want platinum Aubrey James."

Out on the covered porch, watching Juan weed the garden, I sip from a glass of Gina's iced tea. The six o'clock air is hot and stifling. The twilight sky is cloudless, and I decide we could use some rain.

"Still thinking about the meeting?" Piper comes out and sits next to me, hugging her knees to her chest. Her bare toes curl over the edge of the wicker sofa's cushion.

"Yes, trying not to be angry."

"Right, sitting out here alone brooding will accomplish that."

I laugh.

"You smiled a lot today while talking with Scott."

"It was fun," I admit.

"See, we told you." She pats my leg playfully. "Scott's pretty cool, isn't he?"

Brushing her hand away, I shake my head with a snort. "If you like the arrogant jock type."

"What happened between you two? How come I never heard about it?"

Juan is crawling into the garden on his hands and knees, picking weeds and stuffing them into a burlap bag slung over his shoulder.

"Just another incident in the life of Aubrey James." I glance over at my friend of sixteen years. "Have I told you lately what a great friend and assistant you are? Thank you."

She squeezes my hand. "Then dish about Scott. Come on."

I situate myself sideways on the sofa, facing her. "We met last summer. On the Fourth of July. A year ago tomorrow. "

"At Music City Park?"

"Yes, at the concert. He was doing his first piece on the Sandlotters." I wipe the dew from my glass. "He strolled over with his cocky, I'm-a-jock-news-reporter swagger and introduced himself. He didn't even know who I was."

"You're kidding."

"Nope. After a few minutes he figured it out."

"I suppose that's sort of refreshing. He wanted to talk to you for you, not because you're famous. By the way, where was I during all of this?"

I shake my head, then remember. "You were on vacation last year, weren't you?"

"Oh yes, the family reunion from Oz. So, you met Scott Vaughn . . . fell in love, what?"

"No." I shove at her with my foot. "He invited me to a Fourth of July party down in Brentwood. One of his football buddies. Jeff Moore worked security for me all day, so he drove me to the party and waited. When I gave him the okay signal, he went home. You think I'd know better." Recounting the story creates a swirl of anxiety.

"What happened?"

"Scott and I were getting along fabulously. Too good. It seemed surreal, like one of those stories you hear old married couples talk about. 'We just clicked.'"

"So, you started feeling confident and jazzed."

I make a face. "Yep."

"You sang karaoke, didn't you?"

"Of course. And don't imply singing karaoke made Scott weird out. Something else bothered him that night."

"Did you sing your own song? You know when you do that it looks like you're showing off."

"What? No, it doesn't. They begged me to sing."

"Anyway . . ." She swirls her hand, urging me to continue.

"We were talking and laughing, enjoying the party, slow dancing." I still remember the feeling of his arm around me, the scent of his cologne, and the way he pressed his cheek against my hair.

"Then what went wrong?"

"I have no idea. He was going to tell me this morning, but Olivia interrupted. Thinking back, we got separated and ended up in different conversations, then the karaoke started. I never saw him again."

Piper shifts her position, curling her legs under her. "He just left?"

"Just left. I was stranded."

"So he didn't know Jeff dropped you off and went home."

"No, but so what? When is it ever okay to dart out on a date or on a friend without at least saying good-bye?" I stuff my hands under my crossed legs. "When I realized he was gone, terror gripped me. Alone, forty minutes from home, with a half-dozen drunk, defensive linemen."

"Did you ever tell him?"

"When would I? He never called. Today was the first time I'd seen him since that night."

"You should tell him," Piper decides. "The *whole* story."

"Maybe, if it comes up." The evening is warm. I comb back my hair with my fingers and pile it on top of my head. The breeze feels good on my neck. "What I really want to know is *why* he left. By the tone of his apology, I'm sure he didn't intentionally hurt me."

Piper stretches out her legs too. "I'm really proud of you."

"For what?" I laugh softly. "Forgiving Scott? Woo, what a gal I am." I punch the air with an awe-shucks fist.

She laughs. "Yes, and for doing the interview and the Coming Home celebration. About the third year of your career, you became very specific about what you would and wouldn't do. Aggravatingly so at times. But you're softening, considering new things. Even being willing to work with Nathan Brack again."

I stretch my arms along the back of the sofa and rest my head on the top of the cushion. "Don't be impressed about Nathan. I'm sticking with SongTunes because of my history with them. And, I *do* owe them an album. I've done a lot of stupid things in my day, but I want to be a woman of my word. If Daddy taught me anything, he taught me to be trustworthy. Nathan is just a kink in the works."

"Too bad Greg wasn't a better businessman."

"Greg was a frustrated artist who tried to fulfill his dreams by backing a no-talent artist like Shelby Hayward. It bit him in the butt. But Nathan? Only number one Billboard hits will do. Deliver or die. He doesn't care who he crushes."

"Maybe you should spread some forgiveness over Nathan's way."

I lift my head to peer at her. "I've forgiven him."

"Yes, the venom in your voice is proof."

I consider my relationship with Nathan. Have I forgiven him? He tried to hijack my career ten years ago when I was at Mountain Music. Wanted to turn me into Britney Spears with a twang. We fought constantly.

"Forgiveness isn't the issue, Piper. I don't trust him."

Juan finishes in the garden and gathers his tools. He stands back, hands on his hips, and surveys his work.

"Watch." I motion for Piper to look out back. "He's like an artist, but instead of oil and canvas, he paints with flowers and plants."

With his spade, Juan kneels on the ground by the south side of the garden and digs up a wilting plant. From my perch on the porch, the edges seem to be browning. Dirt falls around his feet as he cups the roots with his hand and gingerly walks to the north side of the garden where the shade is rich and thick. He stabs a fresh hole in the ground with the tip of his spade.

A peaceful silence lingers between Piper and me before she scoots off the sofa. "I've got to get going." She swings her hips as she heads for the French doors. "I've got a date."

Hooking my arm over the back of the sofa, I twist around. "Oh yeah?" I smile. "With who?"

"A guy I met on eHarmony. He's an accountant."

Piper's had a series of bad dates with supposedly good-hearted men. It confounds me that someone as beautiful, kind, intelligent, and witty as Piper hasn't found love.

I wrinkle my nose. "An accountant? Online? Really?"

"Yes, an accountant, and don't wrinkle your nose at me. Car's a glorified accountant."

I lift my hands in surrender. "Accountants are good. You've dated enough flakes and weirdos in the music business. A nice, solid, steady bean counter would be a lovely change."

"He seems really nice, and he likes sports. A must for me. So, he's not a total nerd. Goes to a Baptist church."

"He sounds very nice, but be careful, Piper, please. Maybe have Jeff check him out."

She laughs. "Sic your body guard on him? Scare him to death?"

"Good point." I point at her with eyes narrowed. "Don't tell him who you work for."

"Have I ever slipped up?"

"No, but humor me—" I fire off a test question. "What do you do for a living, Piper?"

"Life coach." Not a nanosecond of hesitation.

"Who are your clients?"

"Confidential information."

I give her a thumbs-up. "Perfect. Have fun."

She steps back over to me, grabs my face, and kisses the top of my head. "There, now I have some of your golden charm."

10

The house is way too quiet. I wander the great room wishing I'd made plans to go out or called Vickie to come over for a little jam session. Piper's office area is dark and quiet.

Hope her date is going well. Be nice, Accountant Man.

The kitchen clock tells me it's almost nine, and I'm a little tired, still recovering from the tour. Car's working late, working on his downtown SoBro development project. He asked me again to invest, and when I said no, we argued. I can't seem to make him understand.

George and Ringo hop up from where they were sleeping on the kitchen tile, stretching and yawning.

"What should we do tonight, boys?"

They wag their tails as if to say, "Whatever you want to do."

What do I want to do? I haven't had this much time to myself in quite a while. Guess I could make some popcorn and find a good movie on Lifetime or TMC.

Do I even have popcorn? Checking the pantry, I find the picnic basket I sent home with Juan. There's a note attached.

Gracias, Señorita James. Nos gustó mucho. Tu amiga, Alejandra.

How sweet. A thank-you from Juan's wife, *Your friend, Alejandra*. I set the basket on the counter and turn over Alejandra's note to write one of my own.

Gina, please go to Harris Teeter and fill the basket for Juan and his family. Thanks. XO, Aubrey.

Taping the note to the basket and leaving it on the counter, I resume my quest for popcorn. Can't find any—which kills my movie mood.

Clicking off the pantry light and closing the door behind me, I stare into the great room for a moment. This is my favorite part of the house—the open, flowing lines of the kitchen running into the family room. The high, vaulted ceilings and gleaming hardwood floors. The row of windows overlooking the back lawn and porch.

Gina decorated the great room area two summers ago with warm Tuscan colors. She claimed she couldn't take the starkness anymore.

A year later, Piper begged me to decorate the music room and ended up doing it all herself.

With George and Ringo on my heels, I wander out to the foyer where the ambiance changes—from inviting and serene to cold and stark. Gazing toward the crystal chandelier hanging down from the highest point of the ceiling, I wonder if I'll ever decorate.

"Let's go, boys." I head for the curved stairs, running my hand along the polished, dark-wood banister, listening to the quiet.

On the second-floor landing, I stare down the hall toward the closed library door. This is when I miss *them* the most. Daddy, Momma, and Peter. Wouldn't tonight have been the perfect time to call up and say, "I'm on my way over. Should I rent a movie?"

I try to picture myself calling up prim and proper Grace Carmichael, who is angry with me for declining her Fourth of July soiree, and announcing, "We're on our way over for the evening. See you in a few."

Can't imagine.

At the library door, I brush my fingers along the top of the frame for the key. The library—where all my treasures are stored—is dark and cool. Working my way through the maze of boxes and piles of stuff, I aim for Daddy's old writing desk and lamp, jamming my toe against the side of a box along the way. The dry cardboard crumbles.

Tugging on the lamp's chain, a soft light defeats the darkness.

Don't hide your light, Momma said.

The room is a mess of boxes, piles of clothes, *stuff* scattered helter-skelter over the plush burgundy carpet. The built-in bookcases are bare except for a thin layer of dust.

I fall onto the country sofa that was once Momma's prized possession. The night Daddy brought the new living room set home is a fond but dim memory. Burying my nose against the twenty-year-old fabric, I can still smell the mingling of Chanel N°5 and hot buttered popcorn.

On the other side of the couch, shoved up against the hand-carved cherry bookshelves, is Daddy's leather easy chair and old trunk. On the adjacent wall is Grandma's antique dresser, a plant stand Momma loved, and two oak end tables.

Tucking my arm under my head, I curl up and close my eyes, wishing for the old brown-and-yellow afghan Momma used to fold over the back of the couch. I'd stored it with a bunch of Daddy and Momma's things in Connie's basement, which flooded one monsoon spring and damaged my boxes and caked the afghan with silt.

We salvaged what we could—the photo albums, vinyl records, Daddy's office-supply box, and other mementoes. Clothes and such. But the afghan didn't make it. Connie and I tossed it ceremoniously on a small brush-and-debris fire we staged in her backyard.

A wave of sleep splashes over me. It feels good to exhale and drift off into dreamland. If Momma were here she'd stroke my hair and sing to me. I can't count the number of nights I fell asleep to her lullabies.

But Daddy—now he was a different singer around the house. He'd walk around before dinner with his guitar strapped to his chest making up songs about our evening activities.

There's my sweatheart, Myra / stirring up the fire / cooking vittles for me and the chillens.

Or a song about Peter poring over his homework.

There's my boy a-working hard / don't you know he's gonna be a star / look out Harvard, look out Yale / here comes a southern boy / from Tennessee / Peter.

Every time, Daddy would stop, ponder the ceiling, and mutter, "Should've named you Jesse. Rhymes with Tennessee."

I laugh softly. "I miss you all so much."

"Aubrey?" a cottony voice calls up the staircase. "Are you home?"

Connie? I slip off the couch and maneuver through the maze of boxed memories to the door. Scooting down the hall in my bare feet, I arrive at the rail and peer down into the foyer. "Who let you in?"

My adopted momma holds up her keys. "Let myself in."

"Come on up; I need some company."

Connie takes the stairs, her round hips rolling from side to side with each step. "Is Car working?"

"Yes. His SoBro projects keep him busy."

"How'd your interview with *Inside NashVegas* go today?" Connie lands at the top of the stairs and wraps her arms around me.

"Surprisingly well." Her skin smells like rose petals.

"And your meeting with Nathan Brack?"

I stand back with a curl on my lip. "He's being a hardnose. Stopped our renegotiation, wants his album by the first of September."

Connie follows me into the library. "You're going to give him an album, right? Honor your contract?"

I look over my shoulder at her. "Yes, voice-of-Ray-James." I dive onto the couch, clearing a tall box and an old stereo speaker. "Nathan will get his album. Zach and I called Dave Whitestone on our way home, and we're getting to work next week. I don't feel ready, but I'm doing it."

"If you respect Nathan, despite your past differences, he'll respect you." Connie kicks aside a box to join me on the couch. "Really, Aubrey, why don't you organize this stuff? Throw away what you don't want." She reaches for an old shirt of Daddy's.

"What? No." I snatch the shirt and press its worn cotton softness to my nose. "This is all I have left of them." Folding the shirt on my lap, I set it gently on top of the nearest box.

Connie reaches for my hand. "I suppose it never really goes away, does it?"

"The pain fades, but missing them doesn't." I squeeze Connie's hand. "You've helped me so much, Connie."

Divorced with a grown daughter, Connie fought the courts for guardianship of me when my parents died. During that time, I spent six months in foster care while my eighteen-year-old brother, Peter, lived on his own at our old house.

My foster family, the Fettermans, were lovely people, although hurried and disorganized. They had three children of their own besides me and six-year-old Jennifer Sinclair, who was orphaned two days after me.

Gazing toward the bay windows, I reminisce out loud. "Cuddly, dark-eyed, dark-haired Jennifer. I can still see her standing in the middle of the living room, clutching her doll, trembling. So frightened and alone." The memory stirs my heart.

"I hear from her momma sometimes. Christmas cards now and then." Connie props her feet on top of a box.

"Jen and I chat quite a bit on e-mail."

Connie reaches for something in the box by her leg. "Are you still *Myra* Ray to her?"

Wincing, I nod. "Yeah."

"Are you ever going to tell her the truth?"

My mind races through the pros and cons of confessing my true identity to my little foster sister. In hindsight, it would've been best not to insist on using my mother's name when I went into foster care, but I did.

"Tell her the truth? I should. Fourteen years later, I can't remember why I wanted to change my name when I moved in with the Fettermans, but Myra Ray is Aubrey James's alter ego and I like being a plain, everyday person." I glance at Connie. Does she understand?

"You were grieving, devastated."

My eyes water at the memory of social services dropping me off at the Fettermans two days after the funeral. Peter had disappeared without a word, and Connie had gone to file guardianship papers.

"I thought if I used Momma's name, she'd be close to me. But a year later . . . I couldn't accurately recite one of her everyday sayings. I'd forgotten her funny vocal inflections."

"Forgetting is part of time's healing process."

I reach for Daddy's old shirt again. "I don't want to forget. That's why I keep their albums and costumes, their books and photo albums. Daddy's songbook and box of guitar picks. Momma's old Nikon. I can't, I *won't* get rid of it. I've already forgotten too much."

Connie places her hand over mine, and for a few minutes we sit in contemplation. At last she says, "I could help you organize. Put out the albums and pictures. Find a place for this—" She holds up the bluebird figurine she picked from the box a minute ago. "Whatever it is."

"Oh my gosh." Laughing, I take the squatty, dodo-looking ceramic bird from her. "One of Daddy's friends gave it to him." Turning over the bottom, I read the yellow-taped paper. "May the bluebird of happiness crap all over you."

Connie slaps her thigh as a strong chuckle rolls out of her chest. "Now that's priceless. Ray had some strange friends."

"See, I can't toss this stuff." I position the statue on the sofa cushion between us. "Hello, little bird, have you been flying around me lately? Dropping a few bombs?"

"Oh, pshaw." Connie makes a funny face. "Your little conflicts? What are they compared to your blessings?"

I run my hand over the statue's smooth head. "I *am* blessed."

"The Lord took care of you. And little Jennifer, for that matter. You came to live with me, and she was adopted by her aunt and uncle, raised and corn-fed on an Oklahoma ranch."

Picturing a corn-fed Jennifer makes me smile. "Hard to believe she's a twenty-year-old college woman now."

"Hard to believe she hasn't asked for pictures of you, or to get together."

I wince. "She has. But I'm a *very* busy woman."

Connie frowns. "Fine, but what about pictures."

"Piper."

"Oh, Aubrey."

I rake my fingers through my hair, hating the sound of my confession. "What was I supposed to do? Not send pictures? That would be rude. So I sent Piper's."

"Telling the truth is always a nice option."

"I wasn't ready. I like our relationship. Pure, honest—"

"Honest?"

I shove Connie gently. "You know what I mean. Maybe it's selfish on my part, wanting to dialogue with someone who doesn't care about my celebrity. I just like the fact that my fame doesn't cloud her heart."

Connie pats my leg. "Honey, I understand. But you might consider coming clean one of these days."

"One of these days."

Connie glances at her watch. "Oh, sugar, got to run. I have an early morning art class." She stands. "Why don't you and Car come to dinner soon?"

"That would be lovely."

"Have you set a wedding date?"

"No, though he told all of CMA Fest we were having a spring wedding."

At the library door, she turns back to me, starts to say something, then waves it off. "I love you, you know."

"And I you."

Talking about Jen reminded me to check my private Myra e-mail. I haven't in a few weeks.

Myra,

Guess what? At the end of the summer, I'm moving to Norman to finish my degree at the University of Oklahoma. Go Sooners. I'm very excited. Two more years, and I'm done. Woo hoo.

Dad started grumbling again about retiring. I don't think he likes being a supervisor. Mom rolls her eyes and says, "Whenever you're ready, Tim, but you're going to have to give up the football package. We can't afford all the frills on my salary and you're too young to draw retirement."

That settles him right down. LOL.

Went to a wedding last week. Josh Baldwin. Remember him from my senior year? What a melodrama. Anyway, shotgun wedding. Gotta tell ya, M, he did not make a happy-looking groom. Mom said we should pray for Candy, the girl he married. Mom has a feeling Josh resents Candy and this whole baby-wedding thing and will not be faithful to her. I'm so glad I'm not Candy. Ew, does that sound horrible?

How's your business going? How's it going with Car? That name still makes me laugh, sorry. What if his last name was Horne? Like Lena Horne. Ha ha. Okay, I'm sorry. This is the man you love.

Gotta go to work.

Hugs, Jen

11

"When it's all said and done, Aubrey James won't be remembered for her music. She'll be remembered for her heart for children and the underdogs of this world."

—Gail Snyder, director of Middle Tennessee Youth Athletic League

July 4

In the shade of the dugout, wearing my baseball jersey and Sounds ball cap, I sit with Scott Vaughn for our preconcert interview. The ballgames have been played and won, and now the crew is setting up for the concert.

Scott is relaxed, almost jolly. He looks rugged and a tad sexy in his baseball jersey, baggy khaki shorts, and flip-flops, his wavy hair blowing in the light breeze.

A few feet away, my security henchman, Jeff, stands with his arms crossed, watching the crowd.

"You look nice." Scott slides into the director's chair across from me.

"So do you." I motion to his baseball jersey.

"Ready?" His smile makes me feel warm.

"Hit me with your best shot."

He laughs. "Okay, *Pat Benatar.*"

Scott: *For the last eight years, you've done a Fourth of July benefit concert in Music City Park, carrying on a tradition your father started.*

AJ: This event is a family heritage for me. My father and brother loved Sandlott baseball. Daddy started this Fourth of July Concert in the Park to raise money for the city's youth athletic leagues, but after he died, no one took it up. When I cut my first CD, I offered to start up the concerts again. Actually begged to do the concert again. I really wanted to honor my father by carrying on a tradition he cared about.

Scott: *We talked a little bit about your famous gospel-singing parents the other day, but give me a picture of their life.*

AJ: Their life? [gripping her hands in her lap and angling forward] My parents were caring, loving people. Not perfect, but freely loving. We were the house where all the neighborhood kids gathered.

Scott: *Did they travel a lot with their careers?*

AJ: Dad more than Mom. He had a solo gig going and would travel with guys like Russ Taff. Momma stayed home when we were in school. Then every summer we traveled together.

Scott: *Do you remember your first performance?*

AJ: Certainly. I was six and sang at a church during a Gospel Night or something. Lots of artists were there.

Scott: *Were you scared?*

AJ: [wrinkling her nose] A little. I was too young to realize, "Be scared." Momma and Daddy were on stage singing, so why not me? Oh, you know what I remember about that night? Singing with the Gaither Vocal Band. [laughing] I told Momma, "Those men sing good, don't they?"

Scott: *You have a brother, Peter, who also sang. Where's he now?*

AJ: AWOL

Scott: *AWOL. How long has it been since you've seen him?*

AJ: [hesitating] Too long.

Scott: *Any plans to . . .*

AJ: No.

Scott: *[flipping through his notes] Care to stay on a sports theme?*

AJ: Lead the way. One of my favorite topics.

Scott: *Word on the street is you had one mean three-point shot in high school. Led David Lipscomb high school girls' basketball to a regional championship.*

AJ: [laughing] I refused to lose.

Scott: *You still hold the high school record for most points per game.*

AJ: Well, got to be good at something.

Scott: *Being a multimillion platinum-selling artist must pale in comparison.*

AJ: [serious] Some days, yes. There's nothing like making a great play on the court.

Scott: *Are you still any good?*

AJ: It's been awhile, but I still got game. Why? You wanna take me on?

Rafe: [laughing around side of camera] "She saw you coming, Vaughn."

Scott: *I had a mean three-point shot in my day. How about a little game of one-on-one? Your home court? We have a free day on the schedule. We could make it a basketball shoot-out.*

AJ: Bring it, if you're man enough.

Scott: *[laughing, pointing to himself] I'm bringing it. Better make sure you're bringing it.*

AJ: Like I said, I refuse to lose.

As the hour shifts and the sun slants to the west, concertgoers and reporters begin to cluster around the fence. Photographers aim their big-lens cameras at me. I hear the whirring and clicking of their shutters.

"We love you, Aubrey," someone shouts.

"Miss James, tell us about your engagement."

"Aubrey, why *Inside NashVegas* and Scott Vaughn?"

"Is it true you and Songtunes's new CEO, Nathan Brack, are in a dispute?"

"Aubrey James! I'm your biggest fan. Can I have a kiss?"

Jeff walks toward the fence when an enthusiastic fan tries to climb over, but a hand reaches from the crowd and jerks him back before he can drop over the other side and onto the field. Jeff waits and watches for another second, shoulders square, his feet planted.

Scott: *You're known for your dedication to your fans, holding fan club concerts once a year, but being really distant with the media. Why?*

AJ: My first encounter with the media was when my parents died. We had constant requests for interviews, and it felt like the press cared more about getting a story than honoring my parents. Some of the questions fired at us right after the funeral . . . insane. Since then I've learned the media wants a story, any story. Partial truth is as good as complete truth. Lie now, apologize later. I wanted to avoid Daddy and Momma's story. Ever since then, it's been hide and seek with the media.

Scott: *Some consider any press good press.*

AJ: [nodding] Certainly press and media coverage is good for getting my name out there, but becoming a household name via the tabloids is not my idea of fame.

Scott: *Hurtful?*

AJ: Downright, sometimes. Look, I'm not saying my pain is worse than anyone else's. But when my private life is played out in celeb magazines, entertainment shows, the tabloids, or whatever, it's hard to move past the pain of a broken relationship or an ill-spoken word.

Scott: *Being on the other side, reporters can get so focused on the story, or the inside scoop, they lose sight of people.*

AJ: You have a job to do, I understand.

Scott: *Speaking of relationships in the news, is your fiancé, Car, with you today? We'd like to meet him.*

AJ: No, he couldn't make it. He had a prior commitment.

Jeff taps me on the shoulder. "The band is setting up."

Swerving around, I see my bandmates strolling across the field dressed casually in shorts and tank tops. Seeing them makes me eager to play and sing. The concert is going to be fun.

Vickie notices me and waves. Signaling I'm on my way, I hop down from my chair. "Better go."

He slides down from his chair. "Thanks for today . . . it-it's been fun.""

With a grin, I confess. "More fun than I thought it would be. Thank you."

Scott

*Olivia McConnell, my producer and the goddess of all research, discov-*ered footage of Ray and Myra James performing in concert while digging through the archives Sam inherited from the defunct *Nashville Morning Show*. She sent three videotapes by a runner over to Music City Park in the middle of the Red, White, and Blue Forever fireworks finale.

I glance at the runner as he hands me three cassettes in the glow of exploding rockets. "She has nothing better to do on a holiday?"

He shakes his head. "It's sad."

There is a note taped to the first cassette.

Check out ten-year-old Aubrey on this one. Olivia

Back in my apartment, sunburned, tired, and a little queasy from my sixth hot dog, I twist open a bottle of FRESH! citrus water and drop to the couch with my remote.

"Okay, Olivia, what'd you send me?"

When I press Play, the tape deck whirs and clicks. In the next second, Ray James walks across my TV screen holding onto a light-wood, polished guitar. He's wearing blue jeans with a tucked-in button-down shirt, a wide leather belt, and cowboy boots. Any other day or time I'd guess him to be George Strait without the hat. There's an ease about him, as if being on stage, singing about Jesus, is as right as rain.

Without a doubt, Aubrey inherited his charm. From the moment he smiles and greets the crowd, I can tell he's real and genuine. His character emanates from this twenty-year-old tape.

After he greets the audience—looks like a large church congregation—Ray James introduces his wife, Myra. I jolt forward as she enters.

Aubrey is the image of her mother, right down to her delicate features, long chestnut hair, almond-shaped eyes, and lean body.

Whistling low, I up the volume. The tape is starting to connect the dots for me.

Ray and Myra sing a half dozen songs in a style that seems dated now but was cutting-edge in the day—a country rock sound with a dash of Motown. I swig my water, musing over how much Christian music has morphed since the '80s.

"Now, I'd like to introduce the real stars of the James family." Ray motions stage right. "Our children, Peter and Aubrey."

A tall, gangly boy with dark punked hair walks on stage holding the hand of . . . I put my fist to my lips, trying not to spew water all over my leather couch. Swallowing hard, I gag and cough, then laugh, slapping my knee.

Aubrey is almost as tall as her brother and twice as gangly. Her face sparkles from too much '80s makeup. And her hair . . . oh my. It's like a bomb went off. She looks like . . . No. The camera zooms in on her.

I burst out laughing. Aubrey looks like a mini Rosanne Rosannadanna from *Saturday Night Live*. *Inside NashVegas* fans won't believe this. *The lost tapes of Rosanne Rosannadanna, played by Aubrey James.*

Grabbing my pen and paper, I make notes, rewinding the tape, laughing still.

After a couple of family songs, young Aubrey moves to center stage, alone. The lights go down except for a single spot that falls on the future queen of country soul. My humor over her wild hair dissipates.

The music behind her is subtle and ten-year-old Aubrey sways back and forth, her face to the light, eyes closed. Wearing an oversized pastel-green belted shirt, with black leggings and black flats, she could've been a cast member for *Blossom*. But when she starts to sing, the tall bony kid with too much hair becomes pure magic.

The song feels deep and personal, like a love song. Aubrey holds the last note of the verse, raising her free arm over her head. The drums escalate the dynamic of the song. The electric guitar wails and young Aubrey James leans into the music and belts out the chorus.

And then I saw the Man,
Who hung on that tree,
Wounded, bleeding, all because of me.
Nailed to a cross, dying so I can live,
He loves me eternal. That is why I'm His.

Tears surprise my eyes. I sniff and blink. Cough. Swig my water. Ten-year-old Aubrey is anointed, and capturing me.

As she sings the chorus a second time, the camera pans the audience.

They're on their feet, arms raised, heads tipped back, many with tears streaming down their cheeks. Enraptured, they seem oblivious to the girl on stage pouring out her heart and soul. They don't see Aubrey. They see Jesus.

Salty tears pool in the corner of my mouth, and I don't wipe them away. Snatching up the remote, I rewind. Again. And again.

It's approaching midnight when I fast-forward through the last tape Olivia sent over. Pretty much the same footage as the first, but a different venue, mostly without Peter and Aubrey. Taking out the tape, I slip in the first one again and watch Aubrey one last time. When the song ends, and I cut off the TV, silence rings in my ears.

Collapsing against the back of the couch, I close my eyes, unable to shake the image of Aubrey singing, undone by the love it awakened in me. When did I start to grow cold?

Pressing my hand over my heart, I half expect to feel the chill.

12

"Aubrey James wasn't the greatest basketball player, but she had more heart than the whole team combined. But her three-point shot? Money in the bank every time. And she loved to win."

—*Coach Phoebe King, The Tennessean*

*I shut my office door the next morning and fish out Jeremiah Couch's num*ber. Since watching the James family tapes last night, I can't get Ray, Myra, Peter, and Aubrey out of my head.

What I saw of Peter James, I liked. Fast-forward twenty years, I guess he's about my age, or close to it. Great voice. Excellent guitarist. His interactions with Aubrey seemed sincere, loving, and affectionate.

So why is he AWOL?

I dial Jeremiah. Then press End before the first ring. *Would she want this?* Certainly she has enough resources to take care of the matter herself.

Reaching for my mini bat, I pace around my desk. *Think. What would she want?* I dial again, choosing to be a lion rather than a chicken.

Jeremiah answers.

"Jer, Scott Vaughn here."

"Scott, my man. How are you?"

"Good. You?" I flop down in my chair, knocking my knee against the desk's edge.

"Can't complain. What's up?"

"I wonder if the best private detective in the city could do me a favor?"

He laughs. "Favor? Or job?"

I rub my knee. It still stings from banging against the desk "Job, really. But I can't go too far with this. I've limited funds."

"*You* have limited funds, or that tight wad Sam Watson has limited funds?"

"Me." I'm not ready to take this to Sam yet.

"What's the favor?"

"See if you can find a Peter James, born in Nashville. Current whereabouts unknown."

"Peter James? Holy smokes, Vaughn, which one of the thousands would you like me to track down? Only thing worse is John Smith or Tom Jones."

"Yeah, well, that's why you're the best. Peter James is all I have namewise. He's the son of gospel legends Ray and Myra James, around thirty-two years old. Brother to country superstar Aubrey James."

"No kidding. And she wants me to find him?"

"No . . ."

Jer's exhale is loud. "Scott, what are you doing?" His tone challenges me.

Rocking back in my chair, I stretch out my knee. "I'm doing an exclusive on Aubrey this summer. She mentioned her brother was AWOL, and . . ."

"The last time you tried to help two people connect, *Inside NashVegas* almost got sued."

"Why do you think I'm leaving Sam out? Look, if I can find Peter

James, talk to him, maybe we can arrange a reunion." I still see Aubrey's expression and hear the sad tone in her voice when she said, "AWOL."

"What's your time frame?"

"Yesterday."

Jeremiah whistles. "I'll see what I can do. Listen, consider this a favor for now. We've been slow this summer, but if I start burning too many daylight hours on it, I'm going to have to charge you."

"I understand."

"If you can find out more, like a middle name, social, birth date, city last seen, shoot me an e-mail."

"No paper trail, Jer."

"Have it your way. Call me, then."

Hanging up, I walk over to the window and gaze down into the city street, not sure I've done the right thing, but unwilling to call off the search. I'd envisioned this whole interview with Aubrey as one huge pain in the backside. But now . . .

13

"Scott Vaughn here for Inside the Music's special feature, 'Inside the Diva Life,' an intimate look at the life of Aubrey James. Join us Monday mornings throughout September as I chat with the queen of country soul."

Aubrey

Since the covered porch is airy and open, and the home of my never-used built-in stainless steel grill, *Inside NashVegas* sets up outside for the cooking segment. There's even enough counter space for prepping and chopping.

The July day is blue and beautiful, and slightly cool for midmorning. The ceiling fans spin gently over our heads, stirring the breeze. Around us, Juan's garden blooms with an array of blues, yellows, greens, purples, reds, and pinks, trimming the green, thick lawn like a floral wreath.

I feel rested, even content. Last week's Sandlott concert was a blast—Jennifer Nettles so blows me away with her power pipes—and ticket sales raised over fifty thousand dollars for the city's youth athletic league. An excellent prize for such a comparatively small venue.

Car and I had a nice weekend just hanging around the house. The tension from me missing his parents' Fourth of July party has dissipated.

Then Dave Whitestone and I spent most of Monday discussing my new album and how to record it in a month.

"Nathan is not going to stand for me to do something different. He wants the standard Aubrey James album. Big voice. Drive-time appeal."

Dave shook his head. "I don't want to give up our idea. We can still get Aubrey James, queen of country soul, but with a different type of song. A different feel. I've met a new songwriter, Robin Rivers, and I got a hunch you two will connect. She's your lawyer's cousin, by the way."

"Really? Skyler Banks has a songwriting cousin. She's holding out on me."

"I heard Robin over at James Chastain's place—he's her biological father—and she blew everyone away. She's married to Janie Leeds's ex-fiancé, Lee Rivers."

I gaped at Dave. "James Chastain has a daughter? The same Music Row legend who makes artists weep and songwriters gnash their teeth? How could a guy like that dare to have a daughter?"

Dave laughs. "Robin was raised by her mom and her *dad* in Alabama. Jim is a new development. Anyway, I'd like you to consider her."

So Dave and I mapped out a plan to record an album in a month.

"Hey, you, over there. Daydreaming?" Scott's resonant voice breaks my reminiscing.

"A little." I walk over to the grill where Gina is helping Scott set up. "Are we ready to cook?"

"Almost." He looks into my eyes. "You all right?"

Swallow. The rich tone of his voice sends a warm tingle down the back of my neck. "I'm fine."

Scott stands back and surveys the cooking set up. "Gina, I think we're ready. Chicken? Check. Portabellas, green peppers, scallions, yellow squash? Check. Tinfoil? Check. Spices, extra-virgin olive oil, grill? Check. Knives—"

"Phone to dial 9-1-1?" I hold up the portable. "Check."

"Very funny." Scott tightens the ties of his Kiss the Chef apron. "Who knew the diva had such a sense of humor?"

"Yeah, who knew? She's such a snot." I slip on the only apron I could find. It was hanging on a hook in the back of the pantry. Gina doesn't wear an apron, and I certainly have no need of one.

"Never said that—" Scott stops, wagging his hand toward my off-white burlap apron. "Are you wearing that for the show?"

"Yes, why?"

"You look like a fajita."

I retort by flicking white flour in Scott's face. Gina snickers while Piper laughs outright from her gallery seat—the wicker chair on the far side of the porch.

"Hey, don't shoot the messenger. I'm just saying . . ." Scott gestures to my apron again. "Fajita."

I defend myself with a huff. "I happen to like fajitas."

Scott gives the apron tie a gentle tug. "Yeah, me too."

He makes my insides flutter again. *Scott Vaughn, what is it about you?* With a quick, jerky motion, I snatch up a knife. "What do I do?" My gaze roams the bowls of fresh vegetables.

"Hold on, let me do a little intro for our *Inside NashVegas* audience." Scott smiles at Rafe's camera. "Three, two, one . . . For your Labor Day cookout, Aubrey James and I are going to show you how to make Scott Vaughn's easy fried chicken and veggies *on the grill*. Trust me, you're going to love it. Here's what we're going to do . . ."

I listen as Scott explains how to prepare the meat and the vegetables. He's so natural and confident in front of the camera, witty and real.

That's what I like about you.

He faces me. "Ready, Aubrey?"

With a quick smile, I nod. "Ready."

Gina laughs behind her hand. "Scott, seriously, she burns water."

"Hey, now." I shake my knife at her. "I didn't burn the water, just the pan boiling the water."

"What were you trying to make?" Scott asks.

"Tea," I mumble.

"Tea? In a pan? And you burned it?"

With the camera on his shoulder, Rafe moves gracefully around us.

"She did. I'm telling you, Scott, beware," Gina warns.

Laughing, I wink at her. "Why do you think I keep you around?"

Scott drops a tomato and green pepper onto the cutting board. "Aubrey, cut these into quarters? Can you do *that*?"

I square my shoulders. "I'm not a complete imbecile."

"Just in case . . ." Scott shoves me aside, reaching for the pepper. "Cut like this . . ."

His subtle clean fragrance mingles with the spicy aroma of the pepper, and without much thought, I lean against him to watch. It's crazy, I know, but I like being around him. He makes me feel . . . safe. He's sweet, kind, and funny, with very kissable . . . Stop.

I glance down at Car's ring, feeling ashamed. "S-so what are you saying? I'm sorry, I, um, lost my train of thought."

"You . . . cut out the middle . . . like this . . ." Scott's words are punchy and low. "You . . . um . . . cut . . . like . . . *a-hem* . . . and . . ." He looks over at me. "And . . . Are you getting this . . ." Scott drops the knife and grabs his hand. "Man—"

"What happened? Are you all right?" I pry his hand away to examine his wound. Blood oozes down his finger.

"Here, let me." Gina takes command, walking Scott inside to her mini medical center in the downstairs guest bathroom.

I follow. "Is it bad?"

"The cut is deep, but he won't need stitches," Dr. Gina declares. "You disappoint me, Scott." She dabs the away the blood with gauze before applying ointment and bandaging up the gash. "I expected this of Aubrey. Not you."

Scott leans to see around her. "Yeah, me too." He smiles. My heart jumps.

"I-I'll be on the porch." Whirling around, I shake the image of his white smile from my mind's eye. Okay, I'm attracted to him. No big deal. Passing fancy. Just a pre-wedding crush.

In a few minutes, we're back on track, Scott's wound doctored and his dignity slightly restored. While he preps the meat and talks to the camera, I resume chopping veggies, careful to keep my fingers clear of the sharp blade.

"Scott, you don't mind if I just cut up the vegetables and not my hand, do you?"

He flicks flour at my face. "Coward."

I duck away from the powdery cloud. "What happened to you looked painful."

He laughs. "Never mind, just start cutting."

Rafe zeros in on me as I cut my first veggie. "Here we go Nashville . . . Please, do *not* try this at home." When faced with an uncomfortable situation, a certain goofy *savoir-faire* comes over me.

Setting a green pepper on the cutting board, I raise the knife over my head, and with a samurai warrior cry—"Hiya!"—I whack the pepper, execution style. The knife *thuds* against the cutting board, shooting the pepper halves across the porch like green bullets. One fires at Scott's head. The other wings across the porch, slapping into the wall before landing on the granite floor.

Rafe lowers the camera. "Holy cow, girl."

"Mercy—" Gina inhales.

"Have you gone crazy?" Piper picks up the pepper half from the floor.

I cock my hip to one side. "I hate peppers."

Scott's laughter fills the porch. Catching his breath, he reproves me with a raw chicken breast dangling from his hand. "All right, you, no more executing veggies. Got that?"

I stick my tongue out at him. "Spoilsport."

We fall into a chopping and prepping rhythm while talking about our favorite dishes.

"My mom makes the best biscuits," Scott says.

"My momma made a wonderful chili," I say. "And hot buttery corn bread. We'd come home from school on a wintry day, our noses running, our cheeks red, and she'd have a fire in the fireplace, chili on the stove." Closing my eyes, I breathe in. "The smell was wonderful and the house felt warm and cozy."

The memory strikes me as some odd fairy tale. Wonderful but not true.

Scott draws a sheet of tinfoil from the box and tears it away, explaining to the camera. "Prepare your tinfoil with about two tablespoons of extra-virgin olive oil. Mix finely crushed bread crumbs—or flour, if you prefer—with your favorite spices. I use garlic and rosemary."

He's mixing and rolling. I ask, "What do I do?"

"You're going to make tinfoil boats for the veggies." With quick hands, he demonstrates for me and the *Inside NashVegas* viewers how to make tinfoil boats. "Add the olive oil, salt and pepper, fresh garlic, and seal them shut."

Concentrating on the tinfoil boats, I realize I'm actually enjoying this grill-out day. "Now what?"

"We're ready to grill. Aubrey, why don't you do the honors?" Scott gestures to the shiny grill-beast. "Fire it up."

Fire it up? Sure. Not a problem. Except *how* to fire it up. Wiping my hands down the sides of my apron, I consider the knobs and buttons. Rafe follows me, zooming in on my confusion. Scott watches and waits. Gina and Piper huddle in the corner, holding back their big grins.

For about sixty seconds, I simply stand there, perplexed, then look back at Gina. "How's it work?"

Scott gasps. "You're kidding."

I shake my head. "Wish I was."

He motions for me to step aside, rubbing his hands together. "Let the expert." Facing the grill, he mutters, "Let's see. A grill is a grill."

"It's tricky," Gina calls.

Studying the knobs, Scott points to one. "Turn this to Light, see? And then press this button to ignite."

I nod. "Turn to Light, press this to ignite. Got it."

He stoops down and opens the front panel doors. "I'll open the gas valves."

"Okay. Say when." I poise my finger. Light and ignite.

"The valve is stuck. When did you use this last?"

"Gina?" I ask, my finger still hovering over the button.

"Last summer, maybe. It's been a while," she says.

"The valves are slightly rusted. Don't turn the knob to Light yet."

Scott stoops lower, his face even with the grill rack. "Almost . . . okay, Aubrey, you can—"

I turn the dial to Light.

"Now, just—"

I mash the Ignite switch.

Poof! Fire explodes from the grill bed, consuming the racks . . . and Scott. He falls to the granite floor with his face buried in his hands.

I drop to my knees next to him. "Oh my gosh, are you all right? I'm so sorry!"

"Burns . . ."

I press my hands over my middle, horrified. "Oh, Scott. I'm so sorry. Are you okay?"

Gina gently moves me out of the way. "Put this over your eyes, Scott." She hands him a damp cloth.

"Scott, I didn't mean it—" My apology is punctuated with short gasps. I feel ill. What if he'd been seriously hurt?

"Let me see." Gina pries the cloth away from his face.

A deep pink colors his face, accented with black smudges. And . . .

"Oh, man." Rafe lowers the camera.

"What?" Scott asks, wincing as he shifts his gaze from Rafe's to me. "What?"

Rafe shakes his head with a guttural sound.

Shoving himself off the porch floor, Scott dashes inside. I look at Piper, and try as we might, we cannot hold our laugh.

In the next moment, Scott's broad shoulders fill the porch doorway. "Aubrey James, you seared off my eyebrows."

14

*When Car arrives home after another downtown SoBro development din*ner, I'm in bed, e-mailing.

"Finally . . . home." When he leans to kiss me, jerking his tie loose, George growls low, baring his teeth.

"Stop," I hiss at him, setting my laptop aside, returning Car's kiss. "How'd the dinner go?"

Car tosses his keys and pocket change onto the dresser. "Too many people with too many opinions."

At his closet, he stuffs his white shirt into the dry cleaner bag. "By the way, Mom wants tea with you tomorrow at three."

"What?" I look up from nuzzling George. "Just like that? Come to tea tomorrow?" I point to the clock. "It's after ten p.m., Car."

"Brie—"

"Car, she can't summon me like I'm one of her servants. Tomorrow at three? What if I'm busy?"

"Are you?"

I scrunch down into the pillows. "No, but still."

He steps out of his trousers. "She's concerned about the tabloids and the blogosphere."

"Car, no." I pull the covers over my head. "I'm not discussing my life with your mother." The idea makes me queasy.

The mattress yields as Car sits next to me and yanks back the covers. "Believe me, she's more intimidated by you than you of her."

I sit up. "Hardly. The grand dame of Belle Meade? The queen? I'm a mere entertainer."

Car laughs and kisses my cheek. "You'll be fine. Do what I do: nod your head and mutter, 'Yes, ma'am, you're right' as much as possible."

I bob my head, grinning. "Yes, sir, you're right, sir."

Laughing, Car wraps me in his arms and quiets me with a kiss.

Dear Jen,

I meant to e-mail you days ago. Is this a busy summer or what? Congratulations on deciding to go to the University of Oklahoma. I'm very proud of you!

Funny about your old "flame" Josh. I hope he finds happiness. Anyway, speaking of marriage . . .

I'm engaged. (Ahhhh!) Car asked me to marry him.

Can you believe it? He's a great guy, Jen. Handsome, successful, from an old, established Nashville family.

I've been thinking a lot about family lately. Don't know what it is about this summer, but all points of my life seem to be merging. After fourteen years, I still ache for Daddy and Momma. Peter is who-knows-where. I stopped trying to contact him after the last time. The memory of our conversation, short as it was, still makes me wince.

But with Car, there's hope of gaining a family. His parents are major socialites, members of elite clubs and various charities. He's an only child, but he has family—second, third, and fourth cousins—all over Nashville and middle Tennessee. I've only been to one family get-together, but it was large and fun, if not a tad overwhelming. I think I told you about the lake gathering.

This summer is about change for me. Perhaps finally closing all the doors on my past so I can realize my future. We shall see. Pray for me? Hello to your parents.

Much love,

Myra

Piper insisted I wear a bold orange Tory Burch top and a pair of Prada wedges for my tea with Mrs. Carmichael.

Her theory? "A woman always feels confident in wedges."

As I approach the Carmichael's grand double doors, a maid wearing a gray dress and a starched white apron greets me. "She's waiting for you, ma'am."

"Thank you." Following the woman down a long, dark corridor, I wonder how tea with the queen of Belle Meade can be more nerve-wracking than tea with the very proper and staid queen of England.

Never mind that Prada wedges are doing nothing for my confidence.

"Miss James, ma'am." The maid bows and backs away.

Poised with a fixed smile, Mrs. Carmichael greets me with her manicured hands stretched out. She's beautiful, sophistication wrapped in a pale pink linen suit. Her blonde hair is short and stylish, her figure trim and curved in all the right places.

"Aubrey, dear." She clasps the tips of my fingers with hers and draws me close, kissing the air beside my cheek. Her skin is warm next to mine and, I'm sure, freshly Botoxed.

"Thank you for inviting me to tea, Mrs. Carmichael."

"Ah, now, are we on such formal terms?" She steps back, still holding my fingers. "Call me Grace, please." Her smile is still fixed, but perhaps Car was right. She's as intimidated by me as I am of her.

Moisture coats my hands. "All right, Mrs. Car—Grace."

She releases her grip and returns to her chair at the head of the table. "Let's not beat around the bush, Aubrey. What are you going to do about your bad press and dragging the Carmichael name through the mud?" Her eyes are steely.

I set my purse on the floor by my chair and grip my hands in my lap. "Bad press? I can hardly rein in the media. They print what they want."

Grace spreads a linen napkin across her lap and rings a tiny silver bell. "I realize you showbiz people have your own moral code and way of life"—her tone is patronizing—"and perhaps thrive on being tabloid news, but Aubrey, *you* are marrying a Carmichael. We have our own code of conduct, our own rules and traditions that *must* be observed."

My hands shake as I spread my napkin over my legs. "Grace, being tabloid news is not a value of mine, trust me."

She rings the little bell again. "My friends tell me they see your face every week on the cover of some ragtag magazine. Perhaps this is from your lack of upbringing, but you must learn to be discreet. Let me advise you, cancel the *Inside NashVegas* interview."

Lack of upbringing? My heart thunders at her insult. "The *Inside NashVegas* interview is set and, quite frankly, none of your business—"

"You made it my business when you accepted my son's ring. Such as it was . . ."

"Pardon me?"

A different maid, with freckled skin, appears pushing a cart of tea and pastries. Grace quiets as the woman fills our cups and offers us a treat from a platter. I pick a cinnamon scone, though I'm not sure I can swallow it.

"Anything else, ma'am?" the maid asks.

"You're dismissed, Bonnie." Grace sweetens her tea, adding a drop of cream. "Car assures me the coliseum proposal was his idea."

"Then believe him, Grace." I flick a packet of Splenda against my fingers. "He surprised me. I had no idea. We had barely discussed marriage."

"Nevertheless, the fact remains you'll be my son's wife, my daughter-in-law, a Carmichael."

"I understand, and am honored to become a member of the family."

Her smile is quick, almost as if she doubts me. "Adjustments will need to be made."

"Such as?"

"Avoiding the tabloids and those infernal bloggers."

"Grace, the issue is they don't avoid me."

"Make our family holidays more of a priority."

"I apologize for missing the Fourth, but I have my own tradition."

"And Easter at the beach."

"I can hardly cancel a stadium concert for a beach weekend."

"Something will have to give then, won't it?"

"Yes, on both sides." She can't sincerely believe I'm the only one who must bend.

"The Carmichaels and Beechums were early settlers in these parts—" She continues as if I've said nothing at all. "Founding members of our great city. We've been leaders and business innovators since the Revolutionary War. Both my husband's and my ancestors came to salvation under Sam Jones's preaching. Our men helped build the Ryman. We have a name and honor to protect."

Breaking off a corner of my scone with the tip of my fork, I ponder her implication. "Innovators? I see. Does that include the moonshiners who ran hooch down from the hills? And the Carmichaels' fifty-year feud with the Murdocks?"

Her expression does not change. She appears to be presiding over a grand court. "Before the Second World War, a set of Carmichael sisters married into the Winston family. *They* were the bootleggers."

"Grace, all families have skeletons in the closet. It's no shame. And all families have honor and traditions they uphold. Including mine."

Though I'm not sure of all the James and Roth family traditions, I intend to keep the ones I know.

"Dear," Grace says with a lilt, "which of your family traditions are you upholding, hmm?"

Her tone heightens my defenses. "The traditions of music and serving others."

She sips her tea, tapping the bottom of her cup with her fingernails. "Perhaps you should adhere to your family's gospel roots and stop cavorting around, telling the world about your relations with past lovers and my son."

"Mrs. Carmichael—" Calling her Grace is too intimate in this formal conversation. "You may find this shocking, but your son seduced me."

"You are very sensual and beautiful, Aubrey."

For a moment, my thoughts swirl like a violent wind, and fury grips me. She can't be serious. Implying Car had no control over his actions, that I'm some sort of Helen of Troy.

When I force myself to peer at her, my ire fades. I see her with new eyes. She's confined to the social prejudices in which she was born and raised. She's without freedom to venture out into the world and discover all it's beauty. While I love to discover the rubies and emeralds buried in the heart of others, she only mines for diamonds.

Is this where I push away from the table and bid her good day? Or do I endure for Car's sake? "Mrs. Carmichael, I love your son."

"Do you?"

Is she going to challenge every word?

"As much as I'm marrying a Carmichael, your son is marrying a woman with a public persona. The press, the image, the invasion that comes with a public life cannot be avoided."

The blue-blood southern belle lifts her teacup and stares beyond me. "We all thought Car would marry Tammy Arbuckle." She chortles. "They were such sweethearts all through college. I don't know what happened."

Folding my napkin, I tuck it under my plate and reach down for my handbag. "Thank you for the tea, Mrs. Carmichael."

She looks up, undisturbed by my abrupt departure. "Thank you for coming. And please, don't forget our conversation, dear."

"Not even in my dreams."

15

"Aubrey James stole the D from Demanding and put it in Diva. I love her for it."

—*Zach Roberts, Roberts Management*

Odd. My house is sprouting furniture. There's a new table in the foyer and a plasma TV hanging on the wall in the great room. In the downstairs office, there's a new computer and desk. And a plaque on the wall:

In Appreciation to Brown "Car" Carmichael III

City of Belle Meade

Is he moving in?

Strolling through the foyer to Gina's office, I peer inside. Her redwood desk is neatly cluttered with piles of bills and papers—all the things she does to manage the household. Her nineteen-inch TV is on, but muted. She likes to keep up with her soaps. "Been watching *All My Children* for thirty-five years. They're practically family."

On the other side of the foyer, the formal living room is still white walled and spartan. No sign of new furniture.

The grandfather clock chimes twice. As if on cue, the doorbell rings. I open to Dave standing on the other side with his guitar.

"Come in." I give him a slight hug.

"Ready to write?" He pats his guitar case.

"It's been so long." I wince, motioning down the hall. "We can work in the music room."

"Got any of Gina's chocolate-chip cookies?" Dave asks, grinning. "Didn't have time for lunch."

I tip my head toward the door. "Go check. If she doesn't, I'm sure she'll make some."

Dave returns a second later with Gina shoving his back. "Apparently I'm not allowed in the kitchen."

I look up from tuning my Ovation.

"You work, I'll bring refreshments in a moment. Gee whiz, been here five seconds and you already have your hand in my cookie jar." Gina whirls around with a huff.

Dave rubs his hand as if they were slapped. "Didn't know you had a kitchen gestapo."

"Careful now, they don't come any better than Gina."

Dave settles on the piano bench with his guitar. "I checked Robin's schedule on her MySpace. She's playing at the Bluebird a week from Saturday. We should go."

"If we plan to use her, I suppose we should. You think your instincts are right? She and I will click?"

Dave shrugs. "I don't know her as well as I know you, but my hunch is you are twins separated at birth."

I smile. "Always wanted a sister."

We spend the afternoon playing around with melodies and lyrics, not getting very far song wise, but the process stirs my dormant creativity, and my songwriting confidence eeks to the surface.

Just like that? Without asking me?"

"I'm practically living here anyway." Car sets his laptop down in his new office, flipping through the mail lying on the edge of his desk. "I bought a few pieces of furniture and decided to have them delivered here."

"And, your mail?" I point to the change of address sticker.

"It was a hassle to keep going by my place."

"Car, the United States Post Office knew you were living here before me."

Sitting on the side of the desk, he lifts his hands. "Okay, let's discuss this."

"This sucks, Car. I feel like the whiny baby here, but you're the one who decided to move in without talking to me."

He shrugs. "Are you saying you don't want me to move in?"

His statement sparks a head-splitting debate. We wander down every rabbit trail of our relationship, from my personal bank account to his mother's expectations, from his business dealings to how *my* fame effects *his* life. The argument leaves me cold, feeling abandoned on the other side of the battle line.

"So, where are we here?" I press my fingers to my temples. How could two intelligent people talk so long without finding a resolution.

"Me moving in."

"Right." Full circle. Our words took us nowhere. I look around for a place to sit, but there is none. "You'll need a chair."

"Bringing the furniture from my home office."

"The burgundy suede set?"

"The very same."

"It'll look nice." My headache eases a little. "I suppose you'll want to paint in here."

"Called a guy yesterday." Car stretches out and pulls me into his arms. "Are we okay here?"

I drop my forehead to his shoulder. "Please, don't pull crap like this without talking to me. I would never do this to you."

He brushes my hair off my shoulders. "All right. But sometimes—"

"Car . . ." I gaze into his eyes.

"All right." He wraps his arms around me. "All right."

16

Scott

Thursday, July 12

Sam tosses me a box of new golf balls when he walks into my office after the morning show.

"Nice show this morning with Hannah. Liked your Sandlotter piece." He folds himself into the chair opposite my desk and gestures to my face. "Those things going to grow back soon?"

"Hopefully." I trace the bare skin over my eyes, then hold up the golf balls. "What's the catch?"

"No catch." He leans forward, smiling like a New York gangster. "Just congratulations."

"For . . ."

Sam points. "Read the logo."

I open the package. The golf balls are labled. *Inside NashVegas on CMT*. I grin. "So, it's a done deal?"

Sam reclines in the chair. "We debut during November sweeps with Aubrey's story, 'Inside the Diva Life,' then pick up a time slot the first quarter of next year."

I wrap my fist around the ball and punch the air in silent victory.

"Your interview with Aubrey put us in the pocket."

Glancing at my watch—*Need to leave for Aubrey's in a minute*—I ask, "When do I move into my sports director office?"

Sam gets up and strolls over to the door with his head down and his hands in his pockets. "You're certainly my top candidate."

"Top candidate?" I bolt out of my chair. "Why am I not the only candidate, Sam? *Inside the Game* is my creation. Part of the deal with doing the Aubrey James interview."

He turns the doorknob. "Come on, Vaughn, you weren't born yesterday. You know how these things go. They put us on a national network, we do a little tap dance with talent, producers, directors. Got to give a little."

My eyes narrow. "And why does the giving have to be my sports director job?"

"Hopefully, it won't." He steps into the hallway.

"Sam, don't belly up on me. Sacrifice someone else." I hate the idea of dogging a fellow crew member, but the director job is mine.

"Vaughn, CMT wants us to consider someone else, that's all. And, uh . . ." He can't look at me. "They mentioned a coanchor team they'd like to bring on board." Sam holds up his hands. "All part of the dance. Don't worry. We're still negotiating."

"Who's the coanchor team?"

Sam takes a few steps down the hall like he's in a hurry to leave. "Todd Knight and Chip McGuire."

Knight and McGuire. Perfect. Big names from ESPN. This whole dance scenario is pure bull. "It's a done deal, isn't it?"

Sam ducks his head. "My hands were tied. I didn't have a choice."

"Yeah, right."

"One more thing."

"What? I'm fired?"

"No, you're going to Miami the first week of August. Got a Miami Dolphins player who owns a sports bar, moonlights as a country singer in the off season. CMT thought it would make a good opener in January."

"A singing Dolphin." I fire the CMT golf ball at my wall. "Just great."

In Aubrey's great room, I hold the video of her ten-year-old performance with rippling thoughts on circulating my résumé. Blasted Sam.

But the moment Aubrey walks in, my turbulent thoughts cease, although my heart races. She has this aura about her—graceful and larger than life. If her life's journey had taken her down a simpler road, she would still be a star. Somehow.

"Ready?" I ask, motioning to her chair.

"If you are." She smiles, but I notice the famous light in her blue-green eyes isn't as bright.

"You okay?" I ask.

"I was about to ask you the same thing."

I wave her off. "I'm fine. Long morning."

"What time do you have to wake up for the show?"

"Three." I hand the videocassette to Rafe who walks it over to the player.

She shakes her head. "On the road, that's when I go to bed."

"We have a surprise for you, Aubrey." I take my place in the chair opposite her.

A quizzical expression molds her face. "What kind of surprise?"

"You'll like this one." I check to see if Rafe's ready. "Aubrey, nice plasma TV. Is it new?"

"Yes, a recent *surprise*."

"I see." Plasma TV? *Not* a nice diva surprise. "Ready, Rafe."

Piper comes around and sits on the edge of the couch. "What's this?"

"Something Olivia found," I answer over my shoulder.

A second later, Ray James appears on the screen. Aubrey gasps. "Daddy."

"He looks so young," Piper mutters.

Ray James introduces his son and daughter. Twelve-year-old Peter and ten-year-old Aubrey walk toward him, their faces beaming.

"How old are you there? Ten?" I ask.

"Yes. W-where did you find this?"

"They were in the archives from the old *Nashville Morning Morning Show*."

As soon as Peter starts his guitar solo, Aubrey begins to weep. Piper slips her arm around Aubrey's shoulder. "I miss him so much." Her cheeks are smudged with watery mascara.

"You have an incredible solo coming up," I say, trying to lighten the mood. I didn't count on the tape having this much emotional impact.

"Yes, 'The Man.' The song I wrote with Daddy." As the spotlight zeros in on the young Aubrey James, the older rises from the couch. "I can't . . . I can't . . ."

"Aubrey," Piper calls after her. "Honey . . ."

Jumping up, I follow Aubrey out of the room. "Door at the end of the hall, upstairs." Piper calls to me.

Taking the stairs two at a time, I chastise myself. *Should've warned her.* The heels of my loafers echo down the hall as I approach the closed door.

"Aubrey?" There's no response, so I knock lightly while turning the knob. "Can I come in?" The door eases open.

She's sitting sideways on a country-style blue couch staring toward the bay windows. Her chin is propped in her hand. From the odd angle, I can see the tear tracks in her makeup.

"Interesting décor in here. The whole boxes-everywhere thing. I like it."

She shrugs, chewing on the end of her thumbnail. "I like it."

Since she doesn't order me away, I pick a path through the boxes to where she sits. "I'm sorry. I never imagined seeing them on video would be so emotional."

She faces forward, wiping her face with her fingers. "Me, neither."

"Something was wrong before I got here, though."

Aubrey reaches for a fringed throw pillow. "Car's moving in."

"Darn him." I pound my fist against my palm.

She pinches her lips together, fighting a smile. "You make fun, but we didn't talk about him moving in. He decided on his own. We fought over it, made up, but the tension is still tangible."

Gesturing to a row of boxes, I ask, "What's all this stuff?"

"Memories. Things that belonged to my parents." She points the tip of her shoe at a water-stained box. "I stored them in Connie's basement after we sold my parent's house, and they got caught in a flood."

"So you moved to high, dry ground?" I push back one of the box's flaps to peek inside. Looks like knickknacks.

She hugs the pillow closer. "I had this idea of creating a memorial to my parents, but there's a wide chasm between wanting and doing."

"Best-laid plans . . ." In another box, I find photo albums and pull one free.

"Momma was an only child," she says. "Daddy had a brother in California we rarely saw. Both sets of grandparents had passed away when I was a child, so when my parents were killed, Peter and I were truly alone. A few kooky relatives came out of the woodwork after I became famous, but they were just looking for money."

"Aubrey, I'm sorry about the tape."

She shakes her head. "Don't be—you didn't know."

"Still . . ." I hold her gaze. "I'm sorry."

She wipes away fresh tears, thinking for a moment. "It's fine, really."

"Do you want to call it a day?"

She exhales. "No, but let's invite Rafe up here."

17

"Life dealt her a rough hand. But she played the game and won."

—James Chastain, president of Nashville Noise

Scott: *Your parents were pioneers in gospel music, blending the new contemporary sound of the '80s with soul and country sounds of the '70s. How'd they get started?*

AJ: Daddy grew up in the '60s, playing in garage bands from the time he was young. Thirteen, I think. He was into the '60s psychedelic scene. But he loved sports and music.

One summer, '71 or '72, one of the members of his garage band organized a "tour" and off they went. No guarantees, no manager, just the yee-haw thrill of going on tour. They slept in their VW microbus. Washed in rest-stop bathrooms. Naturally, a bunch of musicians with no manager ended up in the wrong place at the right time. They thought they were doing a rock concert but found themselves playing for a church camp in Georgia.

While waiting to perform his Doors-like rock music, Daddy listened to the preacher and learned for the first time God loved him. It changed his life.

Scott: *How old was he at this time?*

AJ: Twenty-two or -three. The quintessential hippy turned Jesus freak. I love the old pictures of Daddy with his long hair and raggedy bell bottoms. And Momma with a crown of daisies on her head.

Scott: *Your mother was a Jesus freak too?*

AJ: Not the quintessential kind. She was the innocent, goodie-goodie college cheerleader. Such opposites, my parents. Daddy's band played at Momma's church on the invitation of the pastor's son. Little Alliance Baptist was overrun with a bunch of long-haired, antiestablishment, antireligious, rock and roll-loving teens and twenty-somethings. Daddy's band set up drums [gasp] in the sanctuary, and brought in electric guitars and a portable Hammond. They turned Alliance Baptist on its ear.

Scott: *[chuckling] I bet.*

AJ: Momma claimed she fell in love with Daddy the moment he started to sing. But her father was one of the church deacons who helped the pastor run the band offstage midway through their set. "Cut your hair and change your clothes, learn some decent music, and we'll let you come back," they said.

But Daddy always knew it wasn't about the outside, it was about the inside. I remember watching him once during an interview trying to explain how he felt back then. He said cutting their hair wouldn't make them love people or Jesus more. Or make Jesus love *them* more. Their long hair symbolized to them how radical they were about being true to themselves, about not selling out to staid traditions.

Scott: *So being on the edge was second nature to your daddy.*

AJ: He wasn't a rebel for rebel's sake. He felt God gave him melodies and lyrics that were different from what was being played in the churches of the time. But he knew—well, I think he knew—a bunch of ex-rock and rollers would never be comfortable in an organ playing, five-hundred-year-old hymn-singing church. He wanted to worship with the words and music of their day.

Scott: *A lot of great value and theology in hymns.*

AJ: Absolutely. There's great truth in modern songs too. Daddy loved hymns, even made an album of them. But you know he had to do it with new arrangements and, of course, an electric guitar. If he were alive today, he'd be cheering on bands like Reliant K and Switchfoot. He'd love David Crowder, Misty Edwards, Phil Wickman, Matt Redman, Martin Smith, and Charlie Hall. Daddy produced records for some great singers of his day—gospel singers—because he loved the power of gospel music, the power of voice.

Scott: *You spent many of your summer vacations traveling the world.*

AJ: Yes, Europe, Asia, South America, Africa, Australia. I'd been to five continents by the time I was fourteen.

There's a shift in the room's light as the morning surrenders to the afternoon.

Scott: *Tell us about their death.*

AJ: [exhaling] This is the hard part. Okay . . . the summer of '93. I'd just turned sixteen and was not into one more summer on the road with my parents. I mean, please. [rolling her eyes] The year before, I'd fallen in love with playing basketball.

Scott: *Don't forget our one-on-one challenge.*

AJ: Believe me, I'm looking forward to whupping you.

Anyway, I'd missed a lot of summer practice because of being on the road with The James Family, and when I returned to my sophomore year of play, my game was awkward and out of rhythm. I practiced every night in the driveway after dinner until bedtime.

Scott: *All year?*

AJ: All year. Even Thanksgiving and Christmas Day. Daddy and Peter helped by running drills with me, playing offense or defense.

Scott: *You were driven and determined even back then.*

AJ: About some things. Not math. Hated math. But I loved basketball. It was the first thing I'd ever done that was all me. I earned it on my own. No Peter, no Daddy or Momma. Not a family performance. Just me. Singing was something I did because of Ray and Myra James. Without them, I never would've had any notoriety. Peter, like Daddy, loved baseball and played in high school. I followed in his footsteps and found an outside interest.

Scott: *Back to the summer of '93.*

AJ: I wanted to stay home that summer and hang with my friends and the team, play ball every day. Peter had turned eighteen in the spring, was working part time at Kroger, playing Sandlott, and dating a girl named Gailynn.

Scott: *Ah, your parents were fighting a losing battle to get you to go on tour.*

AJ: [smiling] Yeah, in the end they supported us. Daddy reworked our schedule and focused on other projects he had lined up. The only performing dates he kept on the schedule were within a day's drive or short flight.

Scott: *By then, your parents had earned a big name in Christian music.*

AJ: Yes, Ray James was as big a name as Michael W. Smith or Wayne Watson. He'd written a lot of songs for big-name artists. We couldn't turn on the Christian radio station without hearing one of Daddy's songs.

Scott: *Financially, he was doing well?*

AJ: We weren't rich, but songwriting was beginning to pay off for Daddy. We had a nice brick two-story over off Granny White Pike. Took vacations, were spoiled on birthdays and Christmas. Had a nice allowance and frequent trips to the mall.

Scott: *Did you have any idea you would become a music superstar?*

AJ: [big laugh] None whatsoever. Basketball quickly replaced music as my first love, and I wanted a college scholarship to Vandy or UT.

Scott: *What changed?*

AJ: Death changes everything, Scott. And if it hadn't been for Connie Godwin, you wouldn't be sitting here with me today.

Scott: *How does she fit into this picture?*

AJ: Daddy hired Connie as his, our, manager. Connie had managed country artists for years, but she wanted to work with Ray James, so she called him up and convinced him to hire her.

Scott: *Go, Connie.*

AJ: Yeah, she's been a real treasure, and I honestly don't know where I'd be without her. She turned out to be way more than a manager or friend. She probably saved my life.

Scott: *So, the summer of '93 you're all about basketball.*

AJ: [nodding] One of the bookings Daddy didn't cancel that summer was a Gospel Fest in Gatlinburg the first of August. He insisted we all go, do the show, then take a family vacation before Peter went off to college.

But eighteen-year-old Peter would have none of it. He didn't want his dad dictating his life. He had all the pride and arrogance of most young men. The two of them argued off and on throughout July, and then the night before we were to leave, the argument blew up. Pete went ballistic, stormed out, and stayed away all night. Didn't come home to say good-bye to Daddy and Momma.

Momma convinced Daddy I should stay home, be there for Peter when he came back. The whole thing was one of the few really ugly moments in our family's history. Unfortunately, it was our last moment as a family. If I dwell on it too long, it haunts me for days.

Scott: *Are you okay to go on?*

AJ: I'm okay for now. Peter came home the next evening, feeling foolish, but back to his charming self. We ordered pizza and talked out the situation. He felt horrible and anxiously waited for Daddy to call so he could apologize. He jumped up every time the phone rang. Pete is—well, was—a strange mix of temper and sensitivity. The fight with Daddy really ate at him.

We were dishing out ice cream, planning on watching a late movie with our friends, when the phone rang around eleven o'clock.

Peter dashed to answer it. "Dad? It's me, Pete."

I'll never forget his face. First hopeful and expectant. Then crestfallen and ghost white. His whole body convulsed. Then he just start to wail, "No, no, no! You're lying."

Meanwhile, I'm shouting, "What, what, what?" I had no idea what was going on.

Finally, he slumped to the floor, crying—[voice breaking]

Scott: *How incredibly hard. I can't imagine.*

AJ: [moving her hand over her heart] It was sickening and terrifying. Horrible, horrible, horrible. Trapped in our worst nightmare without the hope of waking up. I loved Peter so much, and seeing him balled up on the floor, weeping and wailing, ripped my heart out. "Peter, it's okay. It's okay. What's wrong?"

Scott: *So, you still had no idea what had happened.*

AJ: None. Just something horrible. I could hear a voice through the receiver. "Peter? Peter, hello? Are you there?"

So I answered. "It's Aubrey."

"Honey, it's Connie."

I could tell she'd been crying. In fact, she struggled while talking to me.

"I have something to tell you. It's not easy . . . but . . . honey . . . your mom and dad were in an accident. No one's fault, just . . . an accident."

"Oh my gosh, are they all right?"

Connie paused for a long, long time, sobbing. I guess I knew, but it didn't sink in.

"Honey, they're with Jesus."

Aubrey

Piper finds me in the library after Scott left, sorting through the boxes, reading Daddy's diaries. She crosses her arms and leans against the doorframe.

"Hard day?"

I close the leather-bound book. "At first, but then talking about the death felt sort of freeing, like it really was something in the past."

Piper sinks down to the floor next to me. "I'd be mental if I endured half of what you've endured. The public death of your parents, the public display of your love life, Melanie's betrayal."

"*Now* I'm depressed." I laugh low, nudging her with my elbow. "I had a revelation today."

"What's that?"

"I'm part of the reason Peter left. Remember after a while how he couldn't stay in the old house, or even with Connie. Now, I realize he couldn't even stand to be near me." I gaze into Piper's face. "Just being around me reminded him of the horrible way things were between him and Daddy before he died."

Piper nods. "Makes sense. He's never forgiven himself."

"No." Hugging my knees to my chest, I motion to Piper's Palm Pilot. "Do we need to talk business?"

"If you're ready." She taps the minicomputer's screen with a stylus.

"Go for it."

"New publicity photo shoot is next month on the eighth, *Glamour* and *Self* requesting cover shoots . . ." She looks up. "They heard you're doing interviews now."

"Good news travels fast, I guess."

"FRESH! sent a bouquet of flowers to your business manager's office as a thank you for their record sales during the past two quarters."

"Really? Fantastic. So glad Eli worked in stock holdings as part of my deal."

"A pro-life group e-mailed and asked if you'd sing at a Washington, D.C., rally in the fall."

"Do you know the group?"

"Women For Life. They're legit."

"Make sure. Ask around, check them out. Who else is going to be there? Who's the keynote? If they're aboveboard, I'll do it."

She taps in a note to call the Women For Life. "Last but not least, Eli wants a meeting about your downtown investments. Something about confirming where you want to put the money."

I blink. "What downtown investments?"

She shrugs. "He didn't say. I asked if you could deal with it over the phone, but he said since the amount is so large and involves your name, he wants to meet with you. I told him Friday at eleven."

18

Scott

Aubrey occupies too much of my mind over the weekend. Even when I drive home to Murfreesboro on Sunday for Dad's birthday, I can't shake the sense of her.

Between all the research, interviewing, and helping with the editing, the little girl with the Rosanne Rosannadanna hair turned stunning country diva has gotten under my skin.

And I don't like it. She's out of my league. Engaged, for crying out loud. This assignment can't end soon enough.

Sitting in my folk's backyard under a knotted oak grounds me in *my* reality. I'm simple, albeit charming, Scott Vaughn from Murfreesboro, Tennessee. No match for a beautiful diva.

Dad plops a lounge chair down next to me. "Thanks for coming. I know you're busy."

I grin, shaking my head. "You're thirty minutes away, Dad. How could I not come for your birthday? By the way, your present is in the house."

Twisting open a cold, dripping root beer, he flashes a face-splitting grin. "I saw. Box seats for the Titans' home games." He swigs from his drink. "It pays to have a son with connections."

"I pulled a few strings, irritated a few people, but you're worth it, Pop."

"Payback for putting up with you during your teen years?" He tips up his soda bottle, again.

"Come on, I wasn't so bad."

"Aggressive, ornery, full of yourself. Driven. Did you sleep at all in high school?"

"One or two nights a week."

Dad's deep chuckle rolls out of his chest. "See the redbird flitting over the grass? Reminds me of the time you smacked one out of a tree with your slingshot." He looks over at me. "You'd just gotten good aim."

The memory sickens me all these years later. "It fell to the ground, fighting to fly."

"Never saw a ten-year-old boy cry so hard." Dad pops my knee. "But you nursed her back to health, and she flew again."

The redbird in the yard flutters and hops over the grass, ear cocked to the ground.

"Yeah, she flew. Sideways. Almost boomeranged into the house."

Dad laughs. "One of life's hard lessons." He offers me a swig of root beer. "So, how's it going with Miss James? Ain't a bad job, is it, boy?"

"Somebody's got to do it." I fake a weary sigh, then chug a drink of soda.

"You heard Brit is going to Europe?"

The sound of her name still pings some hollow place in my soul. "London for a year." I pass back the root beer.

"You're better off without her. She was flakey."

"I finally convinced myself." Though Brit broke off our engagement over a year ago, she'd moved in and out of my life every few months until I finally wised up and ended things. Permanently.

"All right, you two, we're ready to eat." Mom sets a serving bowl containing something picnicish on the table. "Chuck, call the kids to come wash up."

Dad anchors his pinkies inside his mouth and lets out a loud, shrill whistle. My nieces and nephews peel toward the house, slamming against each other to get in the back door. I lean over to Mom. "Did you all forget to tell me something, or are there more kids than at Christmas?"

She tee-hees. "The kids brought friends. They want you to organize a baseball game."

Slapping my hands together, I nod. "Sounds like a job I can handle."

My sister Sally unwraps a tub of potato salad. "Is it true?"

I pick an olive off the top. "That the world is round?"

She makes a face. "Are you really so immature? After all this time?"

"I'm a guy. I'm the youngest. I have dibs on immaturity."

My sister Patti leans over Sally's shoulder. "Are you really interviewing Aubrey James?"

I glance at Mom. "Can I not tell you anything?"

She busies herself with stacking napkins, refusing to look me in the eye. "You didn't say it was a secret."

"Did you tell Brit?" Sally asks, stuffing a big wooden spoon into the potato salad. "She'll freak. She *loves* Aubrey James."

"I haven't seen or talked to Brit in three months, and don't intend to start now."

"What's Aubrey like? Is she as beautiful in person?"

I thrust my hand inside an open bag of chips. "More so."

Patti snatches the chips from my hand. "Well, here's what we really want to know."

"What's that?" I gaze at them, my guard up. Nosey sisters. But I'm not dishing on Aubrey. She's sacred territory, for now, until I'm over my crush.

Patti points to my face. "What the heck happened to your eyebrows?"

Aubrey

For a summer that started out to be about resting and recuperating, I've been busy. Monday morning Piper drops me off at the Blackbird Studios where I meet Dave in Studio A with his guitar and SongTunes A&R director Aaron Littleton.

Seeing me, Dave rises from a posh leather chair. "Look, Aaron's here." He makes a face only I can see.

"Aaron, good to see you." I shake his hand, glancing back at Dave. *What is he doing here?*

"Sorry, Aubrey. Nathan wants to know what you're up to—his words not mine."

"Too scared to come down here himself?" I drop my handbag on the table.

"No, he was going to come, but I convinced him I should. You know, do his dirty work for him." He smiles as if to assure me he's joking. "I figured he'd just aggravate you and we'd never get another Aubrey James album."

I twist open my FRESH! bottle. "You're a wise man, Aaron."

"We're just starting the album over," Dave says. "There's nothing to tell Nathan."

Aaron crosses his arms and falls against the wall. "It's okay, Dave. I'll just hang around so I have something to tell him. Besides, it's always fun to watch Aubrey work." He looks around, deciding to sit instead of stand. "Why are you starting over?"

"Aubrey's going to write or cowrite all the songs."

"You're kid—" He stops with a glance at me. "Aubrey, this isn't standard Aubrey James."

"We told you, Aaron," I say.

"You're going to write the songs, record them, and hand it over to Nathan in less than two months." Aaron sounds dubious.

I glance at Dave. "Yes, with the help of a new songwriter, perhaps."

Aaron closes his eyes with a loud exhale. "A *new* songwriter? Aubrey, Aubrey, you're going to give Nathan a heart attack. What's wrong with the *old* songwriters?"

"Nothing, but this album is about doing music a different way. I can't, won't, be boxed in, stuck in one of Nathan's marketing brands."

"Holy cow, it's going to be a showdown."

The floor of my music room is littered with wadded-up paper when Car sticks his head through the door.

His eyes scan the room. "Killing trees?"

I growl and crumple up another page. "Trying to write a song."

"Just *one* song?" Car picks up one of the paper wads.

"Yes, a song." I play the melody that's been running through my head all day, but can't create the lyrics to match. "Gina left you a plate in the warmer."

"I ate downtown." Reading my lyrics, he joins me on the piano bench. "Since when did you write songs?"

"Since I was a kid."

Being the son of Grace Carmichael, he had seven years of piano, so he plays the chords written on the crumpled paper. "Sounds good to me."

"Car." I grab his hands with mine. "I appreciate your encouragement, but it can't just sound 'good to you.'" What was I thinking? I can't write an album of songs. Even half an album of songs. I can't even write one song.

"Why are you doing this? Aubrey, you've become a superstar singing other people's songs. It's the economy of the music business. The writers write, the singers sing. Why are you stressing yourself out over this?"

"Your faith in me is overwhelming," I snap.

Car rears back. "I'm just making a point. You're a huge name, Aubrey. There's not a songwriter in town who wouldn't give his or her eyeteeth to have an Aubrey James cut."

Did I expect him to understand? "Sorry, babe, I'm just ready to do something different."

All evening I'd been racking my brain for a unique way to sing, "I'm in love with you," without rhyming with the words *true*, *blue*, and *new* or sticking in some cliché like "never before" or "first time I've ever felt this way."

Car kisses my forehead. "Don't overthink it, Brie. If you can't come up with something, just go with the familiar."

Go with the familiar. The words hit me like a beam of light. I feel their intent. *Compromise*. Whenever something is hard, I compromise and go with the familiar. Well, not this time.

Car stands at the door. "By the way, the movers are coming Saturday."

"What?" *Love . . . dove . . . above . . . hug?*

"Brie?"

I look up. "Movers. Saturday."

He nods. "Just wanted to make sure you heard me. I'm going to use the library as my den."

This I hear and jump up. "You can't use the library. My boxes are in there."

"Aubrey, you sincerely want to waste that beautiful library storing junk?"

"It's not junk, Car. In those boxes is all I have left of my parents, of my childhood."

"Then do something with them or throw them out." His tone is sharp, making me feel like a troublesome child.

Crossing my arms, I step over to him. "There are plenty of other rooms in this house. Make one of them your den, Car, but the library is mine."

"The library has those beautiful built-in cherrywood bookshelves. You want to hide them with boxes of crap?"

Boxes of crap? "Pick another room, Car."

"Aubrey, if you're going to be territorial, then let's sell this place and buy a new one."

"I'm not being territorial, but you can't come in here and order me around, telling me what I should and shouldn't keep. Whether you like it or not, Car, I was here first."

Car bangs his fist against the door and walks out. My legs feel weak and wobbly, so I sink slowly to the piano bench. *Oh, Car . . .* This is ridiculous. Moving in together shouldn't be this hard, should it?

"Car, wait a minute . . ."

Basketball day. Thursday. Aubrey James versus Scott Vaughn. Piper is coming over early to help me get ready. For all my bragging about whupping Scott, I haven't played basketball in years.

"You came to bed late," Car says, walking out of the bathroom, his skin pink and fresh from a hot shower. The steamy fragrance of his soap fills the bedroom.

"Two a.m. But—" I pull a pair of baggy mesh shorts from the bottom dresser drawer. They're old and winkled. "—I wrote a song."

"One song?" He tugs open his sock drawer. "Are . . . we okay?"

Fighting a yawn, I tighten the short's drawstring and nod. "Yeah, we're okay."

He grabs my hips and tumbles me back onto the bed. "Are you sure? You seem rather quiet."

"I have a lot on my mind. Plus I'm not quite awake yet."

He runs his finger along my jaw line. "You're so beautiful, Brie."

I press my hand to his cheek. "Thank you, Car."

His kiss is passionate as he draws me close and tight, then suddenly releases me, springing off the bed. "Any more of that and I'll be late for work." He winks at me, straightening his tie.

I pat his back on my way to the bathroom. "Have a good day."

Dangling my Nikes from my fingertips, I head down the hall to the library. Piper will be here in a few minutes, but Car's announcement the movers are coming reminds me of something.

My promise to Zach to pray about marrying Car.

Stepping over the boxes and piles of clothes, I land on the couch, pausing a moment to stuff my feet in my shoes. Somewhere in one of these boxes is Daddy's Bible, worn and marked up.

After a brief search, I find it in the box by the door. Returning to my spot on the sofa, I cradle the Good Book to my chest and try to formulate a prayer.

"God, it's me . . ." The conversation feels foreign. "I need to talk about Car and me." Pausing to formulate my next thought, my mind wanders. *What time is it? I wonder if Gina's out with the dogs? I'm going to need breakfast before basketball.*

Stop. Focus. "Is he the right one for me? Is there even such a thing as the 'right one'?"

I wait for an answer, but nothing comes. No audible voice. No thunder or lightning crack. "Do you have an opinion here, God?"

Closing my eyes, I focus on focusing. *How will I know if He answers?* With my thumbs, I separate the Bible pages and let the book fall open on my lap. I jab my finger to some spot on the page and glance down.

"Jesus feeds the four thousand." I laugh. Not exactly the answer I'm looking for except surely if He fed the four thousand with a few loaves of bread, He can take care of me, right?

"I'm going to trust you on this one, God."

"Hey," Piper's voice calls up the stairs. "What's the hold up? Let's go if you want to run drills."

"Coming." I slip Daddy's Bible back in the box and hurry downstairs.

Out on the court, Piper digs bright orange basketballs out of a canvas bag. "Can you believe we never use this court? After all the trouble and expense to build it?"

I pick up the first ball. "We were going to have the old team over and play summer ball on Saturday nights." My nice, easy jump shot hits the rim and bounces high and away.

"Wow, you are out of practice."

"Keep the balls coming." I run to the hoop for a layup. "How's your online boyfriend?"

"Not. He called and invited me for coffee at the Frothy Monkey the other night, then no-showed."

"Pipe, I'm so sorry." I lob up another ball . . . Miss.

She shrugs. "I didn't like him that much anyway."

"You're just too special for these guys." Shoot and miss.

Piper bounces me another ball. "That's the lie I keep telling myself too."

I laugh. "How do any of us know a guy is right?" Dang, missed again.

"Strange question coming from someone who is engaged." She passes me another orange ball. "My new prayer is 'God, if you have a man for me, let him come up and slap me.'"

Pausing with the ball, I make a face. "Kind of drastic, don't you think?"

"Well, if a guy slaps me . . ." She grins. "There'll be no doubt."

"What if he's married?" I set up for a jump shot. *Boing*. The ball bounces off the rim.

"Married? Aubrey, please, it's kind of implied in the whole looking-for-Mr.-Right agreement that he's not married."

"Just in case, better talk to God about a backup plan." Another miss. Crud. I have no game. "I can see this slapping thing going way wrong."

"Speaking of God." Piper jogs around the court to gather up all the loose balls.

"Smooth transition, Cantwell."

She lobs a couple of balls to me. "Did you do what Zach asked you to do?"

I regard her for a second. "What did Zach ask me to do?"

"He told me, Aubrey." She tucks a ball under each arm. "He asked you to pray about marrying Car."

Dribbling up to the basket, I try another layup. And miss. "I've started to work on my promise."

She steps closer, passing me one of the balls from under her arm. "How does one *start* work on a prayer?"

Gripping the ball between my hands, I bounce once. "Do the talking but not the listening." I pause. "Part of me is afraid of what I'll hear."

"Which would be . . ."

"He's disappointed in me."

Piper motions for me to take a shot. "Aubrey, don't you know? God would kill the fatted calf for you."

I shoot and miss, then scurry for the rebound and lob up another shot. The ball rolls right over the rim and falls down the other side. "Scott is going to wipe the court with me."

"Did you hear me?"

"Yes, fatted calf. Prodigal son and all that, right? Prodigal daughter in my case." I stop and stare out over the lawn. "I never really left, Pipe, just wandered away for a while . . . But wouldn't that be lovely? To be back in my Father's house."

"It would." Piper's hand gently caresses my shoulder. "His love never—"

I whirl around. "Never fails. I know."

She jabs my chest. "Don't forget, okay?"

I smile. "You won't let me."

She starts clapping her hands. "All right, enough yapping." Lining up the basketballs on the baseline, Piper instructs me. "Let's get your game back. We're going for a hundred free throws in a row, no misses. Let's go."

"A hundred? Holy schmoly." Bending forward, bouncing on the balls of my feet, the familiar feel of this old drill surfaces. "A hundred in a row, a hundred in a row."

Piper bounces me ball after ball, while I miss shot after shot. After about the thirtieth miss, Piper holds up. "You're rushing. Slow down. Think."

"Slow down." I draw a deep, steadying breath.

"Concentrate." She fires the next ball. "Go."

I fire it up, and miss again.

"Your wrist. Use your wrist."

"Scott is going to kill me," I wail.

"Stop whining, Aubrey. Find your groove."

A few more shots, a few more misses, then it happens. The magic. The rhythm. The groove. *Whoosh.* "Wahoo!" I raise my arms in victory.

"Don't stop, keep going." Piper fires the ball back.

I shoot. Nothing but net.

By the time Scott shows up, Aubrey "Abdul-Jabbar" James is bouncing around the court, mopping sweat from her eyes, ready to take him down.

"Hope you're prepared to lose, 'cause I can't miss."

"No, I didn't come prepared to lose. I hope *you're* prepared to lose."

"Pipe," I call, "from now on, Thursday is staff basketball day."

Gina looks up from where she's stocking a cooler with FRESH! and Gatorade. "Count me out, boss."

"Ah, come on, it'll be fun. Then we can go for a swim."

Gina screeches and hurries away, her fleshy elbows pumping up and down.

"Don't let George and Ringo out!" I holler after her with a glance at Scott. "They like to play chase."

Scott swaggers to the center of the court, his arms and hips in opposite sway. He's wearing a pair of Adidas slides with white socks, a pair of pale blue Melo shorts with a white sleeveless T-shirt. His shoulders are square and thick, his arms muscled.

I stop bouncing as he saunters pass me. "What are you, the basketball mafia?"

Stopping midcourt, he juts one foot forward and lifts his dark shades to his forehead. "I should be able to beat you on this court. No problem."

Laughing, I resume bouncing, circling him Apollo Creed style. "You're going down, Vaughn."

He peers at me over his lowered shades. "Game time."

With that, I buckle over laughing. His pretense of cool is hilarious. Rafe comes over while Scott exchanges his sandals for sneakers and introduces me to a second cameraman. "This is our summer intern, Owen. He's going to run the mini-DV today."

I shake his hand. "Nice to meet you." He's a young twenty-something with an eager expression and sky blue eyes.

His grin stretches across his face. "I love my job. Aubrey James . . ."

Rafe tugs on his shirtsleeve, pulling him aside. "Be cool, man. Be cool."

Back to bouncing. Man, this is going to be fun. Courtside, my fans (aka paid employees) set up lawn chairs. Gina's wearing an oversized floppy hat and sipping something pink from a hurricane glass.

Piper-the-coach leans forward with her elbows on her thighs. "Come on, let's go, Aubrey. You can take him."

Zach, who's just arrived, cups his hands around his mouth, "Take him down, Aubrey."

"What? No one rooting for the winner?" Scott faces them with his arms wide.

"Got to go with the home team," Zach reasons with a laugh.

"We're rooting for you, man." Rafe gives Scott a thumbs-up from behind the camera. "Win this for *Inside NashVegas*." But when Scott looks away, Rafe catches my eye. "Win," he mouths.

I give Rafe a thumbs-up, then challenge Scott. "Are we talking or playing?" Back to bouncing. Man, this feels good.

Scott strides onto the court, palming an orange ball. "Ladies first."

I check to Scott. "First one to twenty-one wins."

He angles forward, shadowing my moves. But when he lunges for a steal, I swerve around him for an easy layup.

"One to zip." I can't stop smiling. Or sweating. The late morning sun is high and hot in a cloudless blue sky.

"I see how it is." Scott takes the ball out, then runs inbounds with a hard drive for the hoop. He stops short for a jump shot and makes his basket.

"One to one, I believe." He backs away, passing me the ball, wearing a goofy, arrogant expression.

Shaking my head, I bounce the ball. "Scott, Scott, Scott."

"Watch her, Scott. She's aggressive."

What? Whose side is she on? "Piper . . ." With my guard down, Scott slaps the ball from my hands for a steal and sinks another basket.

He prances around the court. "Two to one. Two to one."

Game face on, I point to Piper. "Stop aiding the enemy. You distracted me, and now look."

The game is brutal. Thirty minutes later I'm huffing and puffing, and it's very evident I'm not seventeen any more.

The score is nineteen to twenty, Scott.

"He's got you figured out, Aubrey," Piper announces from the sidelines.

"You did some research," I say, dribbling in. "Figured out my best three-pointer."

He mirrors my movements, guarding me. "What can I say? I'm a sports reporter."

More and more, the quirky sportscaster with the cocky grin, lyrical laugh, and soulful eyes captures me. He makes me feel . . . *Never mind. Play ball.*

Keeping my eye on Scott's ball-stealing hand, I drive up the middle. He stumbles, trying to steal, and I shoot an easy fadeaway. The ball swishes through the net.

"Twenty to twenty."

Next, Scott tries his own fadeaway that bounces in, then out. I charge for the ball. "Look who's got the ball. Look who's going to win."

"Pride goes before the fall, Aubrey." He charges me, trying for a steal. "You can't win."

"Come on, Aubrey, finish him off. He can't really play," Rafe taunts. "You should've seen him when we played the Fox 17 sports crew last year. Shewwee, stinker."

"Please, Rafe, he almost beat *me*." I shove past Scott for the final drive and winning shot.

Out of nowhere, Owen-the-intern cuts across the court right in front of me. I eek out a shrill "O-wen!" and swerve sideways, trying to miss him. But my shoulder plows right into him.

The *Inside NashVegas* intern topples backwards, smacking his head against the hard court floor.

"Owen, are you okay?" I drop to my knees next to him.

Zach rushes in from the sideline. "He smacked his head pretty hard."

Doctor Gina bends over the down cameraman, holding up two fingers. "How many fingers do you see?"

"Two."

"Good." Gina reaches for his arm. "Can you get up?"

"Yeah," he mutters, rising up on his elbows with a slow, goofy grin. "I got plowed by Aubrey James."

"Boy, didn't I tell you to be cool?" Rafe mutters.

The rescue squad helps Owen to his feet. Once he's seated with a Ziploc baggie of ice pressed against his head and Gina assures me he's all right, I go back to the court.

Scott stands under the basket, ball poised over his head. "I believe this is twenty-one." He pushes the ball toward the rim.

But instead of sinking down, it rolls around and . . .

"Sink, you stupid ball. Sink." Scott jumps up and down, waving his arms. The ball falls down the other side of the rim and bounces over to me.

The sideline spectators erupt.

"Aubrey, get the ball. Get it."

With two steps forward, I swoop it up for an easy basket and find myself nose to nose with my opponent. "I believe *that* is twenty-one."

19

"Aren't you glad I let you win?" Scott pops a grape into his mouth. He's downed a tall tumbler of Gina's sweet tea and is waiting for a refill.

"Spin it any way you want." I lift my chin to catch the breeze generated by the porch ceiling fans. "We all know the truth."

George and Ringo pace between us, panting, licking knees as they stroll by. Every muscle in my body aches, and I twisted my ankle trying not to trip over Owen.

Poor Owen. He's next to me with ice on his eye, bruised from the camera eyepiece. "How is it?" I ask.

He lowers the ice pack. "Doesn't hurt as much."

"I'm really sorry, Owen."

He replaces his ice pack and smiles. "Not every day a guy can say he got a black eye from Aubrey James."

Scott taps him on the knee. "Next time, be sure to stay out of the way."

Owen's ruddy cheeks flush a deeper red. "Yes, sir."

Scott makes a face. *Sir?* I start to tease him, but Piper taps me on the shoulder. "Phone for you."

"Who is it?"

She shrugs. "He didn't say."

"Hello?"

"It's me."

I rise slowly from the wicker sofa. "H-hello." A stonelike knot catches in my throat, making it hard to breathe. All porch conversation stops.

"What are you trying to do? Just leave it alone." His tone is terse.

"Leave what alone? What are you talking about?" I walk to the edge of the porch; my aching muscles are now trembling.

"We've been down this road before. Leave it alone."

"Peter, I'm not looking for you." There's a collective sigh from the crowd behind me. Now they know. "Why do you think—" There's a click followed by a buzzing dial tone.

Piper takes the phone, pressing End. Chills crawl over my sweat-dried skin. "That was Peter. Someone must be searching for him. He thinks it's me. *Again.*" When I turn around, everyone's expression is serious. I smile with a shaky laugh. "Fun times, huh?"

Zach scoots to the edge of his seat. "Are you searching for him?"

"No. He made his feelings known the last time I tried to get in touch with him: leave him alone. So I did."

Piper sets the phone on the glass table. "How long has it been since you heard from him?"

"Six years." I return to the sofa. "I think we had the same five-second conversation. Some kook who was looking for a payout tried to scare him out of hiding."

Any other day, missing Peter would be a dull, foreign emotion—

one I'd tucked away years ago in the name of self-preservation. But today, the missing is painful. All the talk of Daddy and Momma and our gospel days has scraped the protective coating away from my heart. Zach presses his hand on my arm. "Are you okay?"

"I am, but, if y'all will excuse me . . ." Pausing at the door, I wave to Scott. "Thanks for the game."

Friday evening Car's in bed working on his laptop when I crawl under the covers, still sore from yesterday's game of one-on-one.

Peter's voice clung to my heart most of yesterday afternoon, but by this morning, I'd shaken the impact of his call and resealed my emotions.

However, my business meeting with Eli today brought up a whole new set of issues. Fluffing the covers and plumping my pillows, I watch Car from the corner of my eye.

"Brie, you're shaking the bed. I'm trying to type here."

Hugging my legs to my chest, I ask, "How's the SoBro project?"

"Still frustrating. Working a lot of angles, trying to figure out why investors won't commit."

I rest my chin on the top of my knees. "When were you going to tell me I'm one of your angles?"

His fingers freeze, hovering over the keyboard. "What makes you think I'm using you as one of my angles?" His eyes shift from the computer screen to me.

"I met with my business manager today."

Car shoves his laptop aside with a heavy sigh. "Brie, I called Eli and asked a few questions. What's the big deal?"

"The big deal?" I pound the mattress. "Car, he actually thought I wanted to invest in one of your condos. He spent a lot of time rearranging my accounts, moving money around. Did you not know he'd call me?"

"Then he wasted his own time. I didn't ask him for a commitment."

Car stretches out his long, lean legs and locks his hands behind his head. The air around him is scented with end-of-day cologne and deodorant.

"Then you better rethink how you word things, Car. You had Eli convinced."

He cuts his gaze over to me. "Why won't you trust me and invest, Aubrey?"

"Trust you? When you've gone behind my back three times now?" I slide down under the covers, shivering. I'm both angry and cold. Car sets the air-conditioning so low on summer nights the room has a wintry chill.

He rolls toward me, propping himself up on his elbow. "I went to Eli with our standard proposal. If he liked it, I thought he could bring it to you." He sighs. "Which is ridiculous, considering I share your bed, not Eli."

Buried up to my chin in blankets, I stare at the sculptured swirls in the ceiling. "Car, I need you to tell me you're not out for my money."

His eyes narrow and snap. "I don't need your money."

"Then why are you going behind my back to get me to invest?"

"Because it's a great idea. If *you* invest, I can capitalize on it with other investors."

His confession sends a cold shiver of realization over my body. "Capitalize on my name, Aubrey James?"

He rolls off the bed. "One of the partners dropped your name during dinner with several potential investors. It's amazing what a beautiful face and famous name will do for bored, rich men."

"You cannot use my name." My tone leaves no doubt.

Car paces at the foot, his hands on his hips. "You're going to be my wife and I can't mention your name to my business associates?" He shakes hands with an imaginary man. "Why, yes, Mr. Investor, I *am* married. She's beautiful, talented, and wonderful, but her name is a secret."

"Your cheesy sarcasm pisses me off." I flip over to my side, away from him. But then, in a surge of anger, I sit up. "Car, do you know how damaging it can be for me if something goes wrong with one of these investments? Suppose an investor feels cheated or duped? They'll sue me, not Car Carmichael or Carmichael Financials." I press my hand to my chest. "My name will make the headlines. But all of that aside, I won't risk AubJay Inc."

He chews on his bottom lip, avoiding my gaze for a long, silent moment, then crawls onto the bed next to me. "Aubrey, look, babe. All I wanted was for Eli to hear our plan. It's good and sound. I figured if he pitched it to you, then our agreement to keep our finances separate for a while wouldn't be breeched." Slipping his arms around me, he holds me close, kissing my forehead.

"You make yourself sound very noble, Car. But you knew your actions violated our agreement."

He strokes my hair and slips his finger under my chin with a feathery touch. "Okay, I hear you." His kiss is delicate and sweet, and no matter how hard I resist, I melt a little bit. "How'd I get lucky enough to find you?"

Smoothing my hand over his high, broad cheeks, I remind him. "Your parents lived in the right neighborhood."

He laughs and rolls over to his side of the bed. "Don't forget the movers are coming tomorrow."

I remember. "Don't you forget I'm tied up all day with Dave. Gina will be here to help the movers."

He caresses my arm. "Don't stress over this album, Brie. Why mess with the magic that's always worked?"

"Because I'm thirty, not nineteen." I click off my nightstand light. "We're going to the Bluebird Café tomorrow night to hear a songwriter, Robin Rivers." I scoot over to him and tug on his arm. "Meet me there? Please, Car, it'll be fun."

"Naw, you go ahead. This is your thing."

"My thing," I echo softly. "What happened to all the 'we' stuff when you talked about money?"

He unfastens his watch, setting it on his night table. "I don't know anything about songwriters. They all sound good to me."

"What about being there for me?"

He switches off his night-table lamp and, in the dark, reaches for me. "I have a tee time on Sunday with some clients. I'd planned to get organized Saturday night after the move. Can you meet this songwriter another time? Stay here and help me get settled in."

"You know the time pressure we're under on this album. We're already behind. And if we want to work with Robin, we need to know now."

"And when you come home, your fiancé will be all settled in. You won't have to lift a finger." A wide yawn punctuates his sentence.

"Seems our schedules have us going in opposite directions, doesn't it."

"Two big careers will do that, Brie." Another yawn. The sheets rustle as he moves his legs, getting settled in for sleep.

"I guess so." Laying there in the dark, cradled in his arm, I consider dumping my plans for Saturday and helping my fiancé. But I can't. Time is critical. Actually, I'm looking forward to tomorrow night. Discovering new songs, new sounds. Hearing Robin's music. A twinge of excitement ripples through me.

"Car?"

"Hum . . ."

"I meant to tell you . . ."

"Yeah?"

"If you want the library, you can have it."

"Brie, are you sure?" He rubs my arm with his fingertips.

"You were right. I don't need to keep all those boxes—"

"Thank you, Brie. Really." He tightens his arms around me.

"I'm happy to do it. Just put my boxes in the rec room, okay?"

"Um-hum" His answer is mellow and sleepy.

"Car?" I nudge him gently.

"Library." He turns over, and in another second, I hear the soft sounds of sleep.

Curling up on my side of the bed, I whisper to God. "Car and me . . . What do I do? Please help Dave and me with this new album. And tell Daddy and Momma I miss them."

The Bluebird is a small, seemingly out-of-the-way, café on Hillsboro Road, but a legendary showcase for some of the world's best songwriters. And some of the worst. But every hopeful songwriter can have their day at the Bluebird.

Dave and I arrive well early so I can get in without causing a stir. We find a table in the far, dark corner and weave our way through the tight row of tables and around the four chairs set up "in the round."

"Does Robin know we're coming?" I ask Dave, realizing for the first time this might be a surprise.

"Yes, I called her. She's excited to meet you."

"Good." I glance around at the walls posted with pictures of country music's great songwriters—Dolly Parton, Don Schlitz, Willie Nelson. Two of tonight's songwriters take their seats, tuning their guitars and running a sound check.

A pang of jealousy hits me. They are free to come and go, sing their songs, make their music. Paparazzi don't hide in their bushes; friends don't betray their secrets for fifty thousand dollars.

Maybe they'd give their eyeteeth to trade places with me, but I just might give mine to trade with them. Fame, for all its accolades, comes at a very high price.

Dave nudges me. "There's Robin."

A petite, very pretty redhead with oval green eyes joins our table. Her genuine smile captivates me. I like her.

"Robin Rivers, meet Aubrey James."

I offer my hand. "Very pleased to meet you."

"The pleasure is all mine. I'm a big fan of yours. Before that, I grew up listening to your parents' music."

"You loved my parents' music?"

"Oh yeah, your dad played a mean guitar."

"He did." This might be a perfect partnership.

"So, newlywed." Dave taps her arm. "Is the honeymoon over? Ready to get to work?"

Her cheeks flush. "No, the honeymoon is not over, and yes, I'm ready to work."

"Do you have any songs written that might work for Aubrey?" Dave gets down to business.

Robin's green gaze falls on me. "Every molecule in my body wants to say yes, but to be honest, I don't know. I have some songs I'd love for you to hear."

Impressed with her honesty, I say, "I'm ready to listen."

She laughs. "I just thought of two songs that might work for you. I'll sing them tonight."

"Robin, we're tight on time for this album. If we like what we hear tonight, are you free Monday to do some cowriting?" Dave asks.

"Tell me the time and the place." Robin glances from Dave to me, then to Dave again. I haven't been around Robin's kind of humility in a long time, and it inspires me.

By now, the Bluebird is filling up and the whispers are starting. *Aubrey James . . . No! Where? Really?*

I duck into the shadows, praying against another Boot Corral incident. What a zoo that turned out to be.

Our waitress comes over with warm bread and brie cheese. "On the house."

"Thank you. Tell your boss—" The 'Bird's illustrious owner makes her way through the crowded room toward us. "Guess I'll tell her myself."

"Aubrey, so good to see you."

Standing, I greet her with a hug. "Thanks for the table and the food."

"Anything for you."

We chat for a few minutes, until the lights go down and the show begins. Robin, sitting on the far side of the round, kicks off the evening. "Welcome to the Bluebird, everyone. I'm Robin Rivers. This is a song I wrote a few months ago, and I'm singing it tonight for a new friend of mine."

Her voice is smooth and strong. She's tenuous at first, but her voice steadies after a few measures. She's singing about "life on the river." I love the fun feel of the song, but there's hidden meaning behind the everyday words. Her lyrics are powerful and thought provoking. And all the while, the melody has me tapping my toe.

Our eyes meet, and I recognize the *light* in her eyes. Robin Rivers is a friend of Jesus.

Her third song in the round is exactly the song I was trying to write the other day when Car came into the music room. Saying I love you in a unique, wonderful way.

This stranger is singing my heart. How is it that every major artist in town is not clamoring for her songs?

Smiling, I whisper to Dave, "We've found ourselves a gem, haven't we?"

He nods. "No doubt."

Robin's turn comes around again and she glances my way, hunching up her shoulders. "I might get killed for doing this, but what the heck? No pain, no gain."

She's going to ask me to sing.

"Aubrey James is visiting tonight."

The entire room gasps. Heads whip around. It's the Boot Corral all over again.

"If I play one of your songs, will you sing, Aubrey?" Robin winces, but beckons me with a tip of her red head.

The Bluebird erupts with applause.

I stand. "Only for you, Robin."

Working my way through the tight row of tables, I try to remember when I ever sang so close to the audience. It's a tad unnerving. The woman behind me is doused with a heavy perfume. For a split second, I wish I'd asked my security henchman, Jeff, to join us tonight. But I decided not to mess with his weekend since this was an unscheduled event.

The songwriter sitting left of Robin hops up. "Sit here, Aubrey."

"Thank you." I shake the young man's hand.

Robin strums softly while I take a quick second for a mike check. "Y'all would have to pay a hundred bucks to see Aubrey James this close, and live," she tells the Bluebird crowd.

"Or even this close and dead," I add. Laughter ripples around the room. But that's the Bluebird. Songs and banter. "Thank you for letting me sit in."

Whistles and applause. Someone shouts, "We love you!"

Another, "We love the Bluebird."

Robin looks at me. "Do you have a favorite song?"

"Sure, but what's *your* favorite song of mine?"

She grins. "All of them."

I twist my lips. "Baloney. I can't even make that statement. Come on, name a song."

An audience member shouts, "'And Your Dirty Socks, Too.'"

I turn in the direction of the request. "Really? You want me to sing the dirty socks song?" With a shrug, I nod to Robin. "You know it?"

Without asking me what key, she plays the first measure in perfect rhythm. "Some of you may remember this song won CMT's video of the year," she says.

"Robin, I'm going to hire you to be my publicist."

The Bluebird waitresses hustle between the crowded tables, taking orders and setting down drinks. A few more folks come through the door, squeezing between the folks already lining the wall.

The living room atmosphere of the Bluebird reminds me of singing with Daddy, Momma, and Peter. A peaceful presence swirls around me as I sing, slapping my leg, keeping time. It's strange yet wonderful. While I'm serenading the room with a song about dirty socks, God is reaching out to me, wooing back the Aubrey James who got confused and a little lost along the way.

20

Scott

Saturday, July 21

For the first time since Rafe and I left Nashville in the twilight dawn, I allow myself to think about what I'm doing.

"Her brother wants to be alone," Jeremiah warned me when I told him about Peter James calling Aubrey that day we played one on one. "My guy in Florida spooked him."

"Where can I find Peter?"

"Destin Beach. Runs a deep-sea charter and goes by the name Captain Pete."

"I owe you man."

"Scott, he wants to be left alone."

"Jer, you didn't see her face when he called."

Rafe reaches forward and ups the volume on the radio as my Porsche speeds west along Florida's Gulf Breeze Parkway. Aubrey's voice serenades us.

She wore a big green hat
On top of her red hair
And a pair of blue shoes
I can see from over here

"You're falling in love with her, aren't you?" Rafe says.

"She's engaged. I'm doing this for the story."

"Right, the story." Rafe laughs low.

I glance at him. "You saw her face Thursday."

"Yeah, but I got the feeling she doesn't want you or anyone else bringing her brother home." Rafe taps out the beat of the music on his leg. "At least you're moving on from that chick, what's-her-name."

"Brit."

"Yeah, Brit. Granted, this is the *dumbest* possible way, but at least you're moving on."

I snort a laugh. "This is for Sam and his stupid story."

"Keep lying to yourself, you might just believe it. We've already got the CMT deal." Rafe rolls down his window, and warm salty air rushes in. My Google map slaps against the dash, then flies out the window.

"Rafe!" I snatch at the paper as it whips by. In the next second, it's highway litter.

"Sorry, man, wanted to pour out my Coke." He holds up a gigantic 7-Eleven cup, angling his arm out the window.

"Rafe, wait—" I'm going too fast to empty a drink. Sure enough, the wind jerks the cup out of his hand, and watery Coke sprays all over the leather seats.

"Holy cow, man, can't take you anywhere."

"Simmer down, it's just sticky water." Rafe reaches for a pile of McDonald's napkins. "Leather cleans up easily enough."

I laugh. It's too great a day to be mad. Especially at Rafe. Clicking off the air, I roll down my window, too, and jut out my elbow. The air is hot and muggy, the scene along the highway postcard perfect. Clear horizon, white sandy beach, a pelican flying low over blue-green water. The color reminds me of Aubrey's eyes, but I don't say that out loud. Rafe would never let me live it down.

"Does it get any better than this?" Rafe leans out his window. "Remind me to move here one day."

In the next half hour, we find our Holiday Inn (without the map), check in, and grab a bite to eat at Joe's Crab Shack.

"What's the plan?" Rafe tosses aside his crab legs shell and licks butter from his fingers.

"Find Captain Pete. Jeremiah said he docks at Harborwalk Marina. Vessel's name is *GoneFishing*."

"And if he's not willing to talk to you?" Rafe's eyes widen with doubt.

I crack open my lobster tail. "Figure it out as we go."

After a dinner of too much seafood (as if there is such a thing), Rafe and I hunt for *GoneFishing* and Captain Pete. We find the boat but not the man.

"Let's hang out for a while, see if he comes around," I suggest. It's early evening, and from my limited seafaring experience, my guess is Captain Pete won't go out again until morning. But I'm hoping he'll come around with supplies for the next day.

Rafe and I hang around in the marina's bait and tackle shop for a while, scrutinizing every captain-looking man that comes in.

"Think that's him?"

"No. Do you?"

After a couple of hours, the man behind the counter beckons us. "Can I help you two?"

I flash my TV anchorman smile. "Just looking for Captain Pete."

"Gone for the night."

"Do you know where he might be?" I slide my hand along the counter with the tip of a twenty-dollar bill sticking out. From the corner of my eye, I catch Rafe shaking his head, covering his eyes.

"Home, I reckon." The guy behind the counter moves his toothpick from one side of his mouth to the other. "You want me to break that twenty for you?" He pops open the register and pulls out a ten and two fives.

"Thanks." I hand him the twenty. "Do you know where he lives?"

"Captain Pete? Nope. But he's got a charter Sunday morning at six."

Folding the bills into my pocket, I thank my friend behind the counter and head for the door. Outside, Rafe slaps me on the back.

"Smooth move, man." He mimics me sliding the money across the counter.

"He had no idea I was offering money for information."

"There's hope for humanity after all." Rafe pulls out the mini-DV and faces the golden horizon. "Might as well get some footage of this great sunset."

He activates the camera with an inhale of salty air, films some of the landscape, then lowers the camera and checks with me. "Back here at six a.m.?"

"Guess so." Walking down the dock, we pass Captain Pete's boat again, and in the setting sunlight, I spot a tanned, shirtless man spraying down the deck.

"Rafe," I call low, pointing. He moves alongside me, propping the camera on his shoulder.

"Captain Pete?" I holler.

"Done for the day." He doesn't look around. "Come around in the morning. I have a few openings."

"I'm not interested in a charter." I step to the edge of the dock, anchoring my leg against a pylon. From my below-deck angle, I see he's well-built and tanned a deep brownish red. His sun-bleached hair is buzzed high and tight.

"Then what can I do for you?"

"I'd like to talk to you about your sister, Aubrey James."

Captain Pete's shoulders stiffen, and for a brief moment he stops working. "Did she send you?"

"She doesn't even know I'm here. Can I talk with you?" Here's where I need a plan. But I don't have one. *What do I want from you, Peter James?*

The man resumes working, cleaning his boat in the fading light while Rafe and I stand below. Finding him was easy enough, thanks to Jeremiah, but I have a feeling if I let him go, I won't see him again.

At last, he twists off the water and steps toward the boat's stern. Jumping down to the dock, he looks at me directly for the first time. His skin is leathery with deep lines running across his set, hard features.

"You the one who's been looking for me?"

"Scott Vaughn from *Inside NashVegas*. How you doing?" Offering my hand, I step toward him.

"Doing just fine." He drives his big thick fist into my face.

Aubrey

A dozen wonderful red roses wait for me when I arrive home from Dave's Monday afternoon.

"Robin Rivers is phenomenal," I announce to Gina and the dogs, settling my guitar just inside the great room. "One day into our partnership and we have three fabulous songs."

Gina smiles. "If the light in your eyes is any indication, you're on your way to another platinum album."

I bury my nose in the red-velvet sweetness of the roses. "I'm not after status. I just want to sing from my heart. So, who are these from?"

George and Ringo swirl around me, wagging their tails, sniffing my shoes. "Yes, boys, I was at Dave's. His poodle sends her love."

Gina squirts 409 on the island counter top. "How should I know? Do I read your private notes?" She shudders. "What if it's something about your *bloom*."

I make a face. "I'm sure it's not about my *bloom*."

For the library and our future together.

Love always, Car

"They're from Car." I breathe again the subtle fragrance of the roses.

"Very lovely." Gina turns from where she's unloading the dishwasher. "Guess he's trying to get in on your good side."

I tuck the card under the bottom of the vase. "My good side?" We've had our differences lately, but how would Gina know? Most of our disputes have been behind closed doors.

Piper comes around the corner, papers in her hand. "Good, you're home. How was your day?" She waves the papers at me. "Contracts for the new distributor on your Aubrey Bags. You need to sign them today so I can fax them back. We're backing up on orders already."

"Eli's looked over the contract?"

"Yes, it's straightforward. We pay them to ship the handbags. Period." She holds out a pen and the contract. "Can't get any easier."

We huddle at her desk, reading over the contract one last time, then discuss the possibility of designing a new handbag for the spring. "I'll call the designer tomorrow." Piper taps a note into her Palm Pilot.

I flop down on the couch, humming the melody of the last song Robin and I penned. It has a lot of minor chords and I love the sound. "So, Gina, what do you mean Car's trying to get in on my good side? He didn't paint the library black, did he? Or turn one of the upstairs bedrooms into a putting room? What?"

Piper works the fax machine. "You gave Car the library?"

"I did."

"Guess compromise is key to all relationships, though I wouldn't know." Piper presses the big green Send button and turns to me, hand at her waist.

I nod toward her. "Your day's coming, friend."

Gina comes around with the dogs' leashes. George and Ringo flip and twist around her legs. "I told Car if he threw out all the stuff, you'd be madder than a hornet, but he insisted—"

Rising to my knees, I address Gina over the back of the couch. "What do you mean 'threw out all the stuff'?"

"Your boxes. He said you wanted to get rid of them." Gina snaps a leash onto George's collar, then Ringo's.

My heart nearly stops beating. "He threw out my boxes? I told him to store them in the rec room."

Gina tips her head to one side. "Tried to tell him, but he was a hundred percent convinced you said you didn't need to keep them."

I charge for the stairs, running up two at a time. Piper is close on my heels. Opening the library door, I stop just inside. Light from the southern sun fills the windows and paints the burgundy carpet with golden flecks.

"Oh my gosh, this is beautiful. Where did he get this furniture?" She lightly touches the shelves containing the leather-bound books.

The deep mahogany and leather surroundings speak Car's name. "The question is where did he store my boxes?"

Down the hall, third door on the right, is the rec room. I peer inside. Empty except for the pool table I bought last year. No boxes, no Momma's couch, no Grandma's plant stand.

Piper pulls something from a crate just inside the door. "An old, muddy golf shoe." Wrinkling her nose, she drops the shoe back in the box. "There's a pair of dried-up, sweaty golf gloves too. And a stack of magazines."

"Those have to be Car's." I thunder down the hall, looking in every room for my belongings. *Did he store the boxes in the garage?*

But the garage contains only my antique Mercedes. *I'm surprised he didn't throw it out too. Make room for his Humvee and golf cart.*

A slow, deliberate chill creeps over me. I begin to shake.

"Piper, get your keys, we're going downtown."

I glance at my watch, hoping Car's not in a meeting. It's almost five. His admin, Ilene, jumps from behind her desk as I approach. "A-aubrey. Was Mr. Carmichael expecting you?"

"This is a surprise visit." I walk into Car's big and bright Fourth Avenue corner office.

Car turns from his computer. "Brie, what are you doing here?" He greets me in the middle of the room with a light kiss.

Remain calm. There's a logical explanation. I just know it. "Car, honey, where's my stuff?"

"Your stuff?" His brows knit together. He smoothes his thumb over the back of my hand.

"My stuff. From the library. The boxes, the furniture."

"Oh, y-your stuff . . ." He swallows as the color drains from his face. "Well—" He walks over to his desk, keeping his back to me. "Y-you said you didn't need it. Right?"

"Nooo . . . When would I have said such a thing?"

Car faces me. "Friday night. When we were in bed. You told me I could have the library because you didn't need to keep the boxes."

"Yes. In . . . the . . . library. I asked you to put them in the rec room."

"Aubrey, you said you didn't want to keep the boxes. I heard you."

My heart pounds against my chest. "Then why didn't you hear me ask you to move my things to the rec room?"

"Because you didn't ask me."

"Car, I did ask. You answered."

"How could I answer a question I didn't hear?"

"Oh my gosh." My stomach tightens as I sink down to Car's office sofa. "Where's my stuff?"

He gestures with his hand, his mouth open, but words don't come.

"Did you put it in storage? In your condo?"

"I-I had the movers—I specifically heard you say you didn't want to keep the stuff, Brie. I did."

I rise slowly. "Where did the movers take my things, Car? Where?" My voice rises, demanding an answer.

"They hauled it away. To the dump." His words are clipped, his expression tight.

For a moment, I can't breathe. I can't think. "The dump?" My jaw is clinched so tight I can barely talk. My body trembles. "How could you send my childhood memories, all I have left of my parents, to the dump?" My fist flies at him, landing on the side of his arm.

He snatches me by the shoulders, his face inches from mine. "I would've never thrown away your personal things unless you okayed it."

"You did this on purpose," I say as tears form.

"What? Why would I do such a thing?"

"And why would *I* do such a thing?" I swear. "Why didn't you check with me?"

"I don't know. The movers were moving your boxes from the library, and they asked where to take them—Aubrey, I'm sorry."

I brush the tears from my jaw. "Tell me about the box of old golf gear in the rec room. It's yours, right?"

"Yes."

"And you've kept them because . . . ?"

"Aubrey—"

"Car, answer me?" I stomp my foot.

"Because they are my first golf shoes and gloves." He lifts his head and peers into my eyes. "The gear Dad bought when he taught me to play."

"Old, worn golf gear you keep. But my memories you haul off to the dump." My voice breaks.

Everything's gone. The pictures, the diaries, the bluebird of happiness. I twist the diamond ring around my finger. "I don't know what to do, Car."

"Aubrey, come on." With an awkward step, he pulls me into his arms. "This is a misunderstanding, a mistake." His words touch nothing inside me. I feel odd and empty. "Our relationship is about more than boxes of stuff, right?"

I shove away from him. "But somewhere in the core of our relationship, shouldn't you have an understanding of who I am?"

"Brie, of course. But boxes of junk?"

"Car, call it junk one more time, and you'll wish you hadn't. Those boxes were the only physical evidence remaining of my parents." I feel like a broken record. "Why can't you understand that?"

"Fine, but Aubrey, it's too late now. I can't go dump diving." He looks at me expectantly. "What do you want from me?"

"I—"

A knock interrups my reply. "Car." Ilene's face appears around the door. Two men in dark suits wait behind her. "The Harrington reps are here."

Car glances from me to Ilene, then back to me again. He bends toward my ear. "Can we finish this at home?"

The men stand aside as I leave, mouths agape. When the elevator doors creep open, I hear one mutter, "My gosh, that was Aubrey James."

Connie sets a big glass of sweet tea in front of me, along with a box of Kleenex. "One tough summer for you, girl."

"He makes me so freaking mad." I blow my nose then smash the tissue in my hand.

Driving home from downtown, I asked Piper to drop me off at Connie's. We were stuck in rush-hour traffic and the longer we crept along, the madder I got.

"Honey, did you consider he might have thought you really wanted to get rid of all that stuff?" Connie stores the pitcher of tea in the fridge, then pulls open the drawer by the sink.

"Whose side are you on, anyway?"

"Yours." She scatters silvery-wrapped chocolate kisses across the table. "But you do realize losing your boxes and that old furniture is not the real problem."

Popping a chocolate drop into my mouth, I bite without waiting for it to melt. "What's my real problem?"

She taps her blouse over her heart. "Right here."

I squeeze the tiny tin wrapping into a ball. "My heart? Something is wrong with my heart?" My patience is thin and fragile.

"Sweetie, I'm just trying to get you to see the bigger picture. All the emotion and energy you spent protecting waterlogged boxes proved to be exactly what Jesus taught: perishable things perish. The legacy of your parents is *you*. Aubrey. Who you are. What you've become. The faith they taught you."

Scooting away from the table, I carry my tea over to the sink and pour it out. "I tried to keep the faith for a while, but found no comfort in serving a God who took away my family. By the time I realized being mad at a God who loves me did me no good, I'd become accustomed to ignoring Him. Couldn't figure out the road home." I move over to the refrigerator for a bottle of water. "Besides, He must be pretty angry with me."

Her laugh is high and airy. "Angry with you? Darling, have you seen your life? Maybe you're too close to realize, but you are blessed. Your first album sold four million units."

"What's your point?"

"Your second album, eight million. Third album shot you right into the land of the legends. Aubrey Jo, if God is angry with you"—she rises from her chair, pointing to herself—"I'll take a gallon to go."

Her expression makes me laugh. "No fair. I was on my way to a good meltdown."

She tosses me another chocolate kiss. "Tough being a diva, isn't it?"

"This isn't about me being a diva." I twist the water bottle cap off, then on. "This is about a girl in crisis." A few thin tears slip down my cheeks, and I wipe my face with the back of my hand. "But I can't deny that I've been very blessed."

"Can I say one more thing?"

I peel the silver paper away from the chocolate kiss. "Now you ask permission?"

"Don't go into this marriage with your eyes closed, hoping for the best. If Car's not the one . . . And I'm not saying this because he tossed out your boxes. I'm saying this because I've been watching and listening. I love Car. I love you. But, honey, got to tell you I don't love the two of you together. Please, pray before this thing gets too far. Why don't you talk to Pastor Bolz?"

"I haven't seen Shawn in years. I'd feel ridiculous." Peering into her eyes, I add, "But, Connie, I am praying about Car and me. After today, all the more."

21

"The Coming Home Gospel Celebration is about combining great music with a great faith. This year, we're thrilled to have Aubrey James singing with us at the Ryman, doing a tribute to her parents. If you ask me, it's long overdue."

—*Ralph Lester, The Tennessean*

Dear Myra,

Please remind me I can't fall in love. I'm going off to college. But I just got home from a date with a guy named Buck Carroll and sigh . . .

Maybe there's something to this falling in love, getting married thing. I mean, it's only one date, but I have never felt this way about a guy before. I can literally see myself with him for the rest of my life.

I'm sure that's how you feel about Car, right?

Anyway, Buck is the nicest guy. Very cute in a rodeo rider kind of way. And he works at his daddy's mill. At my suggestion, we went bowling tonight, which is the worst thing to do on a first date. Or any date. Not only am I a terrible bowler, but every time I walked up to the lane, all I could think about was Buck staring at my backside when I went to bowl.

*But, **ahh** we had a great time. Laughed until it hurt. When he dropped me home, he asked if he could kiss me good night. **Blush** I said yes. We're going out again next week, I think.*

Yet, here I am getting ready to go to school. Buck lives here in Claremore. I really want and need to finish college. Meet people, have fun. Not worry about the guy back home. But what if he's the one?

Mom said God would take care of me. He's faithful that way. I wish I had her confidence. Besides, it was only one date. Right?

Got my class schedule yesterday. Holding it in my hand made the reality sink in. In a few weeks, I'll be on OU's campus, going to football games, walking to class, meeting new people. But missing Buck?

Gag, I'm such a girl.

How are you? You know, I was thinking I'd better get an invite to your wedding. LOL. Please let me know as soon as you set a date. I'll put it on my not-to-be missed schedule.

Better go. Work in the morning, then a bunch of us are meeting at the movies tomorrow night.

Love and hugs,
Jen

Scott

"What happened to you?" Aubrey hops off the kitchen stool as I walk into the great room with Rafe Tuesday morning. "I let you out of my sight for a few days, and you managed to get your face punched?"

"Can't leave me alone for a minute." I smile. She looks bright and happy, worth taking a punch from her brother.

Without pausing for permission to touch, she smoothes her finger around the edge of my cheek. "Does it hurt? It looks painful. Worse than Owen's black eye."

"No, it doesn't hurt." Her touch is hot on my skin and makes me think things I don't want to think. I snatch her hand away, hoping she can't hear the drum concert going on inside my chest.

"Are you going to tell me what happened?" she asks again.

"Tried to help a friend."

"Some friend." She's still dangerously close, her soft fragrance floating between us.

"Sh—He doesn't know."

"Sh-he?" Aubrey winks at me. "Scott, did little green men take you away in their spaceship and try to assimilate you?"

A laugh bursts out of me. "No, they were blue men, and I fought them every step of the way." I point to my face. "Exhibit A."

She smiles. "Go down fighting, I always say."

"He went down all right," Rafe puts in.

I shoot him a look. *Quiet.*

Aubrey faces Rafe. "You were there? You didn't help him?"

"Sure, I videoed the whole thing."

Aubrey glances around at me. "I'm confused."

"Me too." I concentrate on booting up my laptop. We need to move away from this conversation. Now. "So, how have you been?"

"Fine. Car finished moving in . . ."

I wait for more, but she seems to have lost her way in the conversation.

"Car's all moved in," I echo. "What else?"

Her focus returns. "I-I wrote a few songs with this great new songwriter, Robin Rivers."

"For your next album?"

She walks around the couch and takes a seat. "Yes."

"Why don't we do a segment teaching Scott how to write a song?" Rafe suggests, the comment almost sounding like an afterthought.

Aubrey's eyes widen. "What a great idea." She sends a visual check for agreement my way.

But I object. "Bad idea."

"Why?" Aubrey asks.

"Yeah, why?" Rafe echoes. "We're scheduled to be in the studio with Aubrey for our next session, anyway. We'll get some footage of Aubrey working and recording, then teaching you how to write a song."

Aubrey claps her hands together. "I love it."

I repeat, "Bad idea."

"And why is it a bad idea, Scott?" Aubrey asks. "I did a cooking segment with you."

"Because I can't carry a tune in a bucket."

She laughs. "Then teaching you to write a song will be hilarious—for Rafe and me."

Rafe chuckles. "And all the CMT viewers."

Aubrey's bright expression fades. "CMT? You mean *Inside NashVegas*."

By the look on Aubrey's face, I know another fact has slipped through the communication cracks. *Get the hint, Rafe. Move on.* But he doesn't.

"Yeah, *Inside NashVegas* is going national. We're joining CMT. Move over *Access Hollywood*. *Inside NashVegas* is here."

Aubrey cocks her head to one side. "Is this new . . . news?"

"No. So, is Connie on her way?" I ask. "She's on the schedule to sit with us this morning."

"She's on her way." Aubrey leans toward me. "So, CMT?"

I confess, "We've known for a while."

"And I'm going to be on CMT?"

"Yep," Rafe answers. "In fact, it's your interview that sealed the deal for us."

Rafe . . . Look up from the camera and see what's going on.

"Aubrey," I sit next to her and explain. "We debut during the November sweeps with our exclusive on you."

She motions to the flat-screen TV on her wall. "So I'm not going to be on *Inside NashVegas* every Monday morning in September and October?"

"You are, but then we'll run about five thirty-minute spots for CMT in November."

"Good grief." She slips off the couch. "Am I always the last to know?"

"Sam's been in negotiations with CMT for a long time, but when you gave us an exclusive, like Rafe said, it sealed the deal."

She opens the door out to the porch. "Hello, Nashville. Anyone else want to get rich on my name?"

"Aubrey, it's a compliment."

She whirls around. "Scott, between Melanie, Car, and now this, I'm a little weary of people using my name to get ahead or broker a deal. And who knows about this person hunting down my brother? Could be somebody trying to make money. It's happened before."

Absently, I touch the bruise on my cheek, quite sure she's heard the last from her brother.

"I'll be back." Aubrey picks up the portable phone from Piper's desk and heads out to the porch. Pacing around the furniture, her arm flails as she speaks. I imagine she's called her manager. After a few minutes, she stops, nods a few times, then lowers the phone.

"Think this gig is up?" Rafe asks, watching her over my shoulder.

"If I know Aubrey, no. She'll work it through."

Sitting on the wicker sofa, Aubrey stares out over the yard where her gardener is motioning to a yellow bloom. She waves, giving him a thumbs-up.

I open the door and step out. "Are you okay?"

"Yes." She doesn't look around.

Should I stand here or take a seat next to her? "Your gardener seems to loves his job."

"He does."

Trying to ascertain her mood, I can't tell if she's tired, subdued, mad, or just plain ole resigned to the situation. "I'm sorry about the show, Aubrey. Sam didn't mean to use you."

"Sure he did."

"Okay." I chuckle softly. "He did, but not in a mean way. He's ambitious and aggressive, insensitive, but not a user."

"You should've told me."

"Me? I'm still recovering from you finding out I was doing the interview instead of Beth."

"For communications professionals, y'all are lousy communicators."

"Touché."

We fall silent. The air between us is comfortable, but I wonder if I should call off the interview. "Aubrey, do you want—"

The phone rings and she nabs it from the glass table. "Zach? Right . . . Well, it would've been nice to know . . . Yes, I understand. Please, all the details next time. Thank you."

She presses End and tosses the phone to the other side of the couch. "Ahhhh," she yells, hands over her face. "What is it about this summer? Everything crashing and colliding." She starts to laugh.

"We don't have to do this today."

"Yes. We do." Aubrey stands, straightening her blue top and propping her hands on her hips. "Connie's on her way. And I'm just going with the flow, see?" She does a hula move. "Shoot, if you all want to put me on national TV, who am I to complain? Maybe I'll sell fifty million albums."

"Fifty million? Did you just pull that figure out of the air?" I laugh. "Sounds like a nice *round* number."

Rafe pokes his head out. "Connie's here."

Aubrey retrieves the phone and walks toward me. "Been one heck of a summer, Scott, and something tells me the rollercoaster hasn't arrived at the station yet."

"Then hold onto the bar."

22

"I've known Aubrey since she was a kid. When she recorded my song 'Always,' I knew we'd hit platinum."

—Songwriter Danny Hayes

Scott: *Your parents were famous gospel singers. Why country music for you?*

AJ: Country happened by accident. In fact, getting into the music business was all a big fluke. During my senior year of high school, Connie signed me up to do a couple of demos for some songwriters she knew, one being Danny Hayes, who was a good friend of Daddy's.

This was back before I was a diva and *people* [nudging Connie] bossed me around. [laughing]

Connie: From the time her parents died, I watched Aubrey's love for music fade. She was still gung-ho for basketball, but I didn't believe it was her true calling. I'd lost Peter to anger and hurt, and I didn't want to lose Aubrey too.

So I staged a musical intervention. Danny had written a great new song and mentioned off the cuff to me he thought it'd be a great song for a voice like Aubrey's.

AJ: He hadn't heard me sing in years.

Connie: His one casual comment gave me the idea to have her sing the demo.

AJ: On the way over to the recording studio, I grumbled and complained. "Why am I doing this? Danny can sing his own dern demo. He doesn't need me." On and on. Connie reminded me I was still saving money for college, plus I needed money for the senior class trip and a basketball camp I wanted to attend. Singing demos paid good money and was way more fun than bagging groceries at Kroger or Harris Teeter.

Scott: Why the aversion to singing, especially a demo?

AJ: Singing brought back too many memories. When a parent dies, so does a part of your past. I could never revisit the memories without realizing, "Daddy and Momma are gone."

Then, once Peter ran off, music completely soured for me. I wanted to play basketball and get on with my "other" life.

Connie: Danny's song fit Aubrey. You should've seen her when she walked in the studio, all stiff with attitude. [laughing] Danny started playing the song, and within a minute, Aubrey completely grasped the melody and understood the lyrics. When the musicians joined in, she stepped up to the mike and belted it out in one take.

AJ: [laughing] I just wanted to get it over with.

Connie: Whatever, but you owned that song, and it became your first number one hit.

Scott: So, that's how we got the song "Always." How'd you go from singing a demo for Danny Hayes to a number one hit?

AJ: Connie, again. [jerking her thumb toward the older woman] She took the demo over to Les Carter, who was then running Mountain Music, and said something like, "Here's your next star."

Connie: Actually, I said, "Call me when you're ready to talk a serious deal." He asked why, who was on the demo, and I said, "Your next star."

Scott: You were a woman on a mission. How did you know Aubrey would sign a deal with Mountain Music?

Connie: I didn't. I spent three weeks convincing her.

Scott: Really? So you held out on her, Aubrey?

AJ: Of course. Never go down without a fight. [winking] About the time of the demo, I found out I'd earned a scholarship to play basketball at Vandy. When Connie came to me with a record deal, I laughed. I knew enough about the business to understand the numbers game. With what little bit of money I had from Daddy and Momma and their continued record sales and songwriting royalties, which we had yet to organize into a business, the money I made singing demos, plus my Vandy scholarship, added up to more than I would make recording an album. And I'd be playing basketball.

Connie: She knew by the time Mountain Music recouped all their expenses for recording, promoting, selling, and marketing a new artist, she'd have to sell gold to see any money other than a tidy advance. Plus, give all of her time and attention to promoting herself and the album.

AJ: Yeah, I think they offered me $100,000, but I had to live on that while recording, and while touring. Pay Connie as my acting manager, pay a lawyer, maybe have to hire an assistant. All these people get paid out of the advance. They get paid whether the album does well or not. And I knew I'd have to sell enough units to pay back the advance to the studio, plus any and all expenses—which add up, trust me. Chances are I wouldn't see any royalties. Not on a first album.

Connie: I still had her lined up to sing demos.

Scott: But your first album went platinum in eight months and sold four million units.

AJ: I'm very blessed, but even that was a fluke. Les at Mountain Music had a friend, Vance Piedmont, who was making an indie romantic comedy. He called Les looking for a theme song. Vance pitched the movie theme, and Les decided to give him "Always." The movie was a hit at the Sundance festival, and next thing you know, "Always" turned my first album, *Willing to Make a Change*, into multiple platinum.

Scott: Got to admit, that is pretty spectacular. But how did you choose Mountain Music over Vandy basketball?

AJ: I got hurt my senior year during the regional playoffs. Pulled my hamstring. The injury sidelined me. Connie took advantage of my weakness and carted me around town for meetings with producers and A&R reps. Between the lot of them, I didn't stand a chance of saying no.

Connie: I told her, "Make the record. At least you can say you did. You can go to college next year."

Scott: The rest, as they say, is history.

AJ: Yes, Connie Godwin history. She's been known to manipulate an artist or two.

Connie: [smiling] And I've never been wrong.

Scott: You have a reputation for being difficult in the studio. Did that start from day one or happen as you grew in the industry?

AJ: First of all, having a reputation is one thing, the truth is another.

Scott: You're not difficult?

AJ: No. Well yes, I am. But not nasty, mean, difficult. And not just *because*. With my first album, I did exactly what Mountain Music wanted: marched to their orders, recorded their songs with their producer, with their musicians. They assigned me a stylist and a media relations person who taught me how to walk, talk, eat, sleep, and wave to the fans.

Connie: Remember, Aubrey thinks this is a one-time thing. She's going to college.

AJ: Right. I gritted my teeth and said, "You can put up with these idiots for one year." [laughing] Then 'Always' became a hit, and six months later three singles from the album were in the top ten, and two hit number one. They had me making videos, singing on Leno and Letterman. It was crazy. The whole time, I'm whispering to Connie, "When I go to Vandy next year, should I live in the dorms or an apartment? Maybe live with you?"

Connie: I'd lie awake in bed at night wondering, *Is this really happening to our little Aubrey James?*

Scott: What finalized your decision to stay with the music business?

AJ: The Garth Brooks tour. That's when I knew this wasn't a one-time album, something fun to pass the time. My destiny had been set.

Connie: She came to me and said, "I'm not going to college, am I?"

AJ: [holding up her hands like a balancing scale] Garth Brooks. College. A sure thing. A not so sure thing. I wanted college, but in the end could not say no to Garth Brooks. Learning from him, watching him, being around him ignited something in me. I forgot all about college. By the end of the tour, I was itching to return to the studio for my next album. And, perhaps, a baby diva was born.

Connie: Les and his team were giddy over a first-time artist doing so well. We had meetings almost every day, preparing for the next album, talking concept, picking songs, listening to demos, discussing songwriters. Aubrey went on photo shoots . . .

AJ: One day, I was in a shoot for eight hours—mind you, there's no album yet; this is a test run—and I changed my clothes four hundred times. Slow but sure, all the lessons I'd learned about music and the business from my parents started to surface. I decided, "This is my career and I'm doing it my way."

First thing I did was fire their producer and hire Dave Whitestone, which caused a *big* ruckus with Les.

Scott: *The baby diva grew up fast.*

AJ: [laughing] Let's just say she found her footing. Connie and I'd known Dave for a long time, and he'd recently worked on some great projects with other artists. I respected him. I didn't have the confidence to write my own material for the country/pop world, but felt Dave and I could find songs that were right for me. With Les's producer, I felt like Johnny Bravo.

Scott: *Johnny Bravo?*

AJ: Yeah, Greg Brady? Johnny Bravo? In one of *The Brady Bunch* episodes, Greg signs with some record label who only wanted him because he fit the costume.

Scott: *Not a big fan of* The Brady Bunch.

AJ: Check it out on TV Land. Anyway, I didn't want to be the Johnny Bravo of Mountain Music: a girl fitting their idea of a country artist, becoming a product of their marketing scheme.

So, this led to my second fight over the album's first single release. We'd agreed on "Get Up, Get Going," but they changed it two days before the release date to, "Listen to the Night," which I felt was too mellow.

Scott: *Did you win?*

AJ: After a lot of bloodshed, yeah. [winking] A year later Les got axed and Nathan Brack came in.

Scott: *What happened between you and Nathan?*

AJ: [looking at Connie] Nathan and I just never clicked. If Les wanted Johnny Bravo, Nathan wanted a robot Johnny Bravo. He's all business, all the time. I was a young, impressionable artist, successful and arrogant. By album three, I'd developed my own style and didn't want any label honcho telling me what to do.

Nathan insisted I look and act like he wanted. Sing the songs his people recommended. But by album three I'd discovered my voice and style was more soulful country than pop country. Nathan hated it. He thought it sounded too much like my gospel roots and would remind fans to be good and not bad, if you know what I mean. Add to that Nathan didn't like being told no by a twenty-two-year-old.

We parted ways after that album. I probably aged five years during the process.

Scott: *And now he's heading up SongTunes.*

AJ: Lucky me. [smiling] Nathan is a good businessman, but he should be on Wall Street, not Music Row.

Greg Leininger headed up SongTunes when I signed with them after Mountain Music. He's a great man, an industry leader, and a friend of artists everywhere. I'm going to miss him.

Scott: *Working with a record label is more complicated than people realize.*

AJ: Much more. Why do you think so many artists create their own labels, forge their own distribution deals? Aside from the money aspect, artists want to create music their way. Not according to drive-time market surveys and packaging. For the label trying to make money, it's all about a commercial product.

And if no one in promotions, marketing, or radio thinks a record is commercial, it doesn't go out the door. Even if your name is Aubrey James or Toby Keith.

Connie: When she came out fighting on her second album, it shocked me. Who is this girl? I knew then her career would go into the stratosphere. So I called Zach Roberts and asked him to take over management. I went back to substitute mom.

AJ: Which I needed more than a manager, really.

Scott: How was it to go from a high school basketball player to a country sensation in a matter of a few years?

AJ: I don't know. Fun at first. Especially when the money started coming and I realized I could buy about anything I wanted. At the same time, my personal freedoms slipped away. Photographers started following me. My friends gave up on me because I was too busy, or they felt I'd changed too much.

Several of us got together to play basketball one summer about five years into my career. We picked a public park, but the paparazzi and fans made it impossible to play. That's why I built a court here. After that day, the friendships really started to fade. Some of them said nasty things that got quoted in the press.

Scott: Like?

AJ: Like how I'd changed and thought I was too good for them. Blah, blah. But getting used to the media took some time. The first time I saw a lying headline about me, I flipped.

Connie: [laughing] Took Zach *and* me to calm her down.

AJ: Tabloid and celeb magazines get it right just enough times to make people believe anything could be true.

Scott: [reading from his notes] Let's talk about some of your tabloid headliners. Your first major relationship was with Hollywood A-lister Jack Mills.

AJ: Ah, you had to go and ruin a good morning interview, didn't you? [laughing]

Scott: *Sorry, but I'm reading from my notes here. It says, "Go for the jugular."*

AJ: [pointing to his cheek] Looks like you already tried . . . with someone.

Scott: *Yeah, well, didn't see it coming . . .*

AJ: So what do you want to know about Jack?

Scott: *Everything, of course. What happened? How old were you when you met?*

AJ: I was twenty-two. Knew it all, of course. We met in LA at Vance Piedmont's party for his next indie film. Jack played the lead, and Vance wanted me to sing the theme song written by Diane Kennedy. Of course, who wouldn't want to record a Diane Kennedy song? It became my biggest hit. Won a Grammy for Best Song. The same year, I was nominated for Top Female Vocalist, but didn't win.

Jack was, and is, incredibly charming and handsome. He swept me off my feet with his dimpled chin and sparkling brown eyes. I never knew what hit me. The night we met, we sat in the corner of Vance's living room, curled on the couch like a couple of old high school friends, and made fun of the drunks. We laughed until we couldn't breathe.

But I was on tour and had to leave the next day for Sacramento. It was torture for my poor twenty-two-year-old heart. I'd fallen in love with Jack, or so I thought. I cried when I had to leave. But got myself together for the show. Then, right before the last number, Jack walked out on stage with a red rose.

The place went nuts. Absolutely nuts. Despite everything else about our relationship, that is one of my all-time favorite touring memories. He was so classy, not like Car and his— [stopping] Pardon me. Rafe, please back up over that last line.

Rafe: Sure, Aubrey.

Scott: *What'd Jack do?*

AJ: Walked out on stage, handed me a rose, kissed my cheek, and walked off waving to the fans. If I wasn't in love before, I was then. He stayed on the tour with me for two weeks before going back to LA. He was my first big love.

By then, we were a discovered couple, and the paparazzi went berserk over us. Thus began the wild, two-year relationship of Jack Mills and Aubrey James.

Scott: *Why'd it end?*

AJ: Jack lived life by a different set of rules. Let me tell you. He'd do these really fun things like spend thousands of dollars to surprise me by flying in from wherever he was filming to wherever I was touring. Or show up here in Nashville out of the blue.

He'd lavish me with expensive jewelry and gifts, flowers. Food would be catered in for a romantic dinner. In those days, I still lived with Connie, so he'd book a suite at the Vanderbilt Loews and play out this incredibly romantic, larger-than-life Don Juan-type of hero. Then he'd have to go back to work, and I'd be heartbroken.

Connie: It was murder watching her go through it. But none of us could talk any sense into her.

AJ: [knocking her head] Always did have to learn the hard way. It was during one of these fly-in-romance episodes he asked me to marry him. I was so in love, so naïve, I thought we were perfect for each other. Until I decided to surprise *him* for once.

He was filming in New York City so I called his assistant and made arrangements for food, flowers, candles, a carriage ride in the park. The works. He'd broken his watch during a fight-scene rehearsal, so I bought him a new one from Tiffany's. Even bought matching his-and-her monogrammed robes.

Scott: *I'm getting the feeling it didn't go well.*

AJ: [shaking her head, rolling her eyes] Not at *all*. Oh gosh, it makes me sick just thinking about it. I was scheduled for my first Barbara Walters interview about this time, but after New York, I cancelled and really started avoiding the press.

Scott: *Pretend I'm Barbara Walters. What would you have said to me back then about you and Jack?*

AJ: [laughing] Pretend you're Barbara Walters? Not even Walt Disney had that much imagination.

Scott: *Oh, I see how it is. [laughing] What happened with Jack?*

AJ: Let's just say when I walked into his suite, he wasn't alone.

Scott: *How'd you get in the room, then?*

AJ: His assistant let me in. She thought he was going over lines with his costar.

Scott: *Ooo, what a shocker.*

AJ: *Big* shocker.

Scott: *Did it all end then?*

AJ: Yes, the relationship had a very emotional, tragic end. I did the whole stomp-around, big-drama, throw-the-engagement-ring across-the-room thing. [covering her face] Really childish.

The next morning news spread of our demise. Tabloids picked up the story, but neither Jack nor I came clean with details. The paparazzi literally camped out on Connie's street, hoping sooner or later Jack Mills would show up. It was horrible.

At first, the media would blame it on me, then Jack if they spotted him with another woman, then me again. Nicole Kidman and Tom Cruise busted up about the same time. If I wasn't in the headlines, Nicole was. It's humiliating having your heartbreak played out before the whole country.

Connie: We organized a mini European-Asian tour just to get her out of the country. Zach and I called her booking agent and said, "Get her in any place you can—pubs, cafés, street corners, whatever. Let's get her out of the country and working."

AJ: Great idea, at first. But the tabloids were worse in England *and* that's how I met Derek Crammer. A very disastrous relationship.

Scott: Derek is one of the most noted drummers of our day.

AJ: He's an amazing musician, and a wonderful person, but we were like fire and water. He's ten years older, from a completely different background and mindset. The only thing we had in common was a broken heart. Me with Jack, and Derek with Candice Laurie, whom he'd been with for five years.

Scott: He was your drummer for the European tour?

AJ: Yes. Derek needed a gig to get his mind off of Candice. We needed a drummer for this slapped-together tour. He called asking for the job. And, in all honesty, he was more than a drummer for the band. His understanding of the industry and touring, giving the fans what they want . . . I learned so much about touring from him, and it's probably part of the reason why I still tour every year. He taught me ways to save money, get media coverage, how to add extra touches to the show to make it shine. I have fans in Europe and Asia today because of him. Garth taught me how to perform. Derek taught me how to tour.

Scott: You were how old at the time you met Derek?

AJ: Twenty-four, almost twenty-five. Met him three months after Jack and I split. We dated for nine months.

After those two very hurtful relationships, I didn't trust anybody. I required these ridiculous artist riders on hotel rooms and dressing rooms regarding privacy. No one but my management could walk within a thousand yards of my bus or my room. Everything cleaned with Clorox, white sheets and towels, bottled water, liquid soap, blah, blah. Salads and grilled meat for meals.

Connie: She got a little crazy on us.

AJ: I reacted the way any person reacts when they lose things: grasp for control. "Isn't going to happen to me again." I still struggle with letting go.

Connie: Zach made her take a vacation and booked her for three weeks in Barcelona on the Mediterranean.

AJ: Heaven on earth. I lay in the sun, slept, read books, forgot about Jack and Derek as much as possible.

Connie: Besides the relationships, she'd been working nonstop for six years.

AJ: I felt like a failure for melting down. There are men and women out there working sixty hours a week to put food on the table, making fifteen bucks an hour, and they don't melt down.

Scott: But there are pressures that come from being in the public eye that can't be compared to a private citizen. When their life goes bad, or their relationships end, they don't get played out on Entertainment Tonight. *They don't pick up a copy of* Globe *and see their ex's face.*

AJ: True, and it's hard and embarrassing. Yet, the whole private-life-versus-public-life excuse feels like a cop-out to me. Heartache is heartache, celebrity or not.

Scott: Did you heal in Barcelona?

AJ: The process got started, and I thought a lot about my life and who I wanted to be.

Scott: Derek wrote a book about your relationship.

AJ: Thank goodness the book landed on the *New York Times* worst-seller list.

Scott: *Guess that's a nice silver lining to your relationship. [glancing at his watch]*

AJ: I suppose so.

"Our time is up." I motion for Rafe to cut.

Aubrey slips off the sofa and motions for me to follow her. "So, feel like a little game of one-on-one? A rematch?"

I stop just outside the porch door. "Now wait a minute; you didn't warn me. I didn't bring my sneakers or a change of clothes."

Aubrey laughs. "Good, all the more reason I can beat you again."

23

"I used to blame her for all the crap in our relationship. But looking back, we were the wrong people for each other at the wrong time. The perfect storm. I wish her well, though I really wanted my book to be on the bestseller list."

—Derek Crammer, author of Drumming for a Diva

Aubrey

*Wednesday night as Car and I dress for dinner with his parents, the ten*sion between us is still thick, even though we've talked out the issue of my discarded boxes.

"I called the movers about your boxes," he says, out of the blue, as he tugs on a Ralph Lauren polo.

"Really?" Slowly, I slip on my engagement ring.

He shakes his head. "They took it to the dump, and like I thought, once it goes there, it's impossible to retrieve."

I lean against the dresser, batting away a swell of tears. "Thank you for trying."

"I thought you'd like to know." He goes to the closet for his shoes. "Mom said the Arbuckles are joining us tonight."

"Lovely." I scan my shoe rack for those Prada wedges. The idea of decades' worth of family history buried among the refuse of Davidson County makes me feel sick.

"Tammy's a big fan of yours." Car's voice is chipper, as if such news should brighten my day.

Finding the Pradas, I sit on the edge of the bed. "I'll take her an Aubrey Bag, then."

He smiles. "Good idea."

The short drive to his parents' house is mixed with small talk followed by silence, then more small talk. Exhaling, I ask, "Car, what's my favorite color?"

He turns into his parents' driveway and parks behind several other cars. "What? Your favorite color?"

I slip my hand through the straps of the Aubrey handbag lying on the seat. "Do you know where I got George and Ringo?"

"The shelter?"

"No, from these cute little kids giving away their puppies in front of Harris Teeter."

"Oh, yeah, right. Did you tell me that before?"

"What's the title of my first number one hit?"

His gaze is wide and surprised. He should know this one. "'Rainy Days'," he blurts.

"'Rainy Days'? Car, that song is from my latest album."

"Aubrey, what are you doing? Why the third degree?"

Gently, I rub my thumb over his hand. "Car, don't you see? We don't know each other, not really. I'm starting to wonder . . ."

He winks and grins. "I think we've *known* each other quite well."

Frustration twists in my chest. "Car, I'm serious."

"Yes, I know. Too serious." He gets out his side of the car and walks around to open my door.

When I step out, I rest my forehead against him. "I'm not sure we're ready for marriage."

He holds me at arm's length. "Sure we are. All couples go through their hard times. My parents did. I'm sure yours did too."

"Hard times, I understand." His square-shaped face is half in the shadows, half in the golden light of the driveway lamps. "We aren't even married yet, and I feel like we're strangers."

He bends down so his eyes are level with mine. "We weren't strangers until I *accidentally* threw away your boxes. So you lost a few family heirlooms. Look at the people in Sri Lanka after the tidal wave. Or the people in New Orleans after Katrina."

He's half right, and I'm irritated at him for it. Those disasters certainly outweigh mine, but our situation is not just about my stuff. It's about Car and me respecting each other.

"Brie, are you going to let this go? Is our relationship worth the price you're trying to pay?"

Absently, I straighten his collar. "Let's go inside and have dinner."

As hostess, Grace Carmichael is in her prime. She's chic and classy in a crisp linen outfit. She links her arm through mine when I walk in with her son and escorts me over to the tan and thin Grayson Arbuckle. I set the Aubrey Bag on the polished end table.

"Gray, you remember Aubrey?"

"Certainly. Nice to see you again." The collar of Grayson's mauve pullover is flipped up around his neck '80s style.

"And you, too, Grayson." He shakes my hand, which he holds too long while trying to gaze into my eyes.

Familiar with *that* handshake and *that* eye gaze, I pull away. Not in a million years, Grayson Arbuckle. Not if we were the last two people on earth.

"Dear Aubrey, good to see you." Sheree Arbuckle eases across the room and presses her cheek to mine as if we're long-standing bridge partners. "Let me see that diamond ring I heard so much about." She grabs my hand. "Tammy, honey, come see."

From the soda bar, Tammy waves. *She's a big fan of yours.* Yes, I can see.

"I saw it, Mother. Remember? I helped Car pick it out."

I glance over at Car. His ex-girlfriend helped him pick out my ring? When Mrs. Arbuckle lets go of my hand, I walk over to him. "Tammy helped you pick out my ring?" I ask in a whisper.

"Um, try these." He hands me a cracker with a cheesy-looking spread. "Very good."

I refuse the cracker. "Babe, my ring?"

He wipes his mouth with a linen napkin. How I long for a stack of Chinet paper plates and matching napkins. "She volunteered to help me, and I thought, why not? Tammy's a woman with excellent taste."

Tipping my head to one side, I quiz him. "Car, I showed you the round solitaire I liked."

"Round. Solitaire. Boring. I wanted to get you something unique. Thousands of women have round solitaries."

"But it's what I like."

Car reaches for another cracker. "Are you saying you don't like the one I bought?"

Closing my eyes, I realize I don't want to have this conversation now. If ever. He chose a ring . . . with Tammy's help . . . and I accepted it. Sort of. "It's a beautiful ring, Car."

"Aubrey." Grace hands me a tall crystal glass filled with something pink and icy. For a moment, I feel like she might share a confidence with me. "I do hope you're being discreet with the Carmichael name while engaging in those interviews."

"C-certainly."

Her slender, tan hand pats mine. "Good, dear. Very good."

Brown calls to her. "Grace, you've got to hear this."

The Arbuckles and the Carmichaels huddle together on the far side of the elegant, wide living room, discussing something that makes them all laugh.

Alone in the middle of the room, I cup my pink drink. The melting ice forms tears on the outside of the carved glass.

"Aubrey, honey, you okay over there?" Car lifts his head from the circle, smiling. "We're just talking about the latest politics at the club. Do you know the Andersons?"

"No, honey, she hasn't met them," Grace says.

"Don't believe I've had the honor." Sipping from my pink drink, I shake water droplets from my chilled hand while the blue bloods continue their conversation.

After another round of laughter, Car slips past me to the snack buffet, tapping my cheek with a kiss. He notices something in the corner. "Dad, why'd you pull out the old dinosaur?"

A smile spreads on Brown Carmichael's face as he walks over to the ornate china hutch. "I found your grandpa's 16-mm movies." He produces two round tin film canisters.

"You're kidding? When? Where were they?" Car's reaches for the tins. "I thought they were lost." He turns to me, his expression like a kid at Christmas. "Brie, you've got to see these family movies. They're priceless."

"Really?" A drop of condensation drips from the bottom of my glass to my foot.

Brown pops his hand on Car's shoulder. "The movies were in the attic all along."

Grace explains with a flip of her wrist. "Car and Brown were frantic when we couldn't find those old movies. Remember, Brown? You even had Gray searching the garage with you."

Gray raises his glass. "I certainly remember."

Car takes one of the antique celluloid tins. "Brie, these are amazing movies. Grandpa set up these little scenes and played the director. The stars were Grandma, Dad and his brothers, and their friends. Being able to see and hear Grandpa and Grandma, see their clothes, hear their voices, watch them move and breathe . . ."

A chill runs over my scalp and down my neck. "Isn't it fortunate to have such a connection to your heritage? Something to remind you of your family, your past, your history?"

"It's invaluable—" Car's posture stiffens. The buried tension between us rises to the surface.

Brown takes the tin from Car. "We have a few minutes before dinner. Let's view this one. I think it's of Dad and his buddies after the war."

With a glance at me, Car helps his father thread the movie through the projector. Car's hypocrisy angers me. How can he be so excited about his family heirlooms and so callous about mine?

Another drop of cold condensation splashes my foot.

Tammy walks over to Grace and me. "Have you seen these movies before? They are wonderful. I love the clothes and the hair."

"No, I haven't seen them." I point to the end table. "I brought you my new Aubrey Bag. Car said—"

"Oh, really? How thoughtful." She doesn't even glance to where I point.

Yeah, she's a *huge* fan, Car.

"Excuse me, please, Tammy."

Setting my drink down, I find the downstairs bathroom, lock the door, and perch on the closed toilet seat. "I can't do this. I can't."

Belonging to this community seemed like the right move for me, an orphan girl who achieved fame. But no matter how I slice it, I'll never be a card-carrying member of Nashville's elite. Even if my last name is Carmichael.

My sigh of relief echoes around the marble and granite bathroom.

"Aubrey, are you all right?" It's Grace, knocking on the door.

Checking my makeup in the mirror, I blow my nose and open the door to her. "I'm fine, actually."

"Oh, well, then." She peers around me into the bathroom as if I might not be alone.

"Thank you for a lovely evening. Please tell Car I needed to go home."

"Shall I get your things?"

I wait in the hall for her to retrieve my purse, but Car returns instead of my future mother-in-law. "Aubrey, Mother said you needed to go home. What's wrong?" He passes me my handbag.

"I don't belong here."

"Ridiculous. Of course you belong here. You're family, my fiancée."

He follows me to the foyer. Our footsteps sound cold and hollow. "I'll see you at home later."

"Aubrey, wait. What's going on? Is this about the ring? Are you walking home?"

"It's not that far. I need to think." I start down the bricked front walk. The July air is sweet, and the velvety night sky is dotted with diamonds.

"Then I'm coming with you."

I press my hands against his chest and kiss his cheek. "Stay. Don't disappoint your dad. I'm fine. We'll talk later."

24

"When you first meet her, there's an innocent air about her, but Aubrey's a tiger woman. She drives herself and everyone else at Mach 10 until the job is done. She's altogether amazing and frightening."

—*David Whitestone, producer of*
Better Left Unsaid, Dandelions & Daffodils
This Way to the Parade, and Borrowed Time

Scott

As planned, Rafe and I drive to the Blackbird Studios Thursday for our session with Aubrey. Playing my macho card on Tuesday when Aubrey challenged me to another game of one-on-one, I made a deal.

If I win, no songwriting lesson. If she wins, I'll howl at the moon. After all, how could she beat me twice? Even if I was wearing loafers and khakis.

Midway through the game, I considered committing hari-kari, but it seemed a rather drastic and messy option just to get out of writing a song.

Then came the slip of my loafers on the slick court surface, followed by a-guy-should-never-do-this-kind-of-split split. Then the horrifying *riiipppp* of my inseam.

Rafe laughed the entire drive back to the *NashVegas* studio. I threatened him with bodily harm if he told anyone. This season with Aubrey is wreaking havoc on my ego. Burnt eyebrows, bruised cheek, losing two games of one-on-one, splits, ripped pants. Next? Impending doom with songwriting.

Yet I woke up this morning wondering how I could keep Aubrey in my life for another month or two.

For a lifetime.

We find Aubrey in Studio A with her producer, Dave Whitestone. "Welcome, *Inside NashVegas*." Dave shakes our hands and quickly introduces us to the studio musicians. "There're a few donuts left over from Donut Den if you want."

I pat my belly. "Love their crullers, but got to watch my figure."

"Not me." Rafe picks out a donut before setting up for the session.

Aubrey spreads her arms wide. "Welcome to my kingdom."

"So, this is where the queen of country soul makes it happen?" I give her a light hug. "How are you today?"

"Can't complain." Her star smile is dim, and I wonder what she's hiding behind her ocean-blue eyes.

"We're going to record a song Aubrey wrote with Robin Rivers. Do you want to film it?" Dave motions to the vocal booth.

"Yeah, give us five minutes."

Aubrey tucks herself away in the vocal booth, eyes closed, lips moving.

"Just so you know, she's nervous."

I regard Dave a second. "She's nervous?"

He nods. "You're really into her private world now." Dave motions to Rafe. "With a camera, no less."

"She makes music videos all the time. Sings before packed stadiums."

Dave chuckles. "Not the same thing. Those are scripted, directed, and rehearsed. A live performance is nothing like recording in the studio. This is the artists at their weakest. Before all the polishing, before the mixing and mastering. Never mind this is a very personal song for Aubrey. One she wrote."

I don't know what my expression says, but Dave pats me on the shoulder. "Don't worry, she'll be fine. Just know Aubrey is a little nervous about you watching."

"Thanks, I'll keep it in mind."

When Rafe indicates we're ready, Dave goes into the control room with the engineer. Aubrey's melodic, soulful voice fills the studio.

I ease down into my chair, captured by the way her soul makes ordinary words come alive. CMT and *Inside NashVegas* viewers are going to love this segment.

After one take, Aubrey comes out of the booth with a jar of peanuts in her hand. Rafe subtly trails her with the mini-DV.

"Was it okay?" she asks Dave, biting her bottom lip, her eyes squinted.

He gives her a thumbs-up, then hugs her shoulders. "Perfect."

She exhales and plops down next to me. "You were making me nervous." Twisting open the jar of peanuts, she pours a small handful.

"Could've fooled me. By the way, I love the song."

Aubrey's smile winkles her nose. "Thank you. Me too."

A diva of divas and she still needs reassurance just like the rest of us. It's all I can do not to pull her into my arms and never let her go.

Scott: *First, I have to ask, what's with the peanuts?*

AJ: [laughing, holding up the jar of Planters] I never even think about it anymore.

Dave: It's her weird quirk.

AJ: I love to munch on peanuts before singing. I don't know why. The salt is good for my throat. I've always eaten them before I record.

Scott: *Doesn't it dry out your mouth?*

AJ: A little, but it helps with the spit factor.

Scott: *Do all artists have weird quirks in the studio?*

Dave: Most of the ones I work with do. Aubrey's tame compared to some.

AJ: We can sing before thousands without batting an eye, but go into the studio where there's nothing but you and your voice, and it's nerve-wracking. Like, "I'm no good, a fraud. This album will expose me. My career is over."

Scott: *To the rest of us it seems like magic.*

Dave: As we intend it, but artists are very insecure people. Maybe more than most.

AJ: One minute, you're the adoration of thousands, the next minute your record label is telling you there's not one radio song on your new album.

Scott: *What makes you want to record a certain song?*

AJ: The feel, mostly. The melody, the lyrics, if the song is saying something that resonates in me.

Dave: We look for songs that say "Aubrey James." A lot of times we love a song, but it doesn't ring true with her. She sings and it just goes flat.

Scott: *The judges on* American Idol *are always telling the contestants about song choice. Is it the same here?*

AJ: [laughing] We're reduced to the advice of Paula Abdul, Dave. But yeah, song choice is extremely critical. Of course, I'm not covering a Mariah Carey tune, but I'd say, for artists who don't write their own material, song selection is one of the most critical components.

Dave: I just want it to be known we knew about song selection well before *American Idol*. [laughing] We've all listened to albums where the songs didn't work. Those are usually the ones that only sell ten thousand units or less, and the label was hoping for platinum. Songs need to resonate with something deep and hidden in the artist.

Scott: *Where do you find these resonating songs?*

AJ: I bought a few on sale at 7-Eleven the other day.

Dave: [laughing] Songwriters we know. Publishers, of course, send their pluggers over to introduce us to new songs and new songwriters. We put a hundred songs on hold for Aubrey's last album, and only twelve made the cut.

Scott: *[whistling] You left a lot of disappointed songwriters in your wake.*

AJ: Too many.

Scott: *For your latest project, you're writing or cowriting most of the material?*

AJ: Yes, with Robin Rivers. Seems I found her at the right time in my career, and hers. Together, we're writing the songs of my heart.

Scott: *You wrote "The Man" with your dad, didn't you?*

AJ: [nodding] When I was ten.

Scott: *Did you ever imagine it would be a gospel cover song?*

AJ: No, I just wanted to survive the experience of writing the song.

Dave: I'd like Aubrey to cover it on this album.

AJ: [looking at Dave] An issue we're still debating. We recorded it this week, but who knows if it'll make the cut. I'm more excited about taking a new direction than singing a twenty-year-old song.

Scott: *Why do you say you wanted to survive the experience of writing the song?*

AJ: [shifting in her chair] It was the first time in my young life I encountered the power of God. I was terrified.

We were in Kentucky somewhere—Bowling Green, maybe—

singing for this old-fashioned revival meeting. A man by the name of Preacher Darrell delivered a fire-and-brimstone message, literally trying to scare the hell out of us. Mission accomplished when it came to me. I refused to get on the stage and sing if Preacher Darrell was anywhere near.

Scott: *I've been in those sorts of meetings.*

AJ: So, I cowered in the back. Then Preacher Darrell barked, "Close your eyes. Everyone. Do you see him? Jesus, coming down the cobblestone road, the heavy, splintered cross on his bleeding back?"

Suddenly, I saw it. Exactly what he described, playing out like a movie. It seemed like forever, but it was probably only ten or fifteen seconds, but it was an encounter I'll never forget. I couldn't stop crying, and when Preacher Darrell called all the sinners to the altar, I stumbled forward.

Kneeling at the altar, I cried and cried. Not sure why or how, but I knew Jesus loved me. After a while, I peeked out from under my arm to see I was the only one at the altar. Daddy and Momma were onstage, singing, watching me. Momma's face was wet with tears.

Preacher Darrell's only convert that night was the little girl in the band. I went back to my seat and wrote what I felt and saw. Those words became the lyrics of "The Man." Later, I sang the melody to Daddy, and we worked on it off and on for the next few months. In fact [pointing at Scott] the old video you saw is the first time I ever sang it live.

Scott: *It was incredible.*

Dave: We're putting it on the album. I'm making an executive decision.

AJ: Yeah, well, we'll see. [whispering to Scott] I like to let him think he's in charge.

Scott: *I'm sure he appreciates it. Several times you've mentioned doing a different kind of Aubrey James album. What do you mean? Aren't you the queen of country soul? Isn't that uniquely Aubrey James?*

AJ: This is my seventh album. I just turned thirty, became engaged, am growing up. I have something different to say than I did when I was twenty or twenty-two. My queen-of-country-soul sound won't really change, but the type of songs I sing—the message, the themes . . . I care less than ever about meeting market demand or the record company's quarterly budget. I suppose that sounds harsh.

Scott: *So you've become a purist. You're about the art, the creative process, not making money.*

Dave: No, we still want to make money.

AJ: But we don't have to make as much. Right?

Dave: But a well-done, unique Aubrey James album will make money. Perhaps not as fast. We decided last year we didn't want to be afraid to try something new. Aubrey's in a good place with her career. If she's going to take a risk, now's the time.

AJ: And hopefully recover from it if the record flops. But I want to be clear about something. Just so folks know, this isn't about arguing with my label or trekking down some navel-gazing, introspective, why-is-there-air philosophical journey. It's about representing my true self in the songs. I don't want to crank out album after album with the same type of songs. I heard a tune on the radio the other day that made me cringe. The artist is a friend of mine, but I could take her melody and plug in the lyrics from another artist's song and sing it perfectly. This is the trap I want to avoid, and it's an easy one to fall into.

Scott: *[smiling] Must be hard to stay cutting edge and original.*

AJ: Yes, but that's the work part, the true artist part. I hear songwriters complaining about no one wanting their music, and it's because Tim McGraw sold a bazillion records with a tune just like the one they're trying to plug. Be fresh, be original, work at it.

Dave: We want to take a chance, but we want to create great music.

Scott: Aubrey, coming from a gospel background, do you pray over your ideas and song choices?

AJ: What a great question. Um, no. I haven't. Which is a shame when I look back and see how incredibly blessed we've been. My parents spent a lot of time committed to the discipline of prayer, but so far, it hasn't been my tradition. [glancing at Dave] We should.

Dave: [shrugging] You're the boss.

Scott: Tell me how someone with your fame and accolades has never won a CMA award?

AJ: Because someone else wins?

Dave: I tell her to buy votes, but she just won't listen.

AJ: [swatting at Dave] Seriously, I have no idea, Scott. You're the reporter, you tell me. I've been nominated ten times for Female Vocalist of the Year, three times for Entertainer of the Year. I've just never won.

Scott: Does it bother you? The CMA is the granddaddy country music award.

AJ: I'm honored to be nominated. Does that sound corny and cliché? Do I want to win? Yes. But I have my share of trophies—Grammys, American Music Awards, Academy of Country Music Awards. So it's not like I'm always invited to the party but never asked to dance. It just hasn't worked out for me and the CMAs.

Scott: Maybe this is your year?

AJ: Who knows? I'm not focused on winning awards. I'd go nuts if I cared too much.

Scott: *[looking at his notes] Well, this is the moment of doom. You teaching me to write a song.*

AJ: [picking up her guitar] I'm ready if you are. Too bad I didn't think to have Robin here today. She's the real songwriter.

Dave: [rising.] This is my cue to cut out. Aubrey, be back in a few hours.

AJ: See you, Dave. Thanks for sitting in.

Scott: *Do you always write with your guitar?*

AJ: [strumming and tuning] Since I haven't done a ton of writing, I can't say I *always* write with my guitar, but it's my preferred instrument at the moment. Here, sing this with me. "Jesus loves me, this I know . . ."

Scott: *[Making a noise.]*

Rafe: [laughing] No, he can't sing. He can't sing.

AJ: [flashing her palm] I didn't believe you, Scott, but you're right. Did you know you're tone deaf?

Scott: *I told you. Good grief.*

AJ: [shaking her head] Never fear. There are some great song-writers who can't sing. We can do this.

Rafe: [Shaking camera as he chuckles.]

AJ: Can you rhyme?

Scott: *Sure. Third graders can rhyme, I can rhyme.*

AJ: Okay, good. [playing again] Usually when I'm writing a song, I think of a theme or a story. Maybe I have a melody to work with, and I add the lyrics. Most of the time I have the lyrics and work out the melody later. I try to avoid cliché scenarios or phrases. [Starting a simple chord progression.]

Scott, think of how this music makes you feel. Close your eyes. Do you see a young couple in love, maybe walking to the movies?

Scott: *[closing eyes] If you say so, sure. He's skinny and she's dropdead gorgeous.*

AJ: [laughing] No, no, no. She's skinny and he's the strong, silent, handsome type.

Scott: *You see what you see, I see what I see.*

AJ: They are a young couple, right after World War II, walking to the movies. [humming softly] The night is chilly as they walk an amber-lit sidewalk, their heels clicking against the cement. He's still in his uniform. Proud, but nervous. His square jaw is cleanly shaven, his dark hair clipped and neat. He thinks she's beautiful with her silky curls falling around her shoulders.

They're together for the first time in two years. Has he changed too much for her? Can he ever explain the terror of bombs exploding over his head on a dark, snowy night, or the horror of killing another man? Will he find the nerve to slip the cool gold-and-diamond ring onto her finger tonight? Does she still love him like she pledged she would when he shipped out?

Meanwhile, she's chatty and lighthearted, thrilled to be able to buy a decent pair of stockings. She leans against him with excitement. "We have chocolate. Would you like to come over after the movies for homemade hot chocolate?"

"Yes, that would be nice." His hands perspire. The memory of her fixing him supper in a bright summer kitchen kept him warm during the snowy trek through the Ardennes. He carried a photograph of her in his pocket, and it steeled his hope when it waned.

Can you see them, Scott? Can you feel his longing for her, his hunger? The ache to take her in his arms and kiss her?

Scott: *[swallowing] Y-yes.*

AJ: Finally, he takes her hand into his. A tingle runs up his arm and across his chest. What are the words here? What is their song?

Scott: *[gently singing, off key] Gee, she sure is pretty. I want to hold her hand, while walking to the movies . . .*

Rafe: [Collapsing to the floor in a fit of laughter.]

AJ: [buttoning her lips] Well . . . that's a start. It almost rhymes . . . [turning away, shoulders shaking, hand over her mouth, snorting]

Scott: *[incredulously] What? It fits the story, and even fits the music.*

Rafe: [Pounding the floor with his big hand, guffawing.]

AJ: Absolutely, it fits the melody and rhythm of the song . . . A-a good start. [surrendering completely to laughter]

Scott: *[muttering] Sure is pretty . . . Walking to the movies.*

25

"Writing with Aubrey James changed the way I approach songwriting. She has this unique view of life and the human heart, and her ideas challenged me to take my lyrics deeper, to the next level."

—*Robin Rivers, Music Row magazine*

Aubrey

Dipping my fry into the ketchup at Noshville Deli, I laugh again at Scott's song. "You are a brave soul, my friend."

"I told you." Scott winks at me, stabbing the air with his salad fork.

"Yes, you did."

"But I saw them, the couple you described. The GI Joe and his girl walking to the movie." He bangs the table. "She *was* pretty."

Rafe slaps him on the back. "I for one am proud of you, man. And I know *Inside NashVegas* viewers are going to love hearing your song."

Scott shoves a forkful of lettuce into his mouth. "You'll be green with envy when I win a Grammy."

The banter around the table continues, and I'm grateful. My heart yearned for a lighthearted, fun day to get my mind off Car and our situation. We've been saying words to each other but not talking.

Dave pays the check, then excuses himself from the table. "Scott, can you give Aubrey a ride home? I need to pick up my kids."

Scott looks at Dave, then me. "Um, sure. No problem."

Rafe pats his belly. "I'm heading back to the studio."

"See you later, Rafe." He walks out, singing, "She sure is pretty, walking to the movies."

"See." Scott gestures to his departing cameraman. "It's a catchy tune."

"Downright hilarious. Maybe we should send a song plugger over to Larry the Cable Guy."

Scott laughs and sips his water, then eyes me seriously. "Why am I driving you home?"

"Because I don't have a car."

"But you do have a car. An antique Mercedes. I've seen it—" His fork clatters against his plate. "Oh my gosh. Of course."

I dip, dip, dip my fry in the ketchup.

"Aubrey, you don't drive, do you?"

I munch on my ketchupped fry. "No."

"Now it all makes sense. The night of the party. When I left—"

"I didn't have a way home. My bodyguard, Jeff—you remember him from the Sandlott game—drove me to meet you. He waited around, but when you and I hit it off, I sent him home."

"Then I abandoned you."

"Pretty much." I shove aside my plate, not hungry anymore.

"I'm sorry." He sits back, running his hand over his thick, coarse hair. "Really sorry. How'd you get home?"

"Cab. One long, angry cab ride."

"Aubrey, why don't you drive?"

"Off the record?"

He nods. "If you want."

Wiping my mouth with my napkin, I wonder how to say this. I sound like a stuck record on the subject of my parents. "When my parents died—"

"Excuse me, Miss James? May we have your autograph?"

Two teenagers smile tentatively at me. "Certainly." Their smiles broaden as they hand me pieces of paper and one of my CDs. "Can you sign the CD too?"

"Absolutely. How are you girls doing today?" We chat while I sign, and when I'm done, they scoot away, giggling.

Scott frowns. "They didn't even recognize me." He looks in their direction. "Hey, *Inside NashVegas* host sitting here."

I roll my eyes. "Wait, my friend, until you're live on CMT."

"You can give me pointers on handling fame."

"First tip: your legendary status is only in your mind."

"Good to know. So, you don't drive?"

"I do *not*."

He whistles low. "I don't know anyone who doesn't drive. Seriously. I mean, what do you do when you crave Ben & Jerry's at midnight?"

"Well, I never crave Ben & Jerry's at midnight, but if I did, I'd ask Car to take me."

He reclines with his arm over the back of the booth. "Before Car, then?"

I shrug. "Midnight runs to Harris Teeter or 7-Eleven are not a part of my routine. Gina keeps the house stocked with stuff she knows I like." Wagging my finger, I remember, "Although, there was no popcorn the other night."

"Why don't you drive?"

Reclining in the corner of the booth, I stretch my legs along the seat. "You've been as much my therapist as my interviewer this summer, Scott."

"Reminiscing helps us understand our lives. Sometimes."

"When my parents were killed in a *car* accident"—I spin my fork on the tabletop—"I was learning to drive. Their accident sort of freaked me out. Then I went to foster care and didn't have a chance to drive."

He expression is soft. "Makes sense."

"My parents were great musicians, and good with money, but had forgotten the little matter of the will and provision for Peter and me if something happened to them. They didn't think in terms of dying. I didn't have money for a car. Or to buy insurance if I did."

"Then you became a recording star."

"Right. Connie drove me to all my appointments and recording sessions since she needed to be there anyway. Next thing you know, I'm living half my life on a tour bus. Then I hired Piper and a bodyguard. They drove me around. Or Gina. Or Derek. Or Car."

"How'd you come to buy the Mercedes?"

The memory of the Mercedes makes me smile. "Jack talked me into buying it. He thought it would motivate me. I do love the car. I'm just too terrified to drive it."

"And no one is challenging you to drive? Not even Car?"

I shake my head. "No. I get where I need to go. He's not burdened by me."

"Don't you want the independence of driving?"

"Again, I've never had it, so I don't miss it."

"Incredible." The corners of Scott's blue eyes crinkle when he smiles. "Since we're doing true confessions . . ."

"Are you finally going to tell me why you left me at the party?"

He laughs. "It's lame . . . but I left because I was having such a great time. Suddenly it hit me that a dog-faced sports anchor like me was on a date with someone like you. One of most beautiful women in the world—"

"According to that *rag, People.*" I roll my eyes in exaggeration and sigh.

"Yeah, what do they know? They think Halle Berry is beautiful."

I flick my hand at him. "Oh, I know. All that smooth caramel skin, perfect features, great body. What's up?"

"Exactly." He flashes his lopsided smile, which makes my stomach do a small somersault. "So, there I am on a *date* with ocean eyes and perfect face." He methodically folds his napkin into a tiny triangle. "We'd danced. You put your head on my shoulder, your hair kept tickling my chin" He looks up at me. "I never wanted to let you go."

"Scott, you're not making sense."

"When I met you, I'd just broken up with my fiancée, Brit, and the ordeal killed my confidence. You were so incredible, I decided you would never want a guy like me."

"I never took you for the self-pity type." I reach for my watery soda.

"Normally, I'm not, but it took me a while to rebound. Unfortunately, you came along a little too soon in the healing process."

"Weren't we an accident waiting to happen that night?" I reach across the table and cover his hand with mine. "An insecure sportscaster and a *de*pendent diva."

"I wanted to call you."

"Why didn't you?" I wonder if my life would be different if he'd called.

"Too much time went by. Then I read about you and Car." Scott tips his head with a click of his tongue. "My loss. His gain."

Next to me, Car sleeps. Golden morning light floods the quiet bedroom. Rolling over onto my side, I stuff the pillow under my head, shove my cold feet under a sleeping Ringo.

The bedside clock tells me there's time . . . if I want to go. Slipping out of bed, I tiptoe down the hall to the wall phone.

"Connie, it's me . . . Yeah, I know it's early on a Sunday . . . *No*, I'm not sick. Are you going to church? Yes, it's really me. Stop! The apocalypse hasn't come . . . Will you pick me up? Faith Community? Sure. Nine thirty . . ."

Car stirs for the first time all morning as I finish getting ready. The sandals in the bottom of my closet will look nice with my blue peasant skirt and white top.

"Where are you going so early?"

"Connie's picking me up for church."

His abrupt laugh startles me. "Seriously, where are you going?"

"Seriously. Church. I'll be home around noon. Remember Gina's off today, so you have to take the dogs out. I'll feed them, but please walk them. Otherwise, they'll terrorize the house and yard."

"Babe, I'm going with Dad to the Music City Motorplex for Funday. Got a client in town with his fifteen-year-old son."

"Fine, but please take the dogs out first."

He swings his feet over the side of the bed, rubbing sleep from his eyes. His hair stands on end, and in the fresh morning light, I can see silver among the thick black strands. "You're really going to church?" He fixes his blue gaze on me.

"Yes." His tone makes me feel defensive, but I don't want to argue.

"What's going on with you?" He reaches for his shorts, neatly folded on the chair. His back is straight, and his bare chest is lean, wiry, and smooth.

"Nothing." *Did I leave my handbag downstairs?*

"You've never mentioned church before." He tugs on my arm, pulling me down onto the bed. "Are we okay?" His eyes search mine.

"I don't know."

"Throwing away your past jeopardized my future?"

I reposition so I can see his face and take his hands in mine. "Remember when you drove by the house last year and saw me outside with the furniture guys?"

"I almost wrecked my Humvee."

I rub my thumbs over the fleshy part of his hand. "You invited me to your parents' for a cookout."

"And you came."

"You treated me like a queen, fixed my plate, and made sure my glass was never empty. Then you drove me home and stumbled up the walk to my door—"

"I was nervous."

"You kissed me good night as we stood in a trail of moonlight." Tears sting my eyes as I peer into his. "Picture perfect."

He brushes my hands with his thumbs. "Are we still picture perfect?"

"Car, I don't know. You amazed me when I met you. You were so what I needed. A normal, down-to-earth guy who didn't make his living playing drums or making movies."

"You . . . you blew me away. Not so much by your fame, but by your beauty. Pictures don't do you justice." He brushes my hair off my shoulder.

"After Derek and Jack, I never imagined I'd trust enough again to love. Then I met you. This handsome, sweet, normal guy."

"But . . ."

"But I'm just not sure we're the same two people we were a year ago."

"We could be if you'd just forgive me."

"Car, I *do* forgive you. This isn't about the boxes. This is about us."

He gets off the bed. "Aubrey, don't play me for the fool, waiting in the wings for you to decide if you want to marry me." The warmth of his early tone evaporates.

I say good-bye to Car with a kiss. "Think about us. Pray, if you have the courage. Then do whatever you have to do. I will."

Connie humors me and drives slow to church so we can arrive late. After being away from the faith for a decade, a prodigal like me wants to arrive home quietly. This is between my Father and me.

The heavy sanctuary doors creak as we enter. Several heads turn to see who's coming to worship so late. I dodge the curious stares by hiding behind my sunglasses and sticking close to Connie.

The sanctuary is packed. I spot Robin Rivers a few rows up and over.

She's leaning against a broad-shouldered man I recognize from my days of hanging out with Janie Leeds. Good for Lee Rivers, finding a gem like Robin. As Connie finds two spare seats, I spot the familiar tilt of Scott's head near the front.

When the man praying at the pulpit says, "Amen," a pretty, bubbly-looking woman with a red Gibson takes center stage. "Let's stand and worship the Lord."

The band kicks in with an up-tempo song, and the congregation begins to clap with the beat. The song is fun and fresh, but I can't help but close my eyes and lower my God barrier. *Here I am. I'm Yours.*

Pastor Bolz teaches about God's kind intentions toward us, reminding us that from the foundation of the earth, He's had a plan. He's not surprised by anything.

Kind intention. I ease forward, listening. *God has a plan for me. Despite all I've done to distance myself from Him, He has a plan.*

Connie leans close. "Doing okay?"

Face in my hands, I nod. "Perfect."

26

"I played the Gaylord Entertainment Center with her when I first signed with SongTunes. She treated me like an equal, goofed around with the crew, came early for her sound check. Just being around her taught me volumes about being an artist and entertainer."

—*Mallory Clark, SongTunes artist*

Jen,

GO TO COLLEGE. If this Buck guy is the right one, he'll be around when you finish school. Don't lose your vision for your life.

I did, for a while, but I've been thinking a lot about God lately and His part in my life. It all started when Connie and some other friends encouraged me to pray about marrying Car.

Not sure if being engaged to this man is right for me. I want stability, I want family, but I can't get married just because I'm thirty and counting.

We had an incident that forced me to look at our relationship. He moved in with me a few weeks ago and inadvertently threw out the boxes of stuff I saved from when Daddy and Momma were alive. Photo albums, records, yearbooks, this and that. Clothes. Daddy's letter jacket.

He claims he thought I wanted him to throw them out, but it was a catalyst in my life and forced me to examine my heart.

I thought I was being silly, making a mountain out of a molehill, until a few days later we go to his parents for dinner and his dad produces old family movies Car thought were lost.

Jen, he flipped. Talked about how great it was to have the old family movies, keep their heritage alive. It hit me how much he regarded his family, but not mine. Dead or not.

I left, pondering my life. I chose the road I'm on, but I wonder if it's time to re-evaluate my journey.

If I could impart any of my wisdom to you, Jen, it'd be to always examine your heart. Don't give in because you can't think of a logical way out.

I accepted an engagement ring before really considering my heart. Before talking to myself or God about it. Not that God and I have been all that close lately . . . But hear what I'm saying. Do as I say, not as I do.

You'll have a blast at college. Make friends you would never make anywhere else in the world. Love and marriage will come. Take this time in your life to discover who you really are.

Enough finger wagging, I guess.

Love, Myra

Car unfolds his napkin and sets his silverware beside his plate. He arrived home early tonight, gathered me in his arms, and with a tender kiss, suggested a drive down West End Avenue for dinner at Amerigo's.

"You were at the studio today?" he asks, reaching for his water.

"All day, but we're getting there. We recorded three songs—one I wrote with Robin, two of her originals. Oh, Car, she's such a magical songwriter." I reach for a slice of Amerigo's warm bread.

"Good, Brie, good. Seems like it's working out fine." He nods, but his eyes search the faces of the dining room. No doubt he's looking for people he knows.

Our server approaches the table. Her eyes are lined with heavy black eyeliner. "Good evening. Welcome to Amerigo's. Are you ready to order?" She stares at me for a lingering moment, then smiles.

With a quick glimpse at her nameplate, Car points to a menu item. "Yes, Carissa, I'll have the flame-grilled salmon."

"Very good." She takes his menu and tucks it under her arm. "For you, Miss James?"

"I'll have the flame-grilled filet with portabella mushrooms."

"Excellent choice. Would either of you like a glass of wine tonight?"

"Not for me, thank you."

"Me, neither." Car shakes his head.

When Carissa leaves, he picks a slice of bread from the basket and absently dabs it in the oil and spices. "Have you thought more about us?"

"Yes." *The* conversation I've been avoiding is starting. Courage, please, God.

"Me, too." His posture is square and stiff, his back pressed against the booth.

"What have you decided?" My taste for the bread vanishes.

"What have you decided?"

"Well, I've been talking to God, but—"

"Is that why you went to church yesterday?" He tears absently at his bread.

"One reason. But with everything that's gone on this summer, it's made me think a lot about my life. Who I am, who I want to be. Church seemed like a safe place to find myself."

"Did *God* say anything?"

My heart beats a little faster. "Maybe."

Our server returns with our salads and the intimate conversation stops until she's gone. "I wish I could offer you more, Car, but I can't."

He stabs at his salad. "You're acting a little like a flake."

I peer at him over the flickering table candle. "I'm trying to keep from making a wrong decision."

Carissa appears around the side of our booth with a fresh glass of tea for Car and a Diet Coke for me.

"Thank you," I mutter.

For a while, the only sound is the clinking of silverware against our salad plates, but my appetite is waning under the sharp tension. As we finish our salads, Carissa arrives with our dinner entrees.

"How's the SoBro project?" I ask, trying to restart our conversation.

"Dad and I are flying to New York next week to meet with the head of an investment firm. They have a branch here in Nashville and want to invest in the city, but we need to meet with the CFO before he'll approve the capital."

"How long will you be gone?" Is now the time? Do I say it in public? *Car, maybe we should take a break . . .*

"Leave Monday, come back Friday. Dad wants to take a few days in the city." He carves a slice from his salmon. "Aubrey, I'm calling the movers to come next week."

The movers? I watch him stir sweetener into his tea. "What movers?"

"The ones coming to move my things." His spoon clinks against the side of the glass over and over while he stirs. "I'd like to ask Gina to supervise their packing, if that's okay with you."

"What are you saying?"

A camera phone flashes from the adjacent table.

Car stops stirring. "I'm making this decision for us."

"I see." Despite my own intentions, his confession stings, and my eyes fill with tears. "I thought I'd be the one to say it."

"I wasn't going to without some kind of indication from you. Your hesitation, confessing you can't give me what I want, is confirmation enough." He slides into the booth next to me. "Be honest. You never said yes when I asked you to marry me."

"You surprised me."

"But you never said yes."

Tell him. "I never said yes."

He leans with his elbows on the table. "I thought we knew each other, but we don't. We're two very different people. You were right that night at my parents'. By the way, your favorite color is purple."

I laugh softly. "No, it's yellow." I hate the mounting sensation of rejection because he said it first.

"Yellow, huh? I should've known from all the decorations at the house."

"My old friend, sarcasm." Under the table, I slip Car's ring from my finger. "So, are we over?"

"Are we over?" he echoes, a watery sheen in his eyes.

I press the ring into the palm of his hand. "This belongs to you." The diamond casts a prism of colors across the linen tablecloth. "I planned more of a three-step approach. Ask you to move out, then get sidetracked with our busy schedules—"

"Then eventually break it off because we drifted apart?" he concludes.

"More or less." My smile is weak. "See, in my plan you can play the jilted lover for a while, and all your friends can hate me and throw out my CDs. After a few months, you fall in love with a lovely and charming Nashville society girl. You'll get married, have five children, and invite me to all their birthday parties. The young Mrs. Carmichael will whisper in her friends' ears, 'Car was once engaged to her.'"

His laugh is sincere, though his eyes are sad. "Spare me your tawdry scenario." Absently, he slips the engagement ring onto his little finger. It stops just below the first knuckle. "And what will you be doing?"

"Oh darling, I'll have become romantically cauterized and added two more dogs and ten cats to the household. I'll do retro albums and entertain on cruise liners trying to recapture my glory days. Piper, of course, will be married to a Music Row exec and whisper to the new artists how not to be like me. Gina will stay with me because she's desperately loyal. And Juan will be the head groundskeeper at Cheekwood."

"Zach? What's become of your manager?"

"Tragic really." I shake my head with an exaggerated exhale. "Managing boy bands out of Orlando."

Car chuckles and squeezes my hand. "You should be a novelist."

I kiss his cheek. "I'm horrible at good-byes, you know."

He kisses my fingers. "No, I didn't." He raises his pinky to me. "Keep the ring if you want."

"How can I? You gave it to me with an intent and a promise, which *we* are now breaking." I close my hand over the ring. "Give it to the future Mrs. Carmichael. When she whispers to her friends you were once engaged to the great Aubrey James, you can whisper to their husbands that your wife is wearing my ring."

His taps the ring against the table. "I didn't even pick out the ring you liked."

"No, but coincidentally you picked out a ring Tammy Arbuckle likes." I wrap my arm around his and rest my head against him. "I'm sorry, Car."

He lays his chin on my head. "I can't say my heart isn't breaking a little."

My tears surface. "Neither can I."

Carissa returns, asking if we want dessert, but we've barely touched our entrees.

"Just the check, please." Car's voice is rough as he flips her his credit card. While we wait for her to return, he tells me a story about his assistant, Ilene.

This is good—to end dinner with laughter instead of tears.

"She had on these spiky heels and caught a thread in the new carpet." He pops his palms together. "Bam, nose-dive to the floor, landing in front of the men's restroom door just as Dad was coming out." Car laughs. "Hilarious."

"Poor Ilene."

"Yeah, she was embarrassed, but laughing about it by the end of the day."

Car signs the bill Carissa brings and, folding my napkin, I pick up my purse. "Guess we should go."

Car lifts my chin with his fingers and kisses me. Our final kiss is good-bye. I can't help it, tears spill down my cheeks. He wipes them away with his thumbs. "This is right, isn't it?" His voice is husky.

I dab the end of my nose with my napkin. "Yes, it is. You know that, don't you?"

"Unfortunately."

When we slide out of the booth to go home, relief mingles with emptiness in my heart. Change is never easy.

As Car holds the door for me, I step into a swarm of blinding paparazzi.

"Miss James, did you end your engagement tonight?"

"Aubrey, this way."

Ducking behind Car, I shove his back. "Go, go, go." We dash around the street corner.

"How do they know already?" Car calls to me.

"My guess is our friend Carissa."

As we dash for the parking lot, Car pulls his Humvee key fob from his pocket. Two more photographers pop out from behind a car.

"Just press through." I grab his hand and move out in front, forging ahead with my head down.

Did *not* see the pothole . . .

27

Associated Press

(Aug. 2) "Diva Down—Aubrey James nose-dives into parking-lot pavement. Fiancé Car Carmichael looks on."

[Click for more of the story]

Scott

Miami Beach. Hot, balmy, and beautiful. Rafe and I cruise south down Collins Avenue, away from Kevin Murphy's Murph's Grill.

"A cowboy-singing defensive lineman. I've seen it all now, Rafe."

"He wasn't all that bad."

A snort escapes my nose. "I've heard better singers auditioning for *Nashville Star*."

Rafe laughs and pounds the console of our rented Explorer. "Did you see how thick his fingers were? How did he press down the right guitar strings?"

A laugh rolls out of my gut as I picture Murphy, whose neck is as thick as a post, who on any given Sunday averages six tackles a game, strumming his guitar while perched on a stool in the middle of the stage. He would squish up his face as he bemoaned and whined some lost love in true country fashion.

"Man, it was like watching Rosie Greer knit."

"Needlepoint," Rafe says.

"Whatever. But I guess two days in Miami is not a bad way to end the week." At least it got me out of Nashville and, for a moment, *her* out of my mind.

We are spending our last night dining on a nice steak and lobster dinner at Shula's. Courtesy of *Inside NashVegas,* I insist.

"Gotta tell you, Rafe, if this is what *Inside NashVegas* and *Inside the Game* is becoming, I'm dubious."

"Hang tight, man. You know how deals like this shake out. The show will change, personnel will change. CMT will figure out you're the one who makes *Inside the Game* work."

"Choose me over their boys? I doubt it. Tell you what, though, I'm not spending my career looking for the musical soul of every jock we interview."

"A nice juicy steak will make you forget the singing Dolphin." Rafe knocks on his window. "Pull over, Kemo Sabe. I need cigarettes."

Waiting for Rafe, I check e-mail on my BlackBerry. Our flight home Saturday morning is confirmed. Thank goodness.

Next is an e-mail from Olivia: *Check this out. On the wire today. Not a big shocker, but I have a feeling you'll find it interesting.*

Opening her attachment, I find a photo of Aubrey facedown on the pavement with a cutline: *Diva Dive. Aubrey James dumps fiancé. Still in love with Jack Mills.*

I hit Reply: *What happened?*

Rafe returns, tapping a pack of Marlboros against his hand. "What's with the goofy grin?"

"Nothing, my man, nothing." I steer the SUV out of the parking lot.

Aubrey's free. "We're in Miami Beach, about to order steak and lobster. It's a good day."

I power down my window, jut out my elbow, and let God's good salty breeze blow against my face.

Aubrey

Hey Myra,

Good advice on Buck and school. You're right. I can't get sidetracked after a few dates. Besides, he hasn't even called me yet this week.

How's it going with Car? This girl I work with got engaged two nights ago. She's driving us all crazy with wedding gown photos. Mom and I were in the grocery store last night, and I admit, I picked up Bride *magazine. I flipped through two pages, then decided I'm not ready for a wedding dress.*

Good reading on the cover of the tabloids, let me tell you. LOL. There was one, the National Inquirer, *with a picture of country singer Aubrey James falling into a pothole. The headline was something about begging her fiancé not to leave her. How humiliating.*

Mom's like, "That poor woman is always in the tabloids. Every time her relationships go in the toilet, the National Inquirer *is there to tell us all about it."*

I can't imagine. What if Buck rejecting me made the local paper? I'd die.

Hey, I'm at work. So better get back to it. Just wanted you to know I'm thinking of you.

Love, Jen

Sunday morning when Connie comes to pick me up for church, the house is quiet and peaceful. Sadness over Car leaving lingers, but the decision was right. I don't regret it.

After our Amerigo's conversation and paparazzi fiasco, he dropped me home, deciding to stay at his parents until he left for New York.

"Do you miss him?" Connie breaks into my thoughts as we drive down Harding Place.

"You're eavesdropping on my thoughts. The past few nights when it gets dark, George and Ringo wait for him in the foyer. I caught myself expecting him once."

"That's understandable."

Absently, I flip through the pages of my new Bible. "Thank you for having the courage to speak the truth to me."

At the end of the service, I spot Scott and sneak up on him. It's been a week since our studio interview and Noshville Deli confession. I miss his irritatingly odd face and quirky personality. "If you keep stalking me, I'll have to get a restraining order."

He spins around, grinning. "I can't help it. You're Aubrey James."

I love how his voice sounds saying my name. I swallow. "Yeah, Aubrey James, and don't you forget it."

He grabs my left hand. "I saw the picture."

"Not my best side." I pull my hand away, tucking my hair behind my ears.

"Is this what you want?"

I raise my chin. "Yes. He wasn't the right man for me."

"Then I'm happy for you."

We stand there a second, quiet, then Scott nudges me. "What are you doing today? Care for a little game of one-on-one?"

"Maybe. Are you up for losing again?" Connie waves at me from the sanctuary doors. "I think she's ready to go." Halfway down the aisle, I turn back to Scott. "Four o'clock? My court?"

He bats a rolled-up bulletin against his palm. "Be prepared to lose."

*Scott and I cool off under the whir of the porch fans after four combat*ive games of one-on-one. "So, how does it feel, loser?" He rolls the *L* off his tongue.

I gawk at him. "Who won three of the four games?" Pointing to myself, I do a little head bob and weave. "Besides, I *let* you win the last game."

He stretches out his legs on the glass table with an exaggerated sigh. "Yep, yep, yep, my game plan is working perfectly."

I flick my water bottle cap at him. "Game plan, my eye."

He's working up some hokey story when the phone rings. I dash inside to answer.

"Aubrey, it's Connie."

"Hey, what's up?"

"Is Scott still there?" Her question is rushed. "Can he drive you over?"

"Why? What's going on?"

"You'll see. Just ask him."

"No, Connie, I don't want to ask him." For the first time in years, I'm aware of how dependent I am on others to take me where I need to go.

"Ask me what?" Scott walks into the kitchen, tossing his water bottle in the recycle bin.

I cradle the phone in my hand. "How do you know we're talking about you?"

He looks around, spreading his arms. "Don't see any other *him*'s around."

I wrinkle my nose. "Maybe we were talking about George and Ringo."

"Just ask."

"Connie wants me to come to her place."

He reaches for his keys on the island counter. "Let's do it."

I've never ridden in a Porsche before, and apparently Scott considers this an opportunity to scare the wits out of me.

"Scott, the car up ahead is braking." My fingers are white as I grip the door handle. Hillsboro Road is not busy for a Sunday evening, but traffic is always stop and start.

"I see, I see." He guns the gas, then stops just shy of the car's bumper.

"Oh my gosh, you're a maniac." My laugh is shaky and my right pinkie has passed out from being pinched against the door.

"You're just now figuring that out?" He revs the gas, making the engine growl so when the light turns green we lurch ahead. Shifting gears, he whips into the right lane and finds some open road.

"Oh, help." My heart pounds and I close my eyes.

Suddenly, the car slows and the engine whines down. "Why are you slowing down?" The cars we were tailing are now several lengths ahead of us.

"Aubrey, I'm sorry," Scott says.

"I'm just a big chicken," I confess, easing my grip on the door handle.

"No, you're not. I have no business racing around town like this." He pries my left hand from where it grips the seat. "I'm sorry I scared you."

"It's okay."

"Now, where do I turn for Connie's?" he asks.

A blue Toyota is parked on the street in front of Connie's house when Scott and I pull up.

"Someone is here." I shove open my door.

"Do you recognize the car?" Scott meets me in the middle of the driveway.

"No. Must be a friend of Connie's." I start up the front walk, but Scott doesn't follow. "You coming?"

"Do you want me to? I'm happy to play the taxi driver."

"Come with me, please?"

"My pleasure." He jogs up the walk.

"Look at us," I say. "We didn't even change." I pick at the sleeve of his T-shirt, still a little damp with sweat. His wiry brown locks stick out in every direction.

"You look perfect." The expression in his blue eyes makes me feel warm and swirly. I'm far from perfect, but in this moment, I am perfect to him.

"How about me?" he asks with his cocky smile that's quickly becoming my favorite smile.

"You look ridic—perfect."

Standing under the eaves of Connie's wide front porch in the early evening light, Scott leans toward me. "Aubrey, can I—"

"Yes." I grab a handful of his loose-fitting T-shirt, my pulse thumping in my ears.

He stops leaning. "I'm nervous."

"Me too. A little." I giggle and don't care that I do.

He slips his arm around my waist, dipping his head toward mine. His breath is warm on my face. "Here goes nothing."

Laughing, I lean away. "Nice. Way to sweet-talk me."

He tightens his arm around me. "Sweet talk? You want some sweet talk?"

The front porch light clicks on and the door swings open. "Are you going to stand out here all night?"

Scott releases me, and I spin around toward Connie. The spell is broken. It takes me a moment to catch my breath. *He was really going to kiss me.* "W-we were just about to knock."

"Knock? Use your key." She stands aside to let us pass. "You didn't clean up from basketball?"

"Well, no, you called and we hurried over." I glance up at Scott as we cross the threshold. His expression tells me, "Maybe this is for the best."

Maybe.

Connie's home is lovely and peaceful, my harbor from life's storms in years past. A candle burns from the tall, dark-wood table in the front hall. Pictures of her daughter and grown grandchildren hang on the wall.

Her little Yorkie, Romeo, scampers toward us yapping. Startled, Scott jumps behind me. "Just an ankle biter, Vaughn."

"Whose ankles?"

Connie scoops up Romeo. "We're in the kitchen eating cookies."

"Who's we, Connie? Is this an emergency cookie-eating meeting?"

Casting a quizzical glance at Scott, I shrug. "Cookies are always a good thing, right?"

Inside the door of her country kitchen, I stop short.

A beautiful young woman with brown hair and large hazel eyes sits at the table with an older, dark-haired woman. The girl's mouth drops open. "Oh my gosh . . ."

Scott stands next to me, his chest against my back. "Hello, I'm—" I offer my hand.

"Aubrey James," she bursts out.

The older woman studies my face, the lines around her brown eyes deepening. Her expression is a mixture of concern, confusion, and wonder. "Myra?"

Myra? Covering my face with my hands, I address the women. "Jen? Mrs. Sinclair?"

"All the way from Oklahoma." Connie moves to my side and swings her arm around my shoulder, gripping me to her side. "Isn't this wonderful?"

"Y-yes. Oh my goodness." I walk over to give Jen a hug. "Sorry, I've been playing basketball with my friend. This is Scott Vaughn." I point to the confused sportscaster.

"How do you do?" He wipes his hand on his shorts before shaking theirs.

This surprise reunion has startled Mrs. Sinclair and Jen. Startled me.

Mrs. Sinclair regards Connie. "I don't get it. Myra Ray is Aubrey James?"

The tension in the room increases. The older Sinclair feels duped. "Aubrey James is my real name. My parents were Ray and Myra James . . ."

"The gospel singers?" A pink hue covers Mrs. Sinclair's cheeks while Jen listens and watches. "They were killed in a car accident."

"Yes." A familiar coating of protection washes over my heart. The same one I've used in the past with fans, the press, and other inquisitors.

Mrs. Sinclair presses her hand to her forehead. "I never expected this."

"Me, neither." Jen's smile is slow but sure. "My foster sister and pen pal is Aubrey James?" She ekes out a tight squeal. "My friends are going to die."

"Why don't we all sit," Connie says over her shoulder as she pulls mason-jar glasses from the cupboard by the sink and picks up a stack of paper plates. "Scott, can you help me with the tea and ice? The tea is sweet, y'all."

I take the chair opposite Jen. "It's really good to see you in person," I start softly. "You're beautiful."

"Why didn't you tell me?"

I lean my elbows. "Selfish, really. I liked our relationship the way it was. Simple. Free. Honest."

"Except the part where you lied about your identity." Mrs. Sinclair has recovered from her shock.

"Yes. Jen, I'm sorry."

"No, it's fine." She shakes her head, brushing off my apology with a wave of her hand. "If I'm going to be surprised, this is the best kind."

Mrs. Sinclair laughs lightly. "I guess it is a fun surprise. But, Aubrey, you sent pictures a few years ago."

"That's right." Jen glances at her mother, then me.

Good grief. At the time, the white lie didn't seem to be a big deal. What's an image of a face when Jen and I could share our hearts? But now the deception makes me hot with shame.

"I sent my assistant Piper Cantwell's picture."

"Oh," Jen says as if it's okay. "I guess I can understand why."

"No, Jen, don't let me off. All this time I convinced myself that a few hidden facts about my life wouldn't change our relationship. After all, I could speak my heart and mind to you. Free to be me. Who cares, really, if I sent you someone else's picture, changed a few names to protect the innocent, or omitted a few details about my career—"

"A few?" Scott murmurs.

I shoot him a glance. *Quiet.* "Forgive me, Jen."

"O-of course. Please, I understand. Given your position, I would've done the same thing." Her laugh is sweet.

The weight of deception is eased by her forgiveness. "Just so you know, I was traveling a lot this spring—on tour. And I do have a business, AubJay, Inc., where I sell—"

"Aubrey Bags," Jen says. "Mom, the one I showed you on the Web site for my birthday."

"Oh, right. Those beautiful handbags."

"Jen, I'll give you as many as you want. You can take some to your friends."

"Really?" Her eyes pop wide.

"Absolutely, and I have a bunch of FRESH! merchandise, too, and, oh, 'Borrowed Time' T-shirts. Didn't those turn out cool?"

"Yeah, the ones with the image of a take-no-guff country girl stealing the watch from her boyfriend's wrist?"

Laughing, I give her thumbs-up. "You got it."

"Aubrey, you don't have to give me things," Jen says, with a voice I recognize from her e-mail.

"I know. But I want to, Jen." I pause. "I'm glad you know. I hope we can keep our friendship."

Jen shakes her head. "You'll always be Myra Ray, my big sister."

My eyes water. "You'll always be Jen Sinclair, my little sister."

28

"She kept me close and warm on the coldest night of my life."

—Jennifer Sinclair,
Inside NashVegas interview

Scott

"Thanks for doing this, you two."

Aubrey and Jen sit with their elbows linked on Aubrey's couch, waiting for Rafe to fire up the camera.

"I can't believe I'm doing an interview with Aubrey James. I mean, last week I didn't even know you."

Aubrey smiles, her countenance peaceful and happy. "Jen, you probably know me better than anyone."

"Except me." I couldn't resist.

"Except you, Scott." Her tone is light, yet mildly sarcastic.

"Let's do it," Rafe says.

"Oh, I'm nervous." Jen shivers, looking up at her mom, who's standing behind the couch.

Mrs. Sinclair taps her daughter's shoulders. "You'll be fine, baby."

"Just remember, we're not live, so we can always stop, go back, do it again." Aubrey's instructions are gentle and big-sister like.

Scott: *Aubrey, you have a double life. Tell us about it.*

AJ: What? I don't have a double life. I had a secret. A foster sister I wrote to using a different name.

Scott: *Why the different name?*

AJ: After my parents died, I was put in foster care for six months until Connie Godwin became my guardian. When I was taken to my foster home, I changed my name to Myra Ray. And I liked it.

Scott: *Didn't your friends at school know you as Aubrey James?*

AJ: Yeah, it was weird. But my foster mom acted like it was no big deal. I'm sure I wasn't the first foster kid to change her name. So, yes, I had two identities for a while. I was trying to hide, yet trying to discover who I was in my postparent world. I hated being identified as an orphaned girl. The cool basketball player was Aubrey James. The orphan was Myra Ray, and not real, if that makes sense.

Scott: *Next to Aubrey is her longtime friend, Jennifer Sinclair. You've been exchanging letters and e-mails for many years. Right?*

Jen: Yes, about ten years now, I guess. But I met Aubrey fourteen years ago. I lived with the same foster family. I was six, she was sixteen.

Scott: *Your mother had also been killed.*

Jen: She was murdered by her boyfriend. And I never knew my father.

Scott: *Murdered. Quite a journey for a six-year-old. Seems a sad set of events brought you two together.*

AJ: Very sad. But I'm realizing more every day, God does work all things together for good.

Scott: *Jen, do you remember meeting Aubrey the first night?*

Jen: I'll never forget. She became my lifeline. I crawled into bed with her because I couldn't sleep. I was frightened and alone, not really sure what was going on. [looking over at Aubrey] She made me feel safe. I thought Mrs. Fetterman, our foster mom, was the meanest lady alive, and I wanted to cling to the pretty girl who'd lost her momma too.

AJ: Jen broke my heart that first night. She came in clutching a baby doll, her face literally lost behind these round, sad eyes. She sat on the edge of the sofa with her toes pressed to the floor so she wouldn't slip off. She didn't say a word, but enormous tears ran down her cheeks.

Jen: My whole life I'd been told to never go into a stranger's house or talk to strangers. Now strange people were leaving me in a strange house, telling me how much fun I'd have and how a nice family wanted to help me.

AJ: Oh my gosh, my heart is breaking all over again. Jen started crying, and no one could console her. Mrs. Fetterman was frantic. It tore all of us up. Finally, Jen wore herself out, and Mrs. Fetterman put her to bed.

Jen: I didn't wear myself out. You rocked me to sleep in that big wooden rocker and sang "Jesus Loves Me" a thousand times.

AJ: Yes, I'd forgotten. [eyeing Jen] How could I forget? Later that night, I woke up with a warm little body snuggling next to me, her fingers wrapped in my hair, her dolly's fingers gouging my back.

Jen: I thought you smelled like flowers.

Scott: *Jen, you were eventually adopted by a family member.*

Jen: My mom's sister and her husband. A year later my uncle got a good job in Oklahoma, so we moved.

Scott: Aubrey and Jen haven't seen each other in . . .

AJ: Thirteen years. But we've been writing for ten years.

Jen: [laughing] But I thought I was writing to Myra Ray.

Scott: Why didn't you tell her, Aubrey?

AJ: When I signed with Mountain Music, Connie took me aside and said, "You need to use your real name. Time to grow up." She was right. Within a year, my career took off and everyone knew my name. Meanwhile, Jen was still young, and we hadn't started regular correspondence. By the time she was a teenager, I was a *name* [rolling her eyes], and being anonymous with Jen felt freeing. So, right or wrong, I decided to hide my identity from her.

Jen: I like to think your fame wouldn't have changed our relationship, but I was young and immature, and finding out my *sister* was a superstar would've impacted me negatively, I think. At least for a while.

Scott: How so?

Jen: [taking a deep breath] I went through a rebellious stage around sixteen, and I know for certain I would've tried to use Aubrey as a way to buck my parents. She would've been caught in the middle. The more I think about it, the more I'm glad I didn't know.

Scott: Okay, the cat is out of the bag. The secret is known. How does it change your relationship?

AJ: On my end, I'm relieved. Jen and I have always talked openly and honestly in our letters except when it came to my career and, of course, actually visiting each other. Now the barriers are gone.

Jen: Well, it helps to know a world-famous person is reading my personal letters. I mean, gee whiz. [laughing] But it really doesn't change anything for me other than I can't go around telling everyone I'm best buds with Aubrey James. [looking at Aubrey] Can I?

AJ: [wrinkling her nose] I prefer not.

Jen: See, no fun for me. [smiling] Really, I don't see anything changing. Maybe get a few passes backstage to her concerts, but that's it. I promise. Everything else stays the same.

Mrs. Sinclair: Except for all the free stuff she's giving you.

Jen: Mom, shhh.

AJ: Actually, this is another really great aspect of the truth. Now I can do more for Jen and her family. I didn't before because I wasn't sure how much my alter ego should flash her cash. But this will make it easier for me to call up and say, "I'm taking a week in the summer to go to the Mediterranean. Want to come?"

Jen: Yes! Double yes.

Mrs. Sinclair: Jen, you can't take advantage of Aubrey.

Scott: Something tells me Aubrey wouldn't mind a little sister abuse.

AJ: [laughing] Probably not. Besides, this is going to be a nationally televised interview. Jen, I guess all your friends are going to find out anyway.

Jen: Can I say something? Despite everything, the Myra Ray aka Aubrey James I know is an amazing, kind woman who wrapped her heart around a frightened little girl and kept her warm and safe. To me, she'll always be my hero.

Scott: Well said, Jen. Thank you.

The interview segment with Jen ends. She rises from the couch, smiling, hugging her mom. I tap Aubrey on the knee. "You're not done yet."

"Okay, whatever." Aubrey peers around at Jen. "She's fab, isn't she?"

"Like her big sister," I say.

Scott: *Ready for some rapid-fire questions?*

AJ: Sure, whatever that means.

Scott: *Dogs or cats.*

AJ: [gesturing toward her pets] Dogs, but I do love cats.

Scott: *Summer or winter?*

AJ: Fall.

Scott: *Okay, not the question, but whatever. Chocolate or vanilla?*

AJ: Are you crazy? Definitely chocolate.

Scott: *Leno or Letterman?*

AJ: Oooh, not fair. I do closing song sets on Letterman a lot, so I'll say Letterman.

Scott: *Reading or television?*

AJ: What is this, "Beat up Aubrey with hard questions"? Um, reading. But I do love old movies.

Scott: *Favorite movie?*

AJ: *Notting Hill, The Way We Were, Never Been Kissed*, and the indie film *Love Like a Rock*, which used my song, "Always."

Scott: *Favorite kind of day?*

AJ: Oh, this I can answer. Fall day. Slightly overcast with the sun filtering through cumulus clouds. A crisp breeze. Walking through fallen leaves with my friends, picturing the bowl of chili that is waiting for me at home.

Scott: *Greatest musical influence?*

AJ: My parents, of course. And my producer, Dave Whitestone. But I'd have to say I really admire Amy Grant. She took some hits for her divorce, but she never lost her faith, unlike some people [pointing to herself] She is an amazing songwriter and performer. I'd love to write and record with her one day.

Scott: *Finish this sentence: "If I could meet anyone, it would be . . ."*

AJ: Dead or alive?

Scott: *"If I could meet anyone, it would be . . ."*

AJ: Okay, okay. Anyone. Cleopatra, or the Queen of Sheba.

Scott: *[grinning] That's two someones, but I'll let you slide. Why Cleo and Sheba?*

AJ: Cleopatra because she sent herself, at twenty-two, to Julius Caesar wrapped in an oriental rug. Sheba, because she exchanged ideas with King Solomon and fell in love.

Scott: *Then why not meet Solomon?*

AJ: I'd rather talk to someone who talked to him. Think about it. Six thousand years ago, or however many years, a woman sat down and exchanged intellectual property with the wisest man whoever lived. Pretty amazing.

Scott: *Feminism wasn't born yesterday, was it?*

AJ: No.

Scott: *Wendy's or McDonald's?*

AJ: Can we go back to Solomon and Sheba?

Scott: *No. Answer the question.*

AJ: Burger King, my final answer.

Scott: *What's on your iPod?*

AJ: Songs.

Scott: *Smart aleck. Whose songs? What kind of songs?*

AJ: Lots of songs. I love to listen to all kinds of music. I recently downloaded Bread's greatest hits, and Journey's. My dad loved their sound. I'm digging Miranda Lambert and Carrie Underwood.

They're two amazing, beautiful artists with a totally different feel and message.

Let's see. Kim Hill and Rita Springer. Glen Campbell. What else? Martina's *Timeless* CD. I'm jealous she did a concept album like that before me. Maybe she won't mind if I cover "Rose Garden" again.

Scott: *No show tunes?*

AJ: [laughing] No, not yet.

Scott: *Final question.*

AJ: Promise?

Scott: *Do you want to go on a date with Scott Vaughn?*

AJ: [hesitating] Someday, maybe, yeah, I might.

29

"Aubrey James returns to her roots Monday night, August 6, as she joins the Ralph Lester Going Home Gospel Tour. This will be the country legend's first gospel performance since her parents' untimely death in '93."

—Brad Schmitt, Brad on 2

Aubrey

August 6, Ryman Auditorium

Scott and Rafe wait for me in the back of the auditorium. Our final interview. As I approach, Scott smiles at me. "Are you going to miss me?"

I snap my fingers. "How'd you know?"

He laughs as I slide in to the pew next to him, then asks, "What's wrong?"

He knows me too well. "I'm nervous."

"More than usual?"

I nod. "It's been a while since I sang gospel."

He takes my hand in his. "You don't see yourself as the rest of us do. And I'm pretty sure you don't see yourself as God does."

"Does anybody?"

He grins. "No, but especially you. Look, forget about labels—gospel, country, rock, whatever. Get up there and believe God will meet you."

I squeeze his hand. "I'm glad we did this *interview* thing. You've . . ." I pick an imaginary piece of lint from my black skirt. "You've helped me realize a lot of things about myself, good and bad." I look into his eyes. "I can't imagine not knowing you."

He coughs, covering his mouth with his fist. "See, I told you. You're going to miss me."

Scott

This is nuts. I can't fall in love with Aubrey James. Can. Not. It's been, what? Four weeks since our first interview segment. In which time she ended a relationship and engagement.

Don't let your heart go there, Vaughn.

Aubrey pulls her hand out of mine. "Guess we should get to the interview."

I clear my throat and nod. "Right, the interview."

Facing the camera, I do a lead-in. "Scott Vaughn for *Inside NashVegas*. I'm inside the historic Ryman Auditorium with country artist Aubrey James. Join us Mondays at seven a.m. for our exclusive look at this exceptional artist."

"Exceptional?" she echoes.

"My lead-in, my adjectives."

She smiles. "I'm not complaining."

Scott: *Tell me about your first performance at the Ryman.*

AJ: I was eight. The James Family was to be a part of a gospel music celebration at the Ryman.

Scott: *Do you think it played a significant part in your career?*

AJ: Certainly, among other things. But how cool to have the spotlight on the Ryman stage at eight? I mean, how many kids can say that? Or adults, for that matter.

Scott: *How old were you when you sang at the Grand Ole Opry?*

AJ: Nineteen. Right after my first country album came out.

Scott: *What do you remember about your first performance in the Ryman?*

AJ: Popcorn. [laughing] When Daddy brought us to the Ryman, concession was preparing for the evening and the whole place smelled like hot, buttery popcorn. [taking a deep breath] From that moment on, the only thing I could *think* about was popcorn. I begged and begged him to buy me a bag, but he refused. I'm pretty sure I came within a hairsbreadth of being grounded for life.

Scott: *I was grounded for life a couple of times.*

AJ: Why does that not surprise me? Anyway, we warmed up, did a sound check, and waited to go on, me still pouting over popcorn. I wore a yellow dress with black patent leather shoes . . . and *no* socks."

Scott: *No socks.*

AJ: No socks. I wanted to wear stockings, but Momma said no. It was nineteen eighty-five, and she still thought stockings were too grown up for an eight-year-old. So I refused to wear anklets because none of the other ladies were wearing them.

Scott: *See, you've been a diva in the making for a long time.*

AJ: Oh my gosh . . . [flicking her wrist] Yeah, you're probably right.

Scott: *Were you nervous?*

AJ: I can't remember. Maybe a little. I didn't understand the magnitude of singing at the Ryman. [stopping to point overhead] Listen. Hear it? The lingering music, the great voices of past performances. Sam Jones preaching. George Hay welcoming listeners to the Grand Ole Opry. That amazing train sound of DeFord Bailey's harmonica. [smiling] I love this place.

Scott: I can see why.

AJ: I forget the incredible history until nights like this when I'm sitting in the quiet sanctuary and history speaks to me.

A commotion in the back of the auditorium nabs our attention. A tour group tromps along the back of the sanctuary. I motion for Rafe to cut. Several of the tourists notice Aubrey and scurry toward us in a synchronized shuffle.

"I can't believe it." A bubbly teen with a blonde ponytail claps her hands over her cheeks. "Please, can I have your autograph?"

I've been with Aubrey several times now when this happens and her graciousness never fails. She makes the conversation feel like neighbors talking over the fence. I signal for Rafe to video this exchange.

"What's your name?" Aubrey asks, poised to sign a Ryman flyer.

"Caitlyn. With a C."

Aubrey smiles. "All right, Caitlyn with a C. Are you coming to the show tonight?"

"No, we couldn't get tickets." The teenager sticks out her lower lip.

Aubrey hands back the pad of paper and pen. "Tell you what, why don't you come as my guests?"

Caitlyn's scream rattles the old stained glass. "Really? Mom, can we please?"

Her mother nods. "Are you sure, Miss James?"

"Absolutely." Aubrey pauses. "Unless you need a hundred tickets."

The mom laughs. "Four would be fine."

"Four I can do. Come to the ticket counter and ask for them in my name." Aubrey turns to me. "Remind me to tell Piper. She's backstage."

Others in the group step up for autographs and digital photos. The crowd is small, so Aubrey complies. Posing and signing, chatting all the while.

Rafe zooms in to capture their faces and banter. The candid moment will add a great touch to our summer interviews, confirming to the world what I've been seeing all summer. A beautiful woman with a sincere heart.

Aubrey talks with the fans, asking questions as if she really cares where they lived, the name of their school and church, and how they liked Nashville. She's nonplussed by their effusive accolades. When the younger fans clear away, clutching their autographs, chatting a mile a minute, a few older ones step up, quietly telling Aubrey they remember her parents.

"Thank you. It's comforting to talk with people who loved their music."

An older, statuesque woman hangs back, eyeing Aubrey from the tip of her raised nose. Her expression causes the hair on the back of my neck to rise.

Aubrey is ending a conversation with a twenty-something woman. "We're in the studio this summer working on a new album. It's different from what I've been doing, so I hope the fans will like it."

"I own all your albums," the woman admits with a small laugh. "I'm sure I'll own the new one too."

The twenty-something fan is gracefully and confidently holding her own with the superstar. From her mannerisms, I can tell Aubrey prefers this kind of self-assured fan. "Listen, I'll send you an advanced copy. I'd love your feedback."

"Really? I'd be honored."

Aubrey instructs the twenty-something how to get in touch with her for the CD, and after a quick hug, she dashes off to join the rest of the tour before the Ryman closes to the public and show prep begins.

But still lurking a few feet away is the statuesque woman. "Would you like an autograph?" Aubrey asks, smiling.

The woman shakes her head, her lips pressed into a tight line. "I knew your people . . . your mother and father." She steps closer, and the tone of her voice is like the sharp edge of a knife.

I slide out from the pew and stand next to Aubrey.

"You knew my parents? Have we met?" Aubrey extends her hand, but the woman doesn't acknowledge the gesture.

"Wouldn't they be ashamed at what their daughter has become?" The woman's accusation is ominous and penetrating.

An adrenaline rush causes my heartbeat to pick up. *What is she up to?* I cross my arms, watching and listening.

"I-I-I," Aubrey stumbles to answer. "I think they'd be very proud of me."

The austere woman shakes her head. "They were *good* Christian people. Don't you imagine they would expect you to live as if they taught you some morals?"

Aubrey blinks, her expression twisted with confusion. "Excuse me, I didn't catch your name?"

"I didn't give it."

This woman is good. Skilled in control and manipulation.

"How did you know my parents?"

"Through church functions, music events around town. I helped coordinate some of their bookings in the early days."

"I see. And that gives you the right to tell me they wouldn't like what I've become?"

"Your parents loved the Lord."

"So do I."

"I'm sure they would be disappointed to see their girl whoring around, living with a man she isn't married to, singing songs about fornicating and drinking."

My fists clench under my crossed arms. *Smack her down, Aubrey. Give it to her.*

But Aubrey doesn't move. Doesn't say a word.

"Don't you feel like the world's biggest hypocrite, singing at a gospel show with all those genuine Christian singers? Paying tribute to your parents while living a life they would never condone?"

Aubrey, tell her to back off. What gives her the right, coming in here, using your parents against you?

A second ticks off, then another. Aubrey is solemn, staring past the woman to another part of the sanctuary.

The accuser can't leave well enough alone. "I just hope you understand how disappointing you are to Christians everywhere."

"Then I'd appreciate your prayers." Aubrey's voice wobbles.

The woman inhales sharply, jerking up her chin. Aubrey's humility knocks her off her high horse. I want to cheer and punch the air with my fist, but I keep my composure. For a split second, the woman appears to soften.

"I'll pray . . . if it's not too late." She walks off, her thick heels thudding against the scarred wood floors.

Rafe looks from around the camera. "What a b—"

"Rafe." I hold up my hand. "Aubrey, you okay?"

She bobs her head once, but won't turn toward me. "I'm fine."

I walk around and lift her chin. "Look at me." Her lower lip quivers, and tears swim in her blue-green eyes.

"I-I . . ." A sob escapes through her pinched lips. ". . . can't . . . She's . . . right . . ."

"She's wrong." Wrapping my arms around her, I hold her while she weeps. "A mean, bitter woman."

Rafe ambles down the aisle and returns in a few minutes with Piper.

"Honey, what's wrong?" Piper leans to see Aubrey's face.

"Rude lady," I say to Piper, starting to explain. Aubrey turns away from us, brushing away her tears.

At the end of my story, Piper folds her arms with a grimace on her face. "Why do you let people like that get to you?"

Aubrey whirls around. "Because she's right. Most of the stuff about me is fabrication, exaggeration, like Car and I didn't break up because I'm still in love with Jack Mills. That's laughable. I can blow it off. But this woman is serious. How have I honored my heritage? How have I honored the vow I made to the Lord when I gave Him my heart? Fifty bucks says this woman is not alone in the way she feels."

"Aubrey." I hand her my handkerchief. "Forget the Frozen Chosen. Let them feel the way they want to feel. All you need to know is you're loved and forgiven. That woman is no less a sinner than you. Go out on the stage tonight and celebrate your parents. Celebrate your own coming home to God. Heck, your Dad got tossed out of a church for doing his own kind of music. Are you better than him? So people criticize. Don't let it get you down."

"Dad got kicked out for playing drums and electric guitar. This woman is calling out my sin."

"Seems I remember a story about a harlot thrown down at Jesus' feet. The mob wanted Him to condemn her to stoning, but He wouldn't. He knew the mob was no better than the woman."

"It's not the same, Scott. Stop."

"It *is* the same, Aubrey. Fine if they want to martyr you, but don't martyr yourself."

"Scott's right," Piper says.

"Aubrey." I hold her by her arms. "Jesus simply told the harlot to go and sin no more. I can't imagine He'd say anything different to you."

Aubrey kicks the floor with her pointy-toed shoe. "Yeah, well, the harlot didn't have to perform in front of several thousand of the Frozen Chosen."

Piper laughs.

"Come on, they're not all the Frozen Chosen," I tease. On impulse, I pull her to me, wrapping her in my arms. "Since when are you afraid of the critics?"

"I hate when you're right." She plants a soft kiss on my cheek. "Thank you."

"Any time," I say, my voice husky, my pulse racing. *Man, I am so gone over her. So gone.*

30

Aubrey

"Ladies and gentlemen . . ."

Waiting in the wings, I listen as Ralph introduces me. I'm still nervous. Very.

". . . we are thrilled to have this great lady of country music with us tonight . . ."

I see *her* austere, judgmental face and hear *her* icy accusation. *What would Daddy and Momma think of me?* "I don't know, I don't know." Momma's face from my dream scrolls across my mind's eye. Her forgiving voice asks, "Why do you hide your light?"

I bat away a fresh batch of tears. My stylist repaired my makeup so

I can't ruin her masterpiece a second time. Exhaling, I choke back the emotion.

". . . We know her as the queen of country soul, but this gal sang right here at the Ryman Auditorium for the first time more than twenty years ago. We're glad to have her here tonight singing the timeless gospel songs of her father and mother, the great Ray and Myra James."

The great Ray and Myra James. Me? The great poser. Sold out when I wasn't even looking to sell. *God, oh God.* I can't go out there, a sinner posing as a believer. *I owe You everything. God, You owe me nothing.*

"Please welcome Aubrey James!" The spot swings to stage right, dropping a circle of white light on the floor in front of me. The Ryman auditorium reverberates with applause.

"Aubrey James . . ." Ralph extends his arm to me.

Shoved from behind—by Piper, I guess—I stand in the center of the spot. The applause grows. Lifting my chin and sculpting my smile, I stride onto the grand old stage. Ralph meets me in the middle and slips his arm around my shoulder.

"What songs are you going to sing tonight?"

"A couple of Daddy's favorites, Ralph. 'Mountain of Myrrh,' 'Baptize Me in the River,' and 'Come, Faithful One.'"

"All my favorites." Ralph backs away. "Once again, Aubrey James."

More cheering and applause. The energy and feel is so different from the CMA Fest. Was it only two months ago I fainted on the coliseum stage?

Tonight's feel is a mixture of encouragement and condemnation. Digging deep for my diva confidence, I make my way to the edge of the stage. Ralph and the band are playing "Mountain of Myrrh."

"Daddy wrote this song during a difficult time in his life. 'A time of pruning,' he said." My eyes scan the audience. "God's been doing some pruning in my life lately. Can anybody relate?"

The audience applauds.

"Yeah, me too." The song evokes a treasure of memories. The ones

Connie challenged me about. The imperishable lessons my parents taught me. Values that can't be carted off to the city dump.

As I start to sing, the first line of the verse catches in my throat. From the third row, center, Piper signals me to keep going by whirling her forefinger in a circle.

Next to Piper, Connie sits like a proud momma. Behind her is the family of four I met earlier. The mother gives me a thumbs-up.

I stumble through the lyrics, my voice weak and wispy, humble but not broken.

I'll never build up to the chorus from here. I wish I could break, breathe, cough, swallow. It's the CMA Fest all over again, I'm failing.

Suddenly a smooth baritone bolsters my weak voice, and I look to see Ralph strolling toward me, his guitar hanging down his side like Daddy's used to do.

I smile and wrap my arm around his. Our voices rise to the top of the auditorium in perfect harmony, and together we go to the "Mountain of Myrrh."

31

Scott

Riding the elevator up to the seventh floor with Aubrey, I take a mental inventory of my loft. For the life of me I can't remember if I finally cleaned up the pile of soggy cereal dishes.

Is there toilet paper in the guest bathroom?

"Do you like living in these lofts?"

Yes, there's toilet paper. I remember putting some in there last shopping trip.

"I do. Great locale." I look down. When did being around her start to feel so right? The first time I met her. Last summer.

"Car was jazzed about increasing downtown residential property."

"It's been a fight, I know. But we'll get there. I sorta like it quiet, but if more residents move in, there will be more shops and restaurants within walking distance."

The elevator slows at my floor. "This way." I unlock my loft door and stand aside for Aubrey to pass, reaching around to flip on the track lighting.

"Scott, this is amazing." She turns a slow circle. "What a great place . . . Oh, your loft has a loft." She points to my upstairs office.

"Yeah, it's a nice perk."

"I can't stand it," she says, hands on her hips. "A bachelor's pad has more ambience and color than my luxurious Belle Meade house."

"Well, my mom—" *Do not talk about your mom.*

"She . . ." Aubrey waits with arched brows.

". . . likes to decorate."

"She's good. Your place is beautiful." Aubrey walks over to the window. "What a great view of the city at night. You can see the Gaylord from here. Don't you love Nashville?"

"More every day." I drop my keys on top of the breakfast counter.

She turns to me. "What do you—"

A knock interrupts her question. My friend and neighbor, Brandon Otis, is on the other side of the door.

"Brandon." I don't open all the way to him. "Kind of late."

"I heard you come in and—" He spies Aubrey. "Didn't know you had company." Brandon shoves past me and my half-opened door. He's a massive man with massive amounts of charm and during our four-year friendship, I've watched him conquer some of Nashville's most beautiful women. Yet in the presence of Aubrey, he's dumbstruck. He can't take his eyes off her.

"Brandon." I follow him like a dutiful wing man. "I'd like you to meet Aubrey James. Aubrey, this is Brandon Otis, the wide receiver for the Nashville Kats."

His blatant gawk doesn't faze her. "Nice to meet you. Brandon, is it?"

"Aubrey James." His charm light clicks on. I recognize his expression. "Have we met before?"

"No, I don't believe we have." Aubrey slips her handbag from her arm and sits on my couch, crossing her legs, shaking her head subtly so her hair falls over her shoulders.

I bite my lips to keep from laughing. She's so playing him.

"And how do you two know each other?" she asks.

"I did some PR work for the Kats before I went to *Inside the Game*," I say.

"Very nice." Her expression and tone are perfect.

Brandon tries to charm her with a few of his classic lines, but she shows not even a flicker of interest. Instead, she toys with the straps of her handbag and gives him one-word answers.

Anyone else, I'd consider her actions rude. But Aubrey is savvy. She pegged him the moment he walked in. Man, it's all I can do to keep from laughing.

I wait another minute, then slap Brandon on the back. "Talk to you tomorrow, dude." I walk him to the door.

In the hall, he whispers, "Get her number for me."

I grin. "No problem."

"How'd I do?" There's a glint in Aubrey's eye.

"You vindicated hundreds of Nashvillian women, and if they knew, they would thank you." I pull a couple of bottles of water from the fridge. "He asked for your number."

Aubrey laughs, taking the water bottle. "If I had a dime for every Brandon Otis I've met in this life . . . What? No FRESH!?"

"Can't afford it."

"Please . . ." She pops me gently on the arm.

"Brandon's not a bad guy under all the bull and good looks." I take a swig of water.

"Thank you for what you did tonight at the Ryman." She twists the cap off her water. "You gave me courage."

"I wanted to punch the old biddy."

"What, and sink to her level? Do to her what she did to me, only with fists instead of words?"

"Point taken." With my thumb, I press in the top part of my water bottle. The plastic crunches. "But she infuriated me."

"And she humiliated me. But come on, Scott, neither of us can deny the ring of truth in her words."

"What ring of truth? That your parents would be disappointed in you?"

"No, that my life does not reflect the values and character they taught me. Being orphaned at sixteen is no excuse." She picks at the water bottle label. "Connie made that clear a few weeks ago."

"How so?"

She sits sideways on the sofa, hugging her legs. "When Car moved in, he threw away the boxes I had in the library"

"You're kidding."

She props her arm on the back of the couch and presses her cheek against her hand. "He claims I told him I didn't want to keep the stuff. But he was half asleep, so who knows what he heard."

"Did it tick you off?"

"Yes. But Connie reminded me the real jewels I have from my parents are the ones they instilled in my character, in my heart."

"Do you think you would have taken the same road if they were alive?"

She thinks for a minute. "I do, and they would've been my biggest fans. My music choice is not the problem, or even being famous. It's my source of inner strength. If my parents were alive, I probably would've made different personal decisions. Like Jack and Derek. Car would've never moved in with me."

"Where to from here?"

"Home." She slips off the couch, grabbing her handbag. "You have to get up early, my friend, and I'm keeping you from a good night's sleep." Walking to the kitchen, she holds up her empty water bottle. "Trash? Recycle?"

"Set it in the sink. I'll get it later."

"Is this your family?" Aubrey wanders down the short hall to her right.

"Yes." I join her, looking at the pictures on the hall table. "My parents, there, and my sisters and their families."

"Where do they live?"

"Murfreesboro. Born and raised. All of us. Got a whole herd of kinfolk. Aunts, uncles, cousins, grandparents. Mom's first-grade friends are still her friends, and Dad still gets with his old high school football buddies."

She shakes her head as if astounded. "I cannot imagine. What are your sisters' names? They're very pretty."

"Older one is Patti." I tap the frame. "And this is Sally."

She chuckles. "You're the baby boy, huh?"

I nod. "Yes, the not-so-spoiled boy. Both Mom and Dad are the oldest children in their families, so for the longest time I was the only boy grandson, cousin, and nephew. Got loaned out for chores and grass cutting. I've probably mowed half the lawns in Murfreesboro. Family, friends of family, you name it."

"Builds character, my dad used to say." Aubrey looks up at me, smiling, her gaze meshing with mine. "Well, I guess . . . we'd . . . better get going."

I touch her arm. She steps closer. I slip my arm around her back. She smoothes her hand over my chest. "Is this a good idea?"

"You tell me." My heart pounds under her hand.

She lifts her face to mine. "Every ounce of me wants to say yes. You are an amazing man, Scott. But I've been here before. Emotions on the surface, hearts connecting, romantic setting . . ."

"I'm not like them."

"Yes, but I'm still me. Broken, wounded, messed up, and impulsive." Her lips quiver. "I don't want to hurt you."

As she looks down, a lock of her hair falls over her face. When I touch her forehead to brush it aside, electricity fires through me. Aubrey cups my hand to her face, then lightly kisses my palm.

"If it took Melanie Daniels' betrayal for me to meet a friend like you, I'd do it all over again." She laces her fingers with mine. "And if it took Car tossing out my past in order for me to realize my future, then it was worth it." Aubrey lifts her face to mine. "I like being here with you. Too much."

Every molecule in my body is urging me to take her in my arms and kiss her. "Yeah, me too—" I clear my throat. "How do you expect a guy not to fall in love when you confess something like that?"

"I'm not playing fair, am I?"

It takes all my strength to pull away from her. Another second, I'd barge past the boundaries she's drawn. "Guess the dog-face boy should drive the gorgeous country girl home."

"I guess he should." She follows me to the kitchen, her fingertips hooked with mine.

Picking up my keys, I turn to her. "Ready?"

"Yes."

Her eyes, her lips, her face, everything about her entices me. "Better go."

It's late. I'm going to hate my alarm when it goes off at three a.m., but I have to do this.

Flipping on my bedroom light, I root through my top dresser drawer. It's in here somewhere, unless Brit took it when she came for her CDs and DVDs. After she left, I discovered half of my media collection missing.

Small price to pay to get her permanently out of my life.

My fingers land against a thick velvet box. Popping open the lid, I regard the half-karat solitaire diamond in the light.

Sheeze. What an ugly piece of jewelry. Brit reset the diamond in a gaudy gold mount when she thought she could dump me but keep the ring.

Riding the elevator down to the street, I jog toward Riverfront Park in the red and amber lights of downtown. The night air is thick and warm. I yank my shirttail from my belt.

This past month with Aubrey has cleared the final Brit cobwebs from my mind. Whether I'm falling in love with Aubrey James or *not*, I'm back in the love game. Come to find out, my heart isn't quite as broken as I thought.

When I arrive at the river, I lean against the sidewalk rail and retrieve the ring box from my pocket. My heart thumps as I wind up for the pitch.

"Here's to you, Brit."

But just before releasing the ring box and chunking my past into the rippling waters, I hesitate.

Six months of Ramen Noodles. Washing and ironing my own shirts instead of taking them to the cleaners. No cable TV or Internet at home. Going to a barber instead of a stylist. Changing my own car oil. Any place I could cut expenses to save for a ring, I did.

Down twenty pounds and mourning the loss of two dress shirts scorched by a rogue iron, I'd finally saved four thousand dollars.

What did it buy me? The world's biggest heartache. I cock my arm back again. "Here's to you, Brit."

The ring box floats out over the river in a nice, high arc, then breaks the water's surface with a tiny splash. I punch the night air with a cleansing yell. "Liberty!"

32

"Back to gospel? Country superstar Aubrey James rocked the Coming Home Gospel Celebration at the Ryman last night. But the country diva is not without her critics.

"Gospel and Aubrey James?" wondered her former musical director Melanie Daniels. "Don't go together."

—*Fox 17 News 7*

Aubrey

Piper and I review the final photos from my latest FRESH! photo shoot, deciding which image we like the best, when the french door jerks open. George and Ringo scamper in, attached to Gina, who is gasping for breath.

"Another rabbit?" I bend down to greet the dogs, taking the leashes from Gina.

"No . . . *(gasp, pant)* A cat. A blame cat."

The dogs lap water then nuzzle my navy capris with their wet noses. I sit on the floor and bury my face in their fur. "Did you have fun with Gina? Hum?"

Gina's cheeks are rosy and her smile wide as she retrieves a pitcher of tea from the fridge. "Fall is in the air. It's a beautiful September morning."

"I can't believe it's September already. The summer is almost gone."

Gina waltzes around the kitchen with her pitcher of tea, singing Neil Diamond. "September morn . . . We da-da-da-da-da-da, something-something brand-new day."

I laugh. "Want me to call Neil for the lyrics?"

"What, don't you like my version?" Gina stops swirling and leans her hands on the kitchen counter. "I am so glad for a dip in the temperature."

"It is a gorgeous day." George nudges Ringo aside so he can give me a slobbery lick.

"So, Aubrey, we're going with these?" Piper slides the contact sheet under my nose, tapping the thumbnail images she's circled with a red-wax pencil.

I review the shots. "Yes, those are the final five."

Piper has an envelope all ready for mailing. "By the way, we're getting a lot of fan mail since the *Inside NashVegas* segments started running. People are watching the show on the Internet. Your fans are loving you for this, Aubrey."

I laugh and hop up for a Diet Coke. "I'm glad it's a hit. Have you seen the ads on CMT for *Inside NashVegas?*" I mimic the announcer's voice. "Premiering in November."

Piper smiles, nodding. "All the shots of Scott and Beth are from the spring, before she went out with her pregnancy. Must be an awkward time for her to be out."

"But what a good reason to be out of work. A baby." I toss ice into a plastic cup Gina keeps by the fridge and twist the cap off my soda.

Piper hands me a stack of printed-out e-mails. "The reviews from your interview are great, Aubrey. Holding out all these years really built curiosity in folks."

I fan the stack of papers through my fingers. "You seriously expect me to read these?"

"Skim them on your way to SongTunes." Piper glances at her watch. "Zach will be here in a few minutes."

Dave and I finished my new album in mid-August. Ten of the twelve cuts were written by Robin and me. The other two are mine alone. The idea sends an electric excitement through me.

I'm anxious to hear the world's reaction. Excitement mixed with dread. Will they like it? What if they don't? What if they do?

But I'm confident in this album—no matter what the reviews. "Someday Love Will Find Me" is my favorite new tune. A soulful ballad with lots of fiddle and steel guitar, and I can't believe I cowrote it. My love for the art of music is renewed.

From the time we recorded the last song, Dave worked night and day to get it mixed, mastered, and submitted to Nathan by his mythological deadline of September first.

Now, a whole two weeks later, we're beckoned.

"Can't believe it took him two weeks to listen to an album he wanted recorded and mastered in eight," I say out of the blue.

Piper looks up. "Are you talking to us?"

I swig my Diet Coke. "Guess I was thinking out loud." I let my thoughts wander from Nathan to Scott and our last interview. It's been over a month, and though I see him at church, I miss him.

Since my first Sunday back at Faith Community in July, I haven't missed a Sunday service. Of course, it's hard to sleep in when I know Connie's on her way to pick me up, but I find myself looking forward to Sundays, noting how empty the weekdays feel.

I can tell the condition of my soul is different. Less cracked and dry. The emotional plane of my life is yielding to the watering and care of the master Gardener.

Which reminds me . . . I look out the window. Juan is working today, preparing the garden for fall.

"Hey Aubrey, what's going on in the foyer?"

I turn to see Zach in the doorway, thumb pointed over his shoulder.

"Aubrey is painting," Piper announces without emotion, though I know she thinks I'm ridiculous.

He furrows his brow. "Painting what?"

I twist my lips. "Um, the foyer?"

He tosses his keys to the counter and reaches for one of Gina's scones. "About time. Who'd you hire to do it? I've heard Baylor Bone is really good."

"I've heard that, too, but I'm doing this myself."

Zach chokes. Crumbs spew from his lips. "You're doing it yourself?"

"Yes," I say, sorta defiantly. "I know how to use a paintbrush."

"Aubrey, hire someone. In case you've forgotten, you can afford it."

"It's not about the money; it's about me pouring myself into my house. Adding my touch. Making it my own."

He shrugs. "Do you think it'll be done by 2010 or 2020?"

"Very funny. My manager, the snark face." I point at the kitchen clock. "Better go. Can't keep the great Nathan Brack waiting."

With my manager, Zach; my lawyer, Skyler; and my producer, Dave, I discuss a game plan before going into SongTunes and the meeting with Nathan.

"Skyler, any feel for what's going on?" I ask as we stand on the sidewalk of Music Row East, shielding our eyes from the late morning sun.

She shakes her head. "SongTunes is being very vague."

Zach motions to me. "What are you thinking?"

"This is the best album I've ever done. Skyler, your cousin is a phenomenal songwriter. She's going to have several hits from this record."

Skyler smiles. "She says you brought out lyrics and melodies in her she didn't know she had. She's really grateful, Aubrey."

"She's grateful? I'm the one. This album wouldn't have happened without her."

Zach's expression is pinched. "Great, we have a fabulous album and mutual admiration society. But what is SongTunes going to say?"

"Do you see them dumping Aubrey when they need their most successful artist to help the bottom line?" Dave shifts his stance from side to side.

"Just be prepared for whatever," Skyler says.

I offer a prediction. "Nathan's going to posture himself as the important label boss, rattle off a bunch of industry buzzwords, say the album is daring and not classic Aubrey James. How could I deviate from the careful branding of SongTunes? Yadda, yadda. And in the end he'll say 'they're' nervous, but marketing is geared up for a January release."

Zach checks his watch and motions for the door. "Let's go find out."

The SongTunes team is gathered when we walk into Nathan's office. He's seated at the head of the conference table with Aaron from A&R and Ian from legal.

"Come in, come in." Nathan's posture is hard to read. "Aubrey, I've been watching *Inside NashVegas* on Monday mornings." He clicks his tongue and winks. "Funny stuff, burning off Scott Vaughn's eyebrows."

"It was an accident." Sitting where Nathan points, I note the absence of a chilled glass of ice and bottle of FRESH!.

The president of SongTunes takes his seat and places his hand over a CD case I can only guess is mine. "You and Carmichael broke up? Did I read it somewhere?"

"Yes, we broke up."

Nathan slides the CD across the table to me. "Don't like it."

I reach for the case. "What don't you like?" My confidence is high, and I feel ready for a fight.

He rocks back in his chair, pressing his fingertips together. "There's not one radio release on the album. Not one. What were you two thinking?" He motions between Dave and me.

"We were thinking we'd like to piss off Nathan Brack," Dave says.

A muffled laugh comes from Nathan's side of the table, but the man himself remains hard with an unyielding demeanor.

"Mission accomplished, then, Aubrey. How did you figure this would be an album I could release to the public? I want hit songs, not this poetry nightclub crap. Radio had a fit when they heard it. Is it country, is it R&B, is it gospel? You're all over the place."

Across from me, Aaron shakes his head. He already told me he loved the album, but can't convince his boss.

"Nathan, I'm sincerely not trying to make you angry or upset. We weren't trying to tick you off." I shoot a glance at Dave. "But *this* is my next album. Do you want to honor our contract or not?"

A red hue creeps up his neck and covers his cheeks. "I want you to honor your contract, go back in the studio, and record something I can sell to the public."

I slide the CD case back across the table. "You have something you can sell to the public."

He shoves it back. "No, I don't."

We shove the CD back and forth one more time before a migraine-sized debate erupts between SongTunes and the Aubrey James camp. My lawyer versus their lawyer. Nathan confronting Zach and Dave.

Aaron and I smile from our opposite sides. "I'll say it again, Aubrey, I loved it. Brilliant work."

"Thanks, Aaron. Robin Rivers is an outstanding songwriter. You should get her to write for the other artists."

He hunts for a scrap of paper. "What's her name again?"

When the debate has raged on long enough, I stand. "This is ridiculous. Nathan, either take the album or we do. Your choice."

Skyler whispers in my ear. "Are you willing to take this leap?"

"I believe in this project," I whisper back.

"You walk out with the album, Aubrey, and we're in a court battle."

"Nathan, I've fulfilled my end of the contract. Delivered an album of great songs. Your choice if you turn it down."

"We can walk, Nathan," Skyler says. "You know it, Ian knows it. And not be in breach of contract."

Nathan fumes in silence with a sharp eye on Ian. His voice is calm when he says, "It's your reputation, Aubrey." He sits, swiping his palms together as if to wash his hands of me.

"Best of luck to you, Nathan." With my little brigade, I leave Nathan's office, ending another chapter of my life this summer. My eight-year run with SongTunes.

33

"SongTunes president Nathan Brack announced his resignation from the label this afternoon during a last-minute press conference. Word on Music Row is his decision came after country superstar Aubrey James parted ways with the label last week."

—*AllAboutCountry.com*

Piper claims I've gone Zen with my garden gazebo, but for the past week I've loved coming out here in the evenings with my guitar and Bible.

George and Ringo accompany me, scampering ahead, circling the red cedar gazebo before leaping the steps and plopping down on the floor, panting. All of this before I'm halfway across the lawn.

This routine makes Juan unhappy. George and Ringo are creating a path across his well-tended yard.

"My work, ruined." He gestures to the smashed grass blades, his brow furrowed. But there's always a glint in his eyes.

"How are Alejandra and the baby?" I ask.

His smile brightens. "Very good. The baby doesn't cry so much now."

It's Friday night, and since Piper is without an e-date, she's decided to hang out with me and play a little guitar. "It's been years."

"Well, this is what back-porch picking is for, messing around with the guitar."

Piper tunes one of the guitars from the music room. "Did you and Zach decide what you're going to do with your album yet?"

"No. Still considering the options. Robin thinks I should sign with Nashville Noise. Zach talked with them, but we are still discussing the independent label option."

"It's a lot of work being independent. Distribution, marketing, promotions, the entire business side of the music business. Which you hate."

"It's my one hesitation, but we can hire *people* to do all of that stuff." Fishing a pick from my guitar case, I play a melody I've had in my head for a few days. Once I started writing again, the creative gates were opened and ideas come often.

"Yeah, but I know you, Aubrey. If you start your own label, you won't be able to let others run it without getting involved. After all, it's your business. You can't divorce yourself from it."

"That's my biggest hesitation."

A fall breeze ushers in the cool, September night. The maple shading the gazebo is already tipped with red and gold.

Piper attempts to play what I'm playing. Concentrating, her quick fingers are accurate with the chords, but after a few measures, she laughs, dropping her hand away from the strings. "I have no calluses. It hurts to keep playing." She spreads her arms along the top of the gazebo bench. "Did you see the latest *Music Row* magazine?"

"No, why?"

Piper shifts the guitar on her knee and starts to play again. "They did a cover story on Melanie Daniels. She's branding herself as the new Aubrey James."

"Good. Now I can be who I want to be. The real me."

Piper sets the guitar against the gazebo bench. "She'll never have your heart or your character."

We continue to talk while I play. The sun sinks behind the treetops and the night air grows cold.

"What's up with you and Scott?" Piper asks.

I shrug. "Nothing. We're through with the interview and—"

"You're into him, aren't you?"

I squint at her in the soft light. "No, I'm not *into him*."

"If you say so, but ever since the Come Home Gospel Celebration, your face lights up every time you hear his name."

Sometimes Piper pays too much attention to detail. "Scott is a great guy."

She laughs. "I sorta had a crush on him."

I stop playing. "You did not."

She nods. "I did."

"Do you want me to fix you up?"

"No. Are you kidding? He's very into you, Aubrey." Piper's attention is drawn toward the house. She stands. "Were you expecting company? Scott is here and . . ." She sucks in a deep breath. "Oh my gosh."

I twist around to see what she's talking about. In the white glow of the yard lanterns, a tall, lean man with dark skin and sun-bleached hair accompanies Scott. The easy sway in his walk reminds me of . . .

I drop my guitar against the gazebo bench. "I can't believe it."

"Is it who I think it is?"

"Yes." I run down the gazebo steps, my bare feet pounding across the lawn. "Peter!"

My hands are still shaking as I fix my big brother a plate of Gina's left- over pot roast and potatoes. *Fix my big brother.* The notion hits me with both excitement and confusion.

Glancing toward the family room, I watch my brother, *my big brother*, talk and laugh with Piper and Scott.

I love seeing him here. But I have so many questions. Why is he here? How did he find me. How does he know Scott?

"Are you surprised?" Scott tugs open the fridge door and looks inside. "Got any root beer?"

"No, just juice, water, and diet."

"Water it is." He taps the fridge closed with his heel.

"Scott, how do you know Peter?" I ask as he twists off the bottle cap and tosses it in the trash, then retrieves the pie plate from the other side of the kitchen.

I pull out the cutting knife from the island drawer and hand it to him. "Are you ignoring me?"

Focused on cutting a large slice of pie, Scott still doesn't answer.

"Scott." I pull on his elbow. "How do you know him?"

"The pie looks good, doesn't it? You want a piece?" He drops his cut onto one of the paper plates Gina leaves out now.

"Great dinner, Aubrey." Peter approaches with his empty plate.

"Would you like a piece of pie?" I feel like a diner waitress, tossing away his used paper plate and asking if he wants dessert.

But we have to start somewhere. The rapport with my brother has been stifled by years of silence.

Peter tucks his hands in his pockets. "Sure, I'd like what Scott is having."

"So," I venture, slicing Peter a big piece of pie. "How do you two know each other?"

There's more than one way to find out information. Scott concentrates on eating, while Peter takes the plate from me.

"I punched him." He chuckles, pointing to Scott with his fork.

"You what?" I regard Peter, then Scott. "Oh my gosh. Your eye. After that one weekend. You were the one looking for Peter."

"He was," my brother says with a swallow of pie. "When the PI first contacted me—"

"PI? What PI?"

"The one Scott hired."

My mind works to make sense of this. "You hired a private eye?"

"I called a friend—"

"So the day Peter called here, after our first one-on-one game . . . You were the one looking for him."

"Yes."

"Why would you do such a thing? Without asking me? You had no right." I slap the island counter. "This is my life, Scott, not yours. My name. Just because you probed into my life and sniffed around my private thoughts for an interview doesn't give you the right to hunt down my long-lost brother. Did you need him to be a part of the story? Part of the big sale to CMT?"

"Whoa, Aubrey, no. Don't assign motives to me."

I shiver and ball my fists. "Isn't that what this is all about? More of the story? A big dramatic homecoming to boost the CMT ratings?"

He swings his arm toward the great room. "Do you see Rafe here? Cameras?"

"Did it ever occur to you I might not want Peter back in my life? You can't go around doing things in my name, Scott."

"Aubrey," Peter interjects with a daddylike tone.

I whirl around to him. "What? *Aubrey* what?"

"He was just trying to help."

My emotions are twisted so I can't make sense of them. Do I cry? Laugh? Hit someone? I lean toward Scott. "Next time, ask first."

He slides his uneaten pie across the island countertop and walks over to the coffee table, snatching up his car keys. "First of all, I looked for him in my name, not yours." He pauses in the foyer doorway. "And I only did it because of the look on your face the day we talked at Music City Park and you said he was AWOL."

"You can't read my expression and make such a huge decision, Scott."

"Wasn't my intent to cause a fight."

Peter whistles low. "I knew I shouldn't have come." He follows Scott into the foyer.

"Then why did you come? Huh? I haven't talked to you in six years, haven't seen you in eight." I trail after them, my formerly staid emotions erupting. "So, tell me. What made you come back? Money? Do you need money?"

Peter stops abruptly. "No, I don't need your money. I came here because I—" He presses his fist to his lips and clears his throat. "I-I missed you."

"You missed me?"

"Yeah, but apparently it was a bad idea." He picks up a small duffle bag by the door.

He missed me? "Peter, wait. Don't go." I step in his way. If he walks out the door, instinct tells me I'll never see him again. "Please stay."

"Coming here was a bad idea, Aubrey. Too much water under the bridge."

"I didn't sleep for a year after you left," I blurt as we stand in the foyer, deciding if Peter should stay or go. "When I toured, I looked for you everywhere—on the city street, at the county fair, among the faces at a concert. I wanted to share my success with you."

Peter drops his duffle bag, pressing his hand to the back of his neck. "I watched you from my place down in Florida. I knew you were doing well, AJ."

"Did you leave because of me?"

"No, no." His face is flushed and his hazel eyes shine. He paces to the edge of the foyer, standing in the residue of light coming from the kitchen. "You reminded me of him, okay?" The confession clicks like an unlocking key. "I couldn't look at you and not remember. I never had the chance to apologize and tell him he was my hero."

His confession sinks into the fresh, God-tilled ground of my heart. "But he knew." I adore my brother.

"Maybe I handled it wrong by leaving, but I had to get out of Nashville."

"Where'd you go?"

"Florida. Destin Beach. I run a deep-sea fishing boat."

I study his profile. My good-looking brother with the sensitive heart and easy manner. "We're a mess, you and me."

He peers into my eyes, and I feel the depths, and his loneliness. Solitude without peace. For a moment, it's almost unbearable.

"But we're blood, family. And we love each other, don't we?"

He bites his bottom lip and nods once.

"Then you'll stay?"

"I reckon."

From the door, Scott clears his voice. "Is my work here done?"

"Once again, you've made me look at my life." I walk over to him. "I'm sorry for being so nasty in there."

"Hey, I understand. Diva's gotta do what a diva's gotta do."

"Yeah, well, a diva should always be gracious." I grin, looking at Scott and my brother. "You know, we left Piper alone in there."

Scott curves his arm around me and walks me to the kitchen. "Shoot, I bet she ate all the pie."

34

"If you haven't been watching Inside NashVegas, set your alarm and wake up Monday mornings at seven fifteen. Yesterday, Aubrey James beat Scott Vaughn in a game of one-on-one. Pretty humbling."

—*Brad Schmitt, Brad on 2*

*Saturday afternoon Peter and I sit outside and talk. He's leaving tomor-*row, and time seems precious.

The crisp breeze blowing through the porch is fragrant with autumn. Though it's Gina's day off, she made us a pot of her chocolate-chocolate hot chocolate when she stopped to take care of a few things in her office.

George and Ringo sniff Peter's hand, unsure of the new man in their momma's life. After a second, George licks his fingers and drops to the floor by his feet.

"You won them over." I motion to the dogs and sip hot chocolate.

"Dogs I can deal with. Women . . . now that's another thing." He falls against the sofa cushion, holding his mug of cocoa in one hand, rubbing his short golden hair with the other.

"No special lady in your life?" The wind whips past. I shiver and curl my feet under me. Peter seems comfortable in khaki shorts and a *GoneFishing* T-shirt.

"Loved and lost a few times. After Mandy, I decided to bag relationships for a while."

"Remember Tracey Bachman from high school?"

He hides his smile, sipping from his mug. "Some things I choose to forget. So, where's this fiancé I read about?"

"Car? We broke up a few months ago."

His gaze is serious. "Why?"

"The relationship had a lot of holes." I try to picture Car and Peter sitting down for a nice Sunday afternoon conversation. *Shudder.* "Remember the people we used to make fun of at the churches we used to visit?"

He nods. "You were about to marry into one of those families?"

"Can you believe it?"

Peter grins. "Oh, the irony," he says, and it's the closest I've felt to him since he arrived. Most of the communication between us is about facts, not feelings. Which is okay. There's no guidebook for "catching up with your long-lost sibling in twenty-four easy hours," so we're figuring it out as we go along.

Last night, Scott asked us to consider sitting for an interview—a *short* interview—but Peter passed. Just didn't seem like the right time to do a Donny and Marie. I agreed.

"Will you come for Christmas?" I ask.

He shrugs. "The holidays are a busy time for me."

"I could visit you," I venture, "in Florida. Great place to visit in winter, right?"

"Right." He doesn't look at me much. Mostly around me. "Might be a fun thing."

The temperature continues to plummet and when the rain starts, we move inside. Without asking, Peter lights the fireplace as if he'd visited a hundred times.

"AJ, if you don't mind, I think I'll visit some of the old haunts."

"Have fun." Home less than a day and my brother seems changed already. Like he faced it, survived, and is finding peace in a place he thought reminded him of terror.

On his way out, he asks if Mike Loudermilk still lives in town. "Last I heard. His parents are in the same place."

He hums and jiggles his keys. "See you later."

"Want to order pizza for dinner?"

His smile is warm. "Sounds good."

While he reconstructs the links to his past, I spend the afternoon at Piper's desk, getting caught up on e-mail and AubJay business.

Zach e-mailed to confirm our business meeting with Eli on Monday about starting my own label. An idea I'm really starting to hate.

Several e-mail discussions have flown back and forth about the new Aubrey handbag design. I filter through those, make my decision, send an e-mail, and end the cyber argument.

Last but not least, I find an e-mail from Jen.

Aubrey,

School is fantastic. I am having a blast. My engineering classes are hard, but I love the challenge, and I'm getting A's in calc and physics.

Football Saturdays are a blast. A couple of us are road tripping it up to Kansas for the next away game.

Mom and I decided living in an apartment would be better than the dorms. Great decision now that I've visited the dorms. A girl I knew from community college moved to OU the same time as me and needed a roommate, so we decided to get a place together.

She's really fun, sweet, clean. And guess what, a huge Aubrey James fan. I had to tell her. Please forgive me. I had to. And a few of my best friends at home. I mean, they are my best friends.

But my roommate wants to meet you. Now look, no pressure, but maybe we could road trip to Nashville on a long break. Up to you. Whatever. I'm just saying. She's really cool. I promise she won't be a stalker.

Down to business. I found a church near campus I like a lot. I had no intentions of meeting anyone other than God there, and wham, the cutest youth pastor this side of heaven walks up to me. Did I mention he's single?

What do you think? Do I grab him by the ears and kiss him or what? Bad idea? Yeah, bad idea. I mean, why start something I can't finish. But every time I see him, my knees go weak. I can tell he's interested, but sorta standing back and watching. I changed clothes three times before church last week. I'm being ridiculous, right?

I do miss my friends from home, but get to see them over Thanksgiving. Oh, remember Buck? Never called me . . . until the night before I was leaving. Goofball. But we have a date the Saturday after Thanksgiving. (Snicker)

Hope you are doing well. Miss you. Write!

Love lots, Jen

I hit Reply and pour out my heart, telling her about the night at the Ryman, the growing emotion between Scott and me, Peter coming home, and my plans to paint the house. Well, the half I can reach, anyway.

. . . I'd love for you to road trip to Nashville. And we can talk about bringing your friend. I want to trust you, but I've been burned before. Had a stalker for a couple of years when a friend brought a friend over. Give me her name and I'll have Jeff check her out. Oooh, does that sound cynical? Know what? I'll leave it up to you, Jen. If you say she's good people, then she is. As for the cute youth pastor . . . just be wise. But don't be afraid.

I'm attaching a gift certificate to the AubJay store. You and your roommate can shop there for whatever you want. Oh, and I'm forwarding you a gift certificate to Target. All college kids need stuff from Target, right?

Love you,
Aubrey

She returns my e-mail right away. Must be hanging out online today. Smiling, I read.

Aubrey,

OMG, a thousand dollars to Target!!!!!! Are you crazy? No, I guess not. Thank you, thank you, thank you. Seriously, it's too much. You shouldn't have. Thank you, thank you, thank you. My roommate is really impressed now. She sends her thanks for the AubJay shopping spree. She's going to look like a walking billboard for you. Actually, we're having fun not telling people, but flashing around your name and stuff. Ha!

Better go. I'm in the library with my study group. On a Saturday, no less. Did I mention there are some things about college I don't like?

Love, and thanks again,
Jen

Shutting down the computer, stretching and collapsing against the back of the chair, I peer out the window at the maple's red and gold leaves clapping in the wind. Juan is steering a wheelbarrow across the lawn toward the gazebo. He stops and lifts out flower boxes of marigolds. How beautiful. Juan. He never leaves my garden unattended.

The phone's ring snaps me out of my mindless stare.

"Want to catch dinner with Ami and me?" Zach asks.

"Um, sure. Hey, Peter showed up last night."

"Your brother Peter?"

"One and the same. Can you believe it?"

"No . . . How are you?"

I smile. "Actually, wonderful."

"Well, then, do you *and* Peter want to join us for dinner?"

"He's out right now. Let me call you when—" I hear the chime of the front door opening and closing. I hear footsteps echoing in the foyer and down the hall. "Pete just came home. What time do you want to meet?"

"Seven thirty at LongHorn."

"See you then." I go find Peter. He chose to sleep in the barren but rather large downstairs master bedroom.

"Peter?" I knock lightly and wait for an answer. I call again, but when he doesn't answer, I inch the door open. "Pete?" No answer.

I know I heard him come in. I check Car's old office to see if he decided to use my old laptop.

"Peter?" I jog upstairs to check the library and the rec room. He's not in either place, or in any of the bedrooms. All right, I'm not crazy; I did hear him come in. Puzzled, I stand at the top of the stairs.

Then I hear music. I cock my ear toward the sound. Peter is singing and playing one of Momma's songs. His voice is still strong, and wrapped with emotion. Leaning my arms on the railing, I close my eyes and sing harmony.

Peter's bag is in the foyer Sunday afternoon when Connie and I arrive home from church. Connie wipes her eyes when he wraps his arm around her shoulders. "You're a sight I've been praying to see for a long time."

I set my bag and Bible on the end table. "Do you want some lunch?"

"Naw," he waves me off. "I'll grab something on the road."

The idea of him leaving sends a pang of loneliness through me. "You'll come back, won't you?"

"Probably." He clears his throat. "I'm proud of you. Momma and Daddy would be proud of you."

My eyes water. "They'd be proud of you too."

"That's debatable." He puts his arm around me as we walk to the foyer. "See you."

"Christmastime?"

He pauses at the door. "Maybe. You could drive down, and I'll string the boat with a few lights and—"

"I still don't drive," I confess with a wince.

At first, he's stunned. Then his rolling laugh bounces off the high ceiling and rains over me. "Holy cow, AJ, learn to freaking drive."

"Spoken like a true brother," Connie says.

He opens the front door. "I'll see you."

"There's money," I blurt.

"I don't want your money."

"Not my money, yours. Around a half a million."

He cocks his head sideways as if I'm speaking a foreign language and steps back inside. "Come again?"

"Half a million. Connie and I finally organized Daddy and Momma's affairs. We've been putting your half of the mechanicals and royalties from their songs into an account. Remember the little publishing company Daddy started the year before he died? Connie keeps it going. 'The Man' was covered again and became a gospel hit."

He circles the room, his hand on his head. "Half million?"

"With your name on it." I run to Piper's desk and find his bank information. "The account is in your name—Peter James's name."

He reviews the bank's info, a slow grin spreading across his face. "Can I access this from Florida?"

"Yes," Connie says, tapping the handwritten pin number and Web site.

He beams, scratching his head. "What a beautiful thing."

35

"Aubrey James is the Susan Lucci of the CMA Awards. Always nominated, never a winner."

—*Country Weekly*

Scott

Oktoberfest. Or, as some in our family call it, Vaughn Fest. The big annual family get-together. All the aunts, uncles, cousins, nieces and nephews, friends, and friends of friends gather at Dad and Mom's the first weekend in October.

Friday afternoon, as I get ready to drive down to Murfreesboro, Mom calls for the fourth time.

"Just had a wild thought. Why don't you bring Aubrey down?"

"Aubrey who?"

She sighs as if the burden of her son's welfare rests on her feeble mom shoulders. "You know Aubrey who."

"Now why would I bring Aubrey?"

"I've been watching the show and . . . well . . . you two have a vibe."

My mother is noticing my vibe? I'm embarrassed. "I see Dad forgot to give you your medication." I pull my duffel bag from the closet floor.

"What medi—Oh, stop. Son, I can tell. Aubrey *is* sweet on you. She's got that look in her eye."

"Mom, that look is for the *NashVegas* audience, her fans."

"Are you saying if you invited her she wouldn't come?"

Tossing the duffel to my bed, I think it over. *Would* she come? "I'm sure she has weekend plans. Aubrey James is a very busy woman."

"Call her. Humor me."

"Can't I just tell you a couple of jokes?" Picking a couple of pairs of socks from the top dresser drawer, I lob them over to my bag. *Vaughn scores a double basket. The crowd goes wild.*

"No. Call her." *Click.*

I jerk the phone away from my ear with a laugh. My mom just hung up on me. *See if I call Aubrey for you now.* I toss the phone onto the bed and finish packing.

But the idea of calling Aubrey nags at me. By the time I zip my bag shut, I'm really annoyed. *Nice going, Mom.*

My logical, thinking, rational side says forget it. She's not going to pack up last minute and go to Murfreesboro for the weekend. What's she going to do with my family all weekend? Listen to stories? Help in the kitchen?

I laugh at the image of Mom watching her kitchen burn down while Aubrey wrings a dish towel in her hands, wailing, "I'll build you a new one."

What if we don't get along and I have to endure rock-hard silence the entire way home? Not to mention she just broke off with Car. She can't be interested in meeting another guy's family.

Last but not least, what if she discovers I'm completely, hopelessly, madly in love with her?

Snatching up the phone before I change my mind, I dial Aubrey's place. Piper answers on the third ring.

"Piper, this is Scott Vaughn—"

"What can I do for you, sir?"

"Is Aubrey around?"

"Yeah, just got back from a meeting with her business manager. Hold on."

This is nuts. She's not going to drop everything and run down to Murfreesboro with me. *Hang up. No, Piper will tell her I called.*

Make up an excuse. *What d'you know? I found the information I needed while waiting for you to come to the phone.*

Nope. She won't buy it. Think of something else.

"Scott, hello."

"Aubrey, how are you?"

"Wonderful. And you?"

"Doing good."

Silence.

"So, is that why you called?" Her laugh is airy and sweet.

"No."

Silence.

"Scott, are you okay?" The airiness is replaced with concern.

"WouldyouliketogotoMurfreesboroformyfamilyOktoberfest?"

"When?"

"Today. In an hour." Here comes the big fat *noooo*.

Silence.

"Fancy or casual?"

Breathe. "Very casual." My heart stops beating so I thump it with my fist.

"Should I bring down some giveaways? Yes, yes I should. The Aubrey Bags are so fabulous. I'll have Piper run down to the warehouse; it's not far. How many people?"

"Hundreds."

"Hundreds? Really?"

I laugh. "Oktoberfest—or, as my sisters and I call it, Vaughn Fest—is a big family-and-friends gathering."

"Okay, then, hundreds. I'll have Piper get some of the AubJay staff to make up kits. Is it okay if they're delivered tomorrow?"

"Aubrey, you don't have to do this." I glance at my reflection in the dresser mirror. Yes, it's true. I'm madly in love with this woman.

"Of course I don't, but I want to. So, tomorrow is good?"

"Tomorrow is more than good." But really, how can it be any better than today?

> **"Inside NashVegas is moving. Starting in January, we'll be a part of the CMT weekly lineup. Watch our November debut with an exclusive look at country superstar Aubrey James."**
>
> —*Scott Vaughn, Inside NashVegas promo*

Vaughn Fest was disturbed when I showed up with Aubrey Friday evening. Big commotion. We hid inside the house until Dad calmed the masses.

We listened to Dad's speech from my old room. "Now, I'm sure Miss James will be delighted to meet everyone, but let's not behave like a bunch of ill-mannered rednecks. Give her space, give each other space, and I'm sure we'll all get a chance to say hello. She came here to relax and have fun just like the rest of us."

"I'm sorry," she says, sinking down to the edge of my bed.

"For what?" I sit next to her.

Her pretty face is pink and lined with concern. She points out the window. "This is the part of being me I hate. Can't show up and blend in."

"Blending in isn't all it's cracked up to be."

She laughs and drops her head against my shoulder. "Sometimes, I feel so tired. Like I can't carry the weight alone for another day."

I'll help you carry the weight. Just ask. Her perfume is subtle and clean, and teasing me. It's fifty degrees outside and I'm sweating. *Lord, help a guy out, would You?*

Dad's speech rolls on. "Now tomorrow, she's going to sign autographs and have a few giveaways, so just be cool—"

I wrap my arm around her and quote Dad, "'Just be cool,'" then laugh. "Didn't he scream the loudest when you showed up at the party?"

She elbows me. "No, that was me. You stepped on the back of my shoe."

I grin. *Aubrey, will you marry me?* "I'm glad you're here."

"Me too."

My sisters torture me all weekend. First, they high-five Aubrey for burning off my eyebrows. Next, they tell her every little stupid, embarrassing story they can remember about me during the Friday-night bonfire.

"Then, when he was twelve he stole the family car—"

"*Borrowed*. I borrowed the family car." If I'm going to be exposed, might as well get the details right.

It's late and the bonfire is burning low, and most of the Vaughn Fest crowd has gone home until tomorrow.

Sally rolls her eyes. "*Borrowed* the family car and lent it to his friend Steve, who drove across town to visit his girlfriend."

Aubrey jabs my ribs with her fingers. "You little thief."

I reach under my crossed arm and grab ahold of her hand. She peeks into my eyes with a shy grin, then urges Sally to tell another one.

Sunday afternoon is sunny and cold. Brown leaves float along in the crisp breeze. Vaughn Fest is officially over, and by four o'clock in the afternoon, everyone has gone home, including my big-mouth sisters.

Aubrey's in the kitchen helping Mom wash up the bowls and pans used this weekend.

I tap her on the shoulder and tip my head toward the door. "Hey, grab your jacket."

"I'm helping your mom," she says.

Mom takes the dish towel from her and gently pushes her toward me. "Go. Have fun." Proud to be playing matchmaker, Mom winks at me, which I find rather disturbing, but if it gets me alone with Aubrey, I'll endure.

"Where are we going?" Aubrey slips on her suede jacket and follows me past Dad, who's snoring on the couch in front of a muted football game.

"Out to the barn."

She stops on the back porch. "Out to the barn? What exactly do you have in mind, Scott?" Her eyebrows are raised.

I make a face. "Come on, you'll see."

While I unlock the barn doors, Aubrey and I reminisce about the weekend and how fun it was to give out the Aubrey Bag gifts.

I swing open the barn doors. "There she blows. In all her glory. Dad's old Jeep Wrangler."

She falls against me, squeezing my arm. "You're kidding. How fun."

Kiss her. "Yeah, the old Jeep is a lot of fun." I wrangle open the passenger-side door for her. "It sticks a little."

Getting behind the wheel, I crank the engine. When it roars to life I look over at Aubrey. "Hang on."

She grabs the roll bar with a rebel yell as I shift into reverse. Cranking up the radio, we careen over the brown, uneven field.

"Dad and Mom own a little over twenty acres. All this is their property. Bought it right after they were married. Poorer than dirt, but wanted a tract of *dirt* to call their own."

Aubrey screams as we hit a ditch and go airborne. Her loose hair whips about her face like mahogany and gold ribbons. "This is amazing."

Her eyes are bright from laughing, her smooth cheeks pink from the chill.

"Dad's tried to sell this old Jeep, but we refuse to let him."

"Is it fun to drive?"

I slam on the brakes and shift into neutral, letting the engine idle. "Why don't you find out?" I hop out and gesture to my seat. "For you, milady."

The excitement in her eyes fades, and her mouth drops open "I-I can't. Besides, this is a stick shift. I couldn't possibly . . . No, Scott, no."

Holding out my hands, I look around. "Why not? There's nothing out here. Can you think of a safer place to try?" I lean against the door. "If you learn to drive this baby, you can drive anything."

"Trees," she says in a panic. "Look at all the trees."

"You mean the ones *waaay* over there? Got to be two miles away. I think we can manage to steer clear."

She faces forward, her posture stiff, her complexion pale. "Scott, you know I can't drive."

"No, I know you *don't* drive. Whoever said you can't? Let's go, James, butt in the driver's seat."

"You're not the boss of me."

I laugh. "Yeah I am."

"Since when?"

"Don't argue with me, diva. Get in the driver's seat. You're burning valuable daylight."

Aubrey tips her sleek nose toward the sky. "No. Why'd you have to go ruin the fun?"

"Me? You're the one being stubborn." I walk around to her side and jerk open her door. She refuses to look at me. Gently, I turn her face to mine. "One last fear. Let's kick it in the rear."

She looks down at her trembling hands. "I'm terrified."

I cover her hands with mine. "I know you are, but, Aubrey, you can't hide behind fear. The longer you do, the more it owns you.

Come on. What do you say?" I lean in and whisper, "Patti and Sally can't drive it."

Her eyes light up. "Really?"

"Honest truth." I nudge her toward the driver's seat.

She pushes back, crossing her arms. "I'm not driving."

"Have it your way, then." I walk off toward the setting sun.

"Vaughn, where are you going? Get back here."

I turn around. Aubrey's standing in the Jeep, looking over the windshield. "Only if you drive," I holler.

"I can't believe you."

"You're thirty years old, Aubrey. Rich, beautiful, famous. But if you want to go to 7-Eleven at nine o'clock at night, you can't. Why? Not because you're famous, but because you're scared."

If I didn't push too hard, she'll cave about—

"Well, don't just stand there. Show me how to drive this rusty piece of junk."

36

"Shift into first," I coach Aubrey after we review the basics of the Jeep. "Slowly let off the clutch; you'll feel it catch. Press gently on the gas."

"Off the clutch . . ." Both her hands grip the wheel. "Give it gas." The Jeep lurches forward. And stalls. She looks devastated.

"You're doing fine. First gear is a little tricky. Start the Jeep again."

She cups her hands around her mouth and blows on them. "I can do this. I've sung before queens and princes, in stadiums of a hundred thousand. What's a stupid Jeep?"

"Exactly. You got it. Be the diva of this Jeep."

Muttering to herself, she lets off the clutch and gives it a little gas. The Jeep creeps forward, not stalling this time.

"I did it. I did it." She laughs and tucks a stray strand of hair behind her ear.

"Now, hear the engine whining? That means you need to shift into second. Same thing. Press in the clutch, shift, ease off the clutch, and give her a little gas."

The Jeep jumps slightly when she moves off the clutch, but we're moving and gaining speed.

"That was easier." She looks over at me. The light is back in her eyes, the pink hue is on her cheeks.

"First gear is always the hardest."

"Oh my gosh, oh my gosh, I'm driving." She lays on the horn. "Out of my way, world, I'm driving."

"See, I told you. Next gear. Hear the whine?"

Aubrey completes a smooth shift from second to third.

"This is the most incredible feeling. Now I know what Alan Jackson was singing about." She whips her cell phone from her belt loop.

"You brought your phone with you?"

"Always, always have my phone. Security team insists . . . Alan! Hey, it's me. Yeah, doing well. Guess what? I'm driving."

After all the coaxing and manipulating to get Aubrey behind the wheel, I can't get her to stop driving. We've covered the width of Dad and Mom's place, crossed over into the neighbor's field, and the neighbor's next to him, before I convince her to turn around and head for home.

"The gas gauge isn't accurate, Aubrey. I don't want to get stranded."

"Spoilsport." She laughs, tapping my leg with her hand. "Thank you."

"Anytime." *Forever, if you're willing.*

"Is that a pond? Let's go over there." Aubrey jerks the wheel to the right.

I grab onto the roll bar. "You're ready for NASCAR."

Aubrey careens toward Dad's fishing hole. She's definitely discovered her need for speed.

Except . . .

One thing we haven't covered much in today's driving lesson: stopping. And the pond nears. "Okay, Aubrey, slow down. Hit the brake and push in the clutch, then downshift."

"Downshift? What do you mean, downshift?"

"Go from fourth to third. Clutch . . . shift . . ."

The gears grind as she tries to change. "Scott!" Her voice is panicked. "What's going on?"

"Just grinding the gears. Keep the clutch in . . . No, don't hit the gas . . . Aubrey, slow down. Brake slowly . . ."

She is now a weird mix of confident-race-car-driver-meets-freaked-out-old-lady. Instead of braking, she guns the gas. We careen toward the pond.

"Aubrey, the brake." I'm trying to stay calm—for her—but the pond isn't going to move out of our way.

She tries to shift without the clutch. "Scott, help me. What—"

"Calm down. Hit the brake, gently." The Jeep slows a little. "Now, clutch. You're just reversing the shift process. Go from fourth to third. . . Good, good. Let out the clutch slowly."

She pops the clutch and we jerk forward, almost stalling.

"Give it some gas, Aubrey."

She hits the gas just as a big jack rabbit streaks across the field in front of us. "Bunny rabbit, no!" Aubrey swerves wide left. The Jeep hits a small grassy mound and goes airborne.

We crash down on the edge of the pond. The front end slowly sinks into the water. For a long time, we say nothing.

"You okay?" I ask low.

"Yes." Aubrey exhales, looking around at me with her wild hair settling over her face. "And that, Scott Vaughn, is how it's done."

Aubrey

*The night is cold, but the bonfire and the company are warm. Scott's sis-*ters and their families returned for a Sunday evening dinner of leftovers and a final night by the fire.

Sitting next to me on the log bench, Scott regales his family with the details of my first driving lesson. Dropping Dad Vaughn's Jeep into the pond was the scariest and funniest thing I've ever done in my life. Bravest, too. I'm quite proud of my pond run.

"Dad comes to pull us out." Scott slaps his knee, pointing at his father. "And he actually checks the ground where the Jeep went in to make sure we didn't splash out any of his precious bass."

His sisters laugh. Patti's close enough to lean over and kiss his cheek. "Dad, you're ridiculous about those fish."

"Aubrey," Sally says, "he stocks the pond, then refuses to let anyone catch and eat. It's all catch and release."

Dad Vaughn props his hands on his thighs so his elbows stick out. "I'm just making sure there's enough fish for the fishing."

His children laugh and counter with, "Right, Dad, that's the reason. Making sure there's fish for everyone to catch. Not. They're your *pets*!"

I cover my laugh when he turns to me. "Did that boy of mine hurt you?"

"No, sir, he didn't." I glance over at Scott. His coarse hair is wild and curly from the open Jeep ride. He looks so rugged and . . . Never mind. "He made me confront my fear."

"Another s'more, Aubrey?" Mom Vaughn holds up graham crackers and a block of chocolate.

"No, thank you, Mrs. Vaughn." I pat my belly. "I've eaten very well—too well—this weekend."

"Here." She passes the ingredients over. "You can diet tomorrow."

I hesitate, not sure she's serious, but when Patti passes over the crackers and chocolate with a wry twist on her lips, I figure I'm eating another s'more.

Scott winds up his story by excusing me. "This was Aubrey's first time driving with a clutch, and come on, Dad, you and I had trouble driving the Jeep at first. The clutch is like a springboard."

"I commend you, Aubrey," Sally says. "You've done the Vaughn women proud since none of us have driven the Jeep."

The Vaughn women? I'm not a Vaughn woman.

I steal a glance at Scott. Men freak when girls they bring home for the first time are included as part of the family.

But Scott is smiling, and he catches me looking at him and scoots a little closer, taking the marshmallow and roasting stick from me. Crouching toward the fire, he rests his elbow on my knee.

I feel safe. Truly safe. Not guarded or controlled like it was with Car. I slip my hand over Scott's and lace my fingers through his.

"Thank you all for a wonderful weekend." My words are filled with emotion. "I haven't had a family weekend like this in years."

Scott squeezes my fingers, his gesture speaking a thousand hot, silent words. "You'll have to come back."

"That would be lovely."

"Here we go," he says, pulling the stick from the fire, "one melted marshmallow."

The browned marshmallow dangles from the stick . . . then plops to the ground. We stare at it, then each other, before bursting into laughter.

"Ah, I didn't need it anyway." I break off a chunk of the Hershey bar and pass it to Scott. "I like my chocolate straight up."

"I hate to be the one, but . . ." Patti stands. "We need to get going, kids. School in the morning."

Sally's husband stretches and agrees. "We need to go too."

Moaning and groaning, the kids drag their feet toward the house, shoulders slumped. Their parents call instructions after them. "Don't forget to put away the PlayStation. Susie, your backpack is in the playroom."

Just before Patti's youngest goes through the back door, she spins around and dashes over to me, wrapping me in a tight, little-girl squeeze. "Thank you for my purse, Aunt Aubrey."

"Lillabeth, hey." Scott touches her arm with a glance up at me. *Sorry*. "Aubrey is not your aunt."

"No, i-i-it's okay," I say, pressing Lillabeth to me. "I don't mind."

We say good-bye to everyone and return to our bench by the fire. "It's getting colder." I rub my hands together.

"I think so." Scott wraps his arm around me. "Better?"

"Much."

He starts to say something, then stops. After a deep breath, he says, "I'm falling in love with you." His confession is quiet but confident. He jams the marshmallow stick in the dirt.

My heartbeat quickens. "Scott, I—"

"Don't say it. I know. Car and the others." He flips the stick into the fire. "I just wanted you to know."

"Hey, you two want some hot chocolate?" Mom hollers from the back door. "It's getting cold out here."

"No, Mom." Scott stands. "It's late and we need to get back. I have to work in the morning."

"I'll pour you some in a thermos."

"Whatever," he mutters with a grin. "She always sends something home with me." He offers his hand and pulls me to my feet, holding my gaze for a second. A haunting loneliness swirls around me when he lets me go. "Ready?"

"Don't give up on me," I whisper.

"Not in a million years."

37

March

*Standing offstage, I watch as Scott Vaughn and Beth Rose tape the open-*ing segment of their new hit show, *Inside NashVegas on CMT.*

Their November debut was a smash, and I've become the coanchors' personal counselor on dealing with fame.

"I didn't think it'd be like this," Scott said one weekend when we drove down to his parents for a weekend getaway.

"You'll get used to it. Believe it or not, the benefits outweigh the hazards."

"I bet I've gotten a dozen marriage proposals." He makes a face. "Let me tell you, there are some sick woman out there. You wouldn't believe what they're offering."

I laugh. "Oh, yeah I would. I get those same sick letters from men."

Scott's become my best friend. Church on Sunday, dinner, movies, weekends on the Vaughn farm. He even drove me down to Destin for Christmas with Peter. And now, he's about to welcome me on to his and Beth's *hit* show.

Scott: *Hi, everyone. I'm Scott Vaughn.*

Beth: *And I'm Beth Rose. Welcome to* Inside NashVegas on CMT.

Scott: *We have a very special guest in the house tonight—*

Beth: *We do. Miss Aubrey James is here. [audience applauding]*

Scott: *She's in the studio, ready to give us an update on her life and perform a cut from her new album,* At Last.

Beth: *So stayed tuned.* Inside NashVegas on CMT *will be back right after this. [more applause]*

The stage manager warns me, "Two minutes, Miss James."

"Thank you."

Scott tips his head with a wink, giving me a thumbs-up. I confessed to him last night that taping in front of a small studio audience was ten times more nerve-wracking than performing in stadiums.

The camera light flashes. Scott and Beth are back on. They banter for a second, then Scott introduces me. "Ladies and gentlemen, please welcome Aubrey James."

I step out to enthusiastic applause, my nerves settling down as I approach the set. I embrace Scott casually, then Beth, and take the empty seat between them.

"We're so glad you're here," Beth says when the applause fades away.

"Me too." I smile and peer out over the crowd, bringing a blur of people into focus, seeing their smiles, catching the glint in their eyes.

Scott: *You've been busy.*

AJ: I have, I have. But it's all good.

Beth: *You released a new CD,* At Last. *Tell us about it.*

AJ: I love this album. It's my coming-of-age project. Robin Rivers and I wrote most of the songs. Two I wrote on my own, making this the first album of my own material. It's both thrilling and frightening.

Scott: *This album has been out for three months, but it's not blowing up the charts like a typical Aubrey James record. Are you concerned?*

AJ: Not really. This album isn't getting as much radio play as previous records, but we're confident Aubrey James fans will find their way to this album and love it.

Beth: *You parted ways with SongTunes last fall after being with the label eight years.*

AJ: Yes, we just didn't see eye to eye on a few things, and Nashville Noise opened their arms to me. So, I made a change. I loved being with SongTunes and have a deep respect for all the people there, but in the end, their idea of Aubrey James and my idea were completely different.

Scott: *Tell us about the CMAs. You were nominated last year, but come November you didn't win, again. It's still the one award that eludes you.*

AJ: [smiling] Must not be my time to win a CMA. I'm very satisfied with my career and the awards I've won. If there's no CMA award in my future, I'm okay with it. Actually, I get more attention and accolades from my fans and peers when I lose. Everyone wants to reassure me.

Scott: *Because of the wait, will it make the award more special when you win?*

AJ: Absolutely. *If* I win. Being denied year after year forces me to understand my career is not defined by ceremonies and awards.

On the other hand, my career took off way too fast and easy. Not winning a CMA teaches me the beauty of the sacrifice. How much more I'll appreciate the award when it comes. Let me tell you, Susan Lucci loves her Emmy way more than the other actresses whose names I can't even recall. Losing made her more famous than winning. We loved her courage and poise year after year. We cheered for her. Not a bad road to take, if you ask me."

Scott: [nodding] Said with true Aubrey James grace.

Beth: *Your name's been missing from the tabloids lately.*

AJ: [applauding, gazing at the audience] For once, and I'm loving it.

Beth: *[touching Aubrey on the arm] So, there's nothing new going on in the love life department. No news?*

AJ: Nothing new, yet. I've been enjoying this season of my life. First time in eleven years I'm not doing a spring tour. We're thinking of going out some over the summer, but wow, I've just been exhaling and getting some things straight in my life. Returning to some core values like my faith. It's very liberating, and I'm having a great time *being* instead of *doing*.

Beth: *Sounds wonderful. I can see the peace in your eyes.*

Scott: *[smiling] So, where's Aubrey James ten years from now?*

AJ: [thinking] Married to the guy who taught her to drive, expecting baby number three.

Scott: *(Cough . . . sputter . . . choke) [gulping water]*

Beth: *Scott, are you all right? [grinning at the audience, patting him on the back]*

So, Aubrey, were you holding out before? Is there a special someone in your life? Who is this man who taught you to drive?

AJ: [smiling, shaking her head] No holding out on you Beth. I'm not sure the guy knows. I just discovered it myself.

The producer signals ten seconds to a break.

Scott: Aubrey, it's always good to have you on Inside NashVegas on CMT. *When we come back from commercial, you're going to sing for us, right?*

AJ: Absolutely. I'm here with my band, and we're going to perform my first single from the new album, but first—[holding up her finger, looking around] Do we have time? I've got to show you all something I'm very proud of, more than the album. [reaching into the back pocket of her jeans, she pulls out a small card] I'm thirty years old and for the first time in my life, I have a driver's license. [flashing license at the camera] Can you see it?

Beth: [applauding with the audience] Congratulations. Good for you.

Scott: [stepping down to kiss her cheek] Very proud of you.

AJ: [staring at her license] I *love* to drive. What have I been doing all these years? The responsibility of driving is so freeing. I need to thank my friend who taught me to drive because he renewed my faith in chivalry and true love. Well, [looking at Beth] he's the love of my life. [slipping her license back into her pocket]

Scott: [clearing his throat] We'll be right back with Aubrey James.

A fire crackles in the family room fireplace as I pace around, untouched by its warmth. George and Ringo watch me, lifting their doggy eyebrows as if to ask, "What's wrong?"

He hasn't called. Confessing my love for him on national TV might have been a little too Julia Roberts in *Notting Hill*, but I had to do it.

The moment I walked onto the set, my feelings for him surfaced and it hit me: "I'm in love with my best friend, Scott Vaughn."

Five months have passed since his Vaughn Fest confession of love. Five months of friendship, laughter, Bible study, late-night heart-to-hearts, and a volcano of smoldering passion. The entire time I kept him at arm's length, waiting for our affection and longing to fade. But it's only increased.

Glancing at the time, I wonder again why he hasn't called. Did I freak him out with my cloaked on-air confession? I run the heel of my hand over my forehead. *Please call.*

When the doorbell rings, George and Ringo jump up, baying and barking, their nails clicking against the marble as they run to the door. The foyer is a lovely, rich burnt-orange glaze now, and the decorator Piper convinced me to hire finished the upstairs last month. The house is beautiful. And very much a reflection of me.

I check the security camera to see who's at the door. My heart nearly stops.

"Are you going to leave me out here all night?"

Taking a moment to catch my breath, I fix my smile and jerk open the door. "Hey."

Scott is leaning against the wall, handsome in his jeans and tweed jacket. "So," he starts, coming in and closing the door behind him. "I was at work today, doing the show with Beth, as usual, and we had this really cool, drop-dead-gorgeous guest on." George and Ringo sniff his feet, panting, eyeing him, waiting for a pet.

"Really? Anyone I know?"

He slips his arms around my waist and kisses my forehead. "Yeah, she's a country artist. Decent singer, pretty good entertainer."

"A B-Lister." I kiss his neck softly. My thoughts are mushy and soft. "I-I don't bother with them. Nothing but trouble."

"Hum, too bad, because"—Scott kisses my cheek, then my neck—"she told me she loves me. So, I'm going to have to go with her to the ends of the earth."

"Wow, really? I guess this is good-bye, then?"

He grips me a little tighter. "Not in a million years." His lips touch mine, soft at first, then with released passion.

My heart beats like a flitting bird and my legs go weak and wobbly. "I love you, Scott. With all my heart."

"So I heard," he says, his breathing deep as he buries his face in my hair. "I love you too. Very much." He lifts his head, cupping my face in his hands. "I'm never leaving you. You're stuck with me for life now."

"A life sentence." I tip my head back with a laugh.

Scott jumps back suddenly and thrusts his fist to his mouth, "Scott Vaughn here for *Inside NashVegas*. We have breaking news."

His deep, fake TV anchorman voice makes me laugh. I bat my hands at him. "Stop, you're creeping me out."

"Ladies and gentleman, we've just learned country sensation Aubrey James is in love." Every other word is enunciated.

"Miss James, what do you have to say for yourself?" He juts the fake mike to my lips.

"That my boyfriend is a loon and I should change my mind."

He lowers his arm and the light in his eye darkens. "Marry me."

"What?"

"Marry me."

"Scott . . . really?"

"Yes. I love you, and I want to start building a life with you. Get working on those three kids." A warm tingle rushes over me. "Please, marry me. Look, I know this is spontaneous and unromantic, but I've never been more sure of any—"

"Yes." I giggle, covering my mouth. "Yes! Absolutely yes."

I hug Momma when she walks into my room. "Momma, I've been thinking of you."

Wrapped in her arms, she rocks me gently from side to side. "I'm so proud of you."

"Are you really? And Daddy?"

Her hands gently grasp the side of my face. "How could you ask such a thing? Of course. Very proud."

"I haven't been the light I should've been."

Momma's laugh is soft yet knowing. "Do any of us shine like we should?"

The afternoon shadows shift and the light in the room fades.

Taking my hands, she leads me to the side of the bed. "Your best years are yet to come, baby girl. Oh, so good. If only you could see."

"But I believe. Momma, I'm in love with the most wonderful man. God is taking care of me."

She brushes her hand over my forehead and down the back of my hair. "I see hope and love in your eyes."

Salty tears blur my vision. "I'm not holding on so tight anymore," I confess. "I let go."

"See there, and you worried about spiraling off into space."

Laughing, I rest my head against her shoulder. "Look, Momma, no hands."

"That's my girl."

I throw my arms around her neck as the tears slip down my cheeks. "I'll miss you until I see you again . . ."

"We'll be watching from the cloud of witnesses."

Closing my eyes, I take Momma's hand in mine and quietly begin to sing. "All to Jesus, I surrender . . ."

Billboard Top 100

March 23

Track	Title	Composer	Time
100	What You're Looking For	James/Rivers	4:01

ALBUM REVIEW—*At Last* by Aubrey James

She's earned the title of diva with her powerful, soulful vocals; demanding artist riders; and record-label disputes. Crowned the Queen of Country Soul, Aubrey James is all about making music her way.

At Last is a drastic change from her previous albums—stylized around her big voice, belting out big melodies and soulful lyrics.

Writing with new songwriter Robin Rivers, James ventured down a new creative path, writing thought-provoking lyrics surrounded by daring melodies.

James also shares the album's production credits with her longtime friend and producer, Dave Whitestone. She put her reputation on the line with songs like "Ragtime" and covering the gospel hit "The Man," written by James with her father, the late Ray James.

At Last is intense but peaceful and moving, perhaps a reflection of James's life in the past year. Lyrics like *In the doorway, I waited for you / But as the day drifted toward night / The reality sank in / You were gone, This time for good / So I turned out the light, and climbed the old stairs* make us realize she's writing about more than a broken heart—a journey into life.

James triumphs with this album, picking the right time in her career and life to show us her heart and soul. You'll want this album as part of your collection for years to come.

—Grace Myers, All Music Guide

"Aubrey James announced her engagement today to Inside NashVegas on CMT cohost Scott Vaughn. 'This is one of the happiest seasons of my life,' James said."

—*Inside Access*

LINER NOTES

Aubrey James would like to thank:

Dave Whitestone for giving this project wings.

FRESH! for a great sponsorship.

Robin Rivers for the amazing songs.

James Chastain and Nashville Noise for welcoming me home.

Scott Vaughn for asking questions that caused me to look inside myself and reconcile my lifestyle with the deeper desires of my heart. I can't wait to marry you.

Peter James, my brother. I'm so glad we're family again.

My posse: Zach Roberts, Piper Cantwell, Connie Godwin, Gina Lacy, Skyler Banks, and everyone at AubJay Inc. Thank you for keeping me from drowning! Bonuses all around.

Melanie Daniels for doing what I should've done years ago: tell my story. I wish you well.

Jen, the best little sister, you are a true star!

Jesus, my Friend. You waited for me in the secret place, and when I finally arrived, You showered me with unconditional love.

LINER NOTES

Rachel Hauck would like to thank:

Aubrey James for introducing yourself to me, being difficult, then becoming my friend.

Ami McConnell for being a writer's friend, fabulous editor, and for believing in me.

Leslie Peterson for your great insight and encouragement in this manuscript.

Allen Arnold and everyone on the fiction team at Thomas Nelson for creating a launching pad for faith-based fiction.

Tony Hauck, my husband and best friend, for putting up with deadline craziness. I can't imagine a life without you.

Diann Hunt, Christine Lynxwiler, Colleen Coble, Allison Wilson, Susie Warren, and Tracey Bateman for the advice, critique, encouragement, and ideas during the process of writing this book. But mostly for your friendship.

Rebekah Gunter for your honest feedback when I was in panic mode, and for being the best baby sister. I love you.

Kim Hill for saying yes to lunch with a stranger. Your insight and wisdom were invaluable. Best of all, I loved meeting you and hanging out. I'm a big fan!

Matt Bronleewe for being my resident record producer.

Chris Oglesby for taking time to sit and talk.

Kelly Sutton at *Good Morning, Tennessee* for your insights and advice.

Molly Day at Fox 17 for a glimpse into the life of a producer.

Chelle Tapper for praying.

Denise Hildreth for dessert and information at Greenhills Grille.

Davis (and Mark) for Sun Shoppe talks.

Skip Rudsenske of JSR Law in Nashville for the great legal help and advice.

Sharon Hayes, my mom, for always loving and always encouraging. And my brothers, Danny, Joel, and Peter-John Hayes.

Saving the best for last, thank you, Jesus, for speaking to my heart that You would help me write this book. And You did. One day, we'll talk about it face-to-face. Isaiah 41:13

READING GROUP GUIDE

1. In the beginning of the book, Aubrey drove herself to the point of exhaustion. Have you ever become so involved in a project you've neglected your health?

2. Aubrey accepts Car's engagement ring. What was the significance behind her acceptance? Do you think she was really in love with him?

3. What signaled to Aubrey that Car did not really "know" her?

4. Piper said Aubrey was more than the collection of boxes left in the library. What did she mean? Is there "stuff" in your life you're clinging to?

5. What legacy did Aubrey's parents leave? What is the significance of the song Aubrey's mother sings to her in her dreams?

6. Why was Aubrey able to be vulnerable with Scott during the interviews?

7. What did Car's family represent to Aubrey? What did Scott's family represent? Which was more important?

8. Why did Aubrey lie to Jennifer about her name? Why did Aubrey want to use a false name for foster care then perpetuate the lie? Do you know anyone who is hiding behind a label?

9. Peter refused to acknowledge his sister because of his painful memories. Is there someone in your life you avoid because of the past? Do you consider seeking them out so you can reconcile?

10. The most common fear people share in America is the fear of public speaking. Nearly everyone has fears and phobias. In the novel, Aubrey won't drive. From where do you think her fear stems?

11. Melanie betrays Aubrey's friendship when she talks to the tabloids, yet at the end of the book Aubrey forgives her. Have you ever felt betrayed? How did you (or how would you like to) handle it?

12. We are a society of consumerism and convenience. We often think we need more. Aubrey appeared to have it all: success, fame, and fortune. What did she lack?

13. Did Aubrey remind you of someone in your life? Did this story compel you to take any action that you heretofore hadn't considered?

Excerpt from *Lost in NashVegas*

★ ★ ★

How I let Daddy and Granddaddy Lukeman talk me into singing a "couple" of my songs at the Spring Sing, *again*, is beyond me. I can't do it. I can barely breathe, let alone sing.

Blood thumps from my heart up to my ears, over my scalp, and down to my toes. Cold sweat beads on the back of my neck and under my arms. My feet burn as if I'm standing on Florida sand in mid-July.

"Gonna chicken out again, Robin?" Smiley Canyon nudges me with his pointy elbow.

"Nooo," I lie, gripping my old Taylor guitar for security.

Smiley laughs at me. "Let's see—last year you broke out in hives the night before the show, didn't ya?"

"I had a rash from stem to stern. You saw me the next morning."

"And the year before that you couldn't find the keys to your truck." He plucks the strings of his beat-up Gibson, trying to tune. Smart aleck. No wonder Nashville kicked him back home to Alabama.

"And didn't you get lost driving across town once?"

I ball my fist. One pop, right in the kisser. Come on, Lord, look the other way, just for a second.

But when I look Smiley in the eye, I see what I don't care to see: the truth. I relax my fingers and attempt to deflect attention. "Your song was real good. Was it a new one?"

"Naw, wrote it a few years back."

I nod. "Good for you."

He tips the brim of his cowboy hat my way. "Better go get my seat. Don't want to miss your debut." He says *debut* like "de-butt"—as if I'm going to fall flat on mine—and walks off snickering.

With a tiny step forward, I peer around the stage curtain. Freedom Music Hall is packed. An electric twinge constricts my middle, and I take two giant steps back. Let Smiley be right. Let him laugh at me again. It's better than public humiliation.

Turning to flee, I bump smack dab into Jeeter Perkins, the Hall's emcee.

"Get ready, Robin Rae. You're up next." He grins and adjusts his bolo tie.

Hello, Robin. What'll it be? Anxiety attack in front of a thousand of your closest friends and family? Yes? Right this way.

"Jeeter, I changed my mind. I'm not singing."

He rolls his eyes. "Now, Robin Rae—"

"How about you let old Paul Whitestone go on with his Dixie Dos?" Behind Jeeter, the former bluegrass icon waits with his round-faced, rosy-cheeked granddaughters—Elvira, Elmira, and Eldora. (Identical triplets. Tall, big girls.)

"Listen, girl, I've heard your songs a hundred times on your granddaddy's porch. You got a gift. A gift." Jeeter pinches my arms in his bony grip and bugs out his eyes. "Sometimes you have to face your fears."

I squint. "And sometimes ya don't."

This isn't like the first day of school or one of Momma's Saturday night dinners. Nope. Singing in the Hall is optional.

And I'm opting out.

Jeeter shakes his head and brushes past me as the Blues Street Boys finish and exit stage left to mild applause. "Thank you, boys," he says into the mike. "I don't think I've ever heard such unique, *ahem*, harmonies." He glances over at me and raises one bushy brow.

Shaking my head, I step backward and poke Paul Whitestone, who's nodded off. "You and the girls are on, Paul."

The old man sputters to life. "Huh? Oh, we're on?" He waves his long arm at the triplets. "Girls, come on. We're up."

Jeeter rouses the crowd with a big call into the microphone, waving his hat in the air. "How y'all doing?" They give Jeeter what he wants—hoots and hollers, whistles and cheers.

"The hills are alive with the sound of music!" Jeeter cuts a glance at me. "We got a real treat for you folks tonight . . ."

Hand on my guitar, I tip my head in the direction of the ladies' room and mouth, "Got to go."

"Next up," Jeeter's voice trails after me, "Paul Whitestone and the Dixie Dos."

Ducking into the ladies' room, I push the lock and fall against the door. My stomach feels like a firecracker just exploded in it. My heart is racing at top NASCAR speed, and my legs are trembling like Granddaddy's old hound, Bruno, when it thunders.

Go out there . . . Sing in front of folks . . . Who'm I kidding? Freedom, Alabama, and their *Nashville* tradition have haunted me for the last time.

I shift my guitar so it hangs down my back and dampen a wad of paper towels. Patting the sweat beads from my forehead, I wonder if I'll make it out of the Hall alive. Blue spots flicker before my eyes.

"Should've stayed home where you belong," I scold my reflection in the mirror. "At twenty-five, you should know better." Grandpa McAfee is right: if you can't run with the big dogs, stay on the porch. Drawing a shaky breath, I adjust my guitar strap so that it's not cutting into my shoulder and unlock the door. But before I can jerk on the knob, the door flies open, bonking me on the head.

"Ouch!" My hand goes to my forehead as Arizona Parish shoves her way inside.

"What're you doing?" She tilts her soft blond head to one side and props her hands on her skinny waist. I pop her on the shoulder.

"What are *you* doing? There's only room for one in here."

"I came to find out what *you're* doing." She looks down at me with her eyebrows pinched and her lips tight. "So, what are you doing?"

"Hiding. My palms are sweating, my heart's racing, and my stomach feels like the finale of the Fourth of July show."

"Robin, it's just performance anxiety. Stage fright." She grabs me by the arms. "Take a deep breath, say 'Help me, Jesus,' and get on out there." She gives me a quick shove toward the stage entrance. "Wow 'em."

"Your sympathy is overwhelming."

"I'm not here to be sympathetic, Robin. I'm here to tell you the time has come to face your fears. You sing like an angel, and your sappy lyrics have ruined my mascara more times than I can count."

"Well, hot diggity dog for me. I don't care what my lyrics have done to your mascara, I'm not going out there." I jab my finger toward the stage door. "I'm going home."

My boot heels thud across Freedom Music Hall's ancient wood floor. The floor that has borne the soles of Garth Brooks, Tammy Wynette, Lionel Richie, and the great Billy Graham. Center stage, old Paul is plunking his banjo while the triplets clog on top of a three-tiered platform, shaking their ruffled skirts, shaking the entire Hall.

Arizona follows me to my guitar case. "How three pudgy girls move their feet so fast is beyond me."

"They've been clogging and eating since they were born." I settle my guitar in its case.

She sighs. "Got to admit, they have the best legs in Freedom."

This makes me laugh. "Can't argue there."

"Robin, don't lock up your guitar. Get out there. Beat this stage fright. If those triplets have the best legs in Freedom, you have the best voice and the best songs. Please. For me." Arizona clasps her hands under her chin and bats her eyes. I stop buckling up my guitar case. Arizona Parish has a way of getting under my skin, forcing me to dig deep and dream big. She introduced herself to me a few years ago as "the girl from Miami." Her journey to Freedom is still a mystery.

"There was a situation," she said.

"Promise me the law ain't after you."

"Promise." She crossed her heart and flashed the Girl Scout salute.

Now, backstage at the Hall, Arizona kneels beside me.

"Please. Go out there."

Standing, I look toward the stage with a shake of my head. "Why I let Daddy and Granddaddy talk me into this every year is crazy. Plumb crazy."

"You know why." She pokes me in the chest with her bony

finger. "Deep inside, you know." Before I can rouse up a crushing reply, a loud crack comes from center stage. Followed by three very distinct thuds.

Elvira.

Elmira.

Eldora.

"What in the world . . ." My first glimpse of three whiteruffled bottoms shaking in the spotlight takes my breath away. It's followed by a *spppti* as I choke back a laugh. "Holy clogging platform, Batman."

The girls' three-tiered clogging platform has broken clean through.

For about ten seconds, there's a heavy hush over the auditorium and a collective holding of breaths. Are they all right? Then, a snort. A muffled guffaw. A fading tee-hee behind someone's hand.

But when Elvira—or is it Elmira—sticks her round hand in the air and says in a high-pitched voice, "We're all right, Papa," it's over. Laughter explodes like water balloons and douses every one of us.

Arizona hides her face behind her hand. "This is terrible. Oh, the humiliation." She ducks behind the stage curtain, pressing her face against the cold wall, honking and gasping for air.

"See?" I say, pointing. "This is what I'm talking about. What if that happens to me?"